Gemini Twins in the Land of the Gods

Lillith Carrie

This book is dedicated to all of my readers who have helped to make dreams of
being an author a reality.
None of this would be possible without you.
I hope you love this book as much as I do.
Remember, never stop believing in what you want to accomplish.
Anything is possible. Even for a small town girl like me.

Love Always,
Lillith Carrie

Prologue

Ivy

Fifteen years...

Fifteen years since the war, and every day, I tried to atone for the shit I had done prior. I could play innocent and act like I hadn't done anything to cause it all, but I'd be fucking lying. Not only to those around me but also to myself.

The day Kara told me my children were to be sent to the land of the gods when they turned eighteen, I made a silent pact to prevent it. They were my children, and I was determined to make sure their lives were their own.

Even if I wanted to strangle them on more than one occasion for their defiance, among other things. "Damn it, Pollux! Where are you?"

Storming through the house, I looked for the eldest of my six children and found, while gifted and the future of our pack, he never seemed to be where he was supposed to be.

"James, have you seen Pollux?" My words seemed to fall on deaf ears as James continued grading the papers before him. After all the hell we had gone through, he decided ten years ago to get into teaching, and he hadn't looked back.

Which honestly was shocking, considering he taught ninth-grade biology.

"James..." I repeated with a groan of frustration. "James!"

"Huh?" His eyes gazed up to meet mine with a clueless look. He had aged so much since I had first met him. Gray hairs now streaked his head, and with it, wrinkles crested the corners of his eyes. "Sorry, sweetie. The end of the grading period is next week, and I have to get these done."

"I know, I know," I replied as I rolled my eyes and walked towards him. No matter how much he had changed physically, he was still the sweet man I once knew. He always thought of others before himself and took pride in his work. "I just haven't seen Pollux since he came home from school, and he promised to take Dillon to practice."

"Practice?" James glanced down at his watch and furrowed his brows. "Babe, that started twenty minutes ago. Why didn't you tell me I would have taken him?"

Smiling, I shook my head. "It's okay. Talon was done with his rounds and offered. He was excited to take him this week. You know how much he hates missing out on stuff."

With all the changes we had undergone, some were harder than others.

Damian had refused to take back his Alpha position, and in doing so, Hale took over as the Alpha of the pack, allowing Damian to spend more time with the business aspects of our world. As for Talon, his obsession with security grew increasingly urgent with every child we had.

Running the training grounds and managing the borders became his calling. One the entire pack was grateful for.

"I know. Let him enjoy it. Dillon's twelve now. He isn't going to be young forever."

Nodding my head, I leaned down, kissing him gently. "I know. I'm glad that he has been coming around lately. When little Sylvia got hurt a few years ago, I never thought he would leave the borders." Thinking about the memory of that day made my chest burn with anguish, but forcing the feeling away, I pushed my mind forward. "If only I can find your son."

James chuckled, shrugging his shoulders. This was a usual thing for the twins. Now that they were about to be sixteen, they thought they could do whatever they wanted, and out of the two... Pollux wasn't the worst.

No, he may have had his moments, but Cassie was very different from her brother.

"Why don't you go ask Cassie where he went? She has her way of finding him," James suggested, causing me to groan in irritation.

There was no way I would let her do something like that. The thought of her using her powers for any reason was out of the question. "James—"

"Don't start, Ivy. You can't make her stop being who she is. Just... go ask."

James didn't give me much chance to reply before quickly going back to the papers before him, and by that point, I was already regretting even asking Pollux to help with his brother. I should have just taken him myself and saved the headache of this entire conversation.

Taking a moment to think about what James suggested, I huffed with irritation before walking towards the staircase headed for Cassie's room. There was no way I was going to ask her to use her powers to find her brother, but I could simply ask if she had seen him.

Her bright white door appeared before me. The acrylic-painted green flames and intertwining vines upon her door were her own design. She was the most artistic person I knew, and many pieces of her original work hung not just around our home but around the pack.

"Cassie..." Knocking on her door, I turned the knob and walked into her room. The white drapes bellowed from the window, blowing through the open window. The twinkling night sky glistened from the balcony where the moon shone upon the world.

It was just like her to leave it open all the time, claiming the fresh air helped to enhance her creative ability. Gazing around the room, I took in the clothes scattered about her unmade bed and littered dresser of makeup and jewelry.

"Cassie?" I called out again as I looked around for where she could be. The softness of her voice called me towards the open balcony doors.

"No, I'm coming, God. Just wait for me."

As soon as my hand pushed back the drape, she quickly hung up the phone and spun to look at me. Her dark brown hair hung in waves over her shoulders as the same celestial blue eyes I once held looked back at me. "Hey, Mom."

"Cassie, who were you on the phone with?" Raising a brow, I crossed my arms over my chest and sighed. She was up to something, and even though she thought she was smarter than me, she wasn't.

"Oh—just Melissa," she replied quickly as she pushed past me back into her bedroom. "She wants me to come over to her house tonight."

"She does, huh?" I smirked as I watched her move around her room. She seemed to think I was stupid regarding her acts of rebellion. There was no way she was simply going to stay at Melissa's house, especially during homecoming. There was definitely something else going on. "So, you're just going to go without asking permission?"

Shoving a few pieces of clothing into her backpack, she stopped with a sigh and looked over her shoulder at me. "I already asked daddy, he said it was okay."

"Oh, really... which daddy did you ask?"

With wide eyes and a disgusted look, she scoffed, "Why do you have to say it like that?"

"Because I want the truth," I replied with my hands on my hips as I stared at her. "Cassie, do you think I'm stupid? Do you honestly think I don't know what you're doing?"

"Oh my god, mom!" she groaned. "I'm literally not doing anything. Just going to Melissa's and hanging out for the night since she is like, one of the very few friends I have. Or am I not supposed to have any friends?"

This was her usual MO. She would sit there and pretend she was disgusted with the mention of her doing something wrong and then try to backtrack to have me trust her.

The moment Cassie came into her powers almost three years ago, I thought the world was going to end. I didn't understand why she had to be difficult, but my mother told me all the time it was just a phase and she would grow out of it. I just wished that would happen sooner rather than later.

Anger surged through me at her tone. "You need to watch how you speak to me, young lady."

She quickly realized I wasn't going to put up with her tone, and with a sigh, she crossed her arms over her chest. "I'm sorry, I just don't like how you act like this to me, but Pollux can do whatever he wants. It's not fair."

The soft pitter-patter of footsteps behind me in the hallway caught my attention, and as I turned, I spotted Raya walking down the hallway with a book in her hand. She was only a year younger than the twins, and while they had a particular way about them, Raya was more of a mother hen, making sure her younger siblings were staying in check at all times.

A child quite often capable of telling me exactly what I wanted to know. Glancing back over at Cassie, I watched her eyes dart to where Raya had just walked by, and her face paled.

"Raya," I called out softly, stepping through the doorway into the hallway, watching as my dark brown-haired beauty turned to me with a confused glance.

"Yes, ma'am."

"Raya, do you know where Pollux went tonight? I can't seem to find him, and he was supposed to take Dillon to practice earlier," I said with a very nonchalant attitude as Raya shrugged her shoulders.

"The homecoming bonfire is tonight. All the kids are going. It's supposed to be seniors only, but you know how Pollux is. He plays on the football team, so he's kind of friends with all of them."

"Is that right? And what kind of stuff will be at these parties?"

I wasn't that old. I knew exactly what would be at these parties, but after I asked, I turned my gaze to Cassie, watching as fear crossed her eyes. She had been caught, and while I had hoped she would have told me the truth, she decided not to.

"Well, there's a lot of drinking and dancing and stuff, and sometimes the boys play pranks on each other, from what I've heard. I mean, Cassie should know more about it. Melissa is going tonight."

"You fucking bitch!" Cassie screamed as she stormed towards Raya, who quickly jumped backward. My arm reached out, snatching Cassie by the waist as she tried to attack her sister.

"Castor Alexandra, that is enough. If you think for one second I didn't know what was going on at these parties or that you thought you were actually going, you were sadly mistaken." I was seething in anger, and I had every right to be. She had lied to me, just like she had tried to lie so many times before, and I couldn't understand why she kept acting like this.

Pulling away from me, she stepped back, her eyes filled with tears as she clenched her fists at her side. "Why are you always ruining everything? I can't wait to get out of here. Maybe my grandfather will have a better time teaching me to be who I am in the other realm than you would ever be able to do for me. You're not a mother, you're a dictator."

Like a dagger to my heart, I broke slowly. Whenever we got into an argument, she would say things she didn't mean, but never had she said anything this hurtful to me. Before I could even speak, a voice sounded behind me.

"Cassie, apologize to your mother right now." The sound of the voice belonged to Damien, and from the cologne I smelt, he wasn't alone. In fact, Hale was with him as well.

"I'm sorry, sweetie. I didn't mean to bother you both," I sighed, turning to face Damian and Hale. They had obviously been in the study down the hall, and while I was trying to get to the bottom of this, I didn't expect it to take the turn it had.

"Ivy, why are you apologizing?" Hale chuckled as he pulled me close to him. "Let Damian handle her, and then when Talon gets home, we can fill him in."

Over the years, it was clear that most of her traits came from Talon. Honestly, while we never actually tested who their fathers biologically were, we could tell Pollux and Castor were a mix of Hale and Talon.

God knows Cassie had Talon's temper.

"Dad, this isn't fair." She began to sob. "All I wanted to do was go to the party with everybody else. Why does Pollux get to do whatever he wants, and I don't?"

"Perhaps because Pollux is honest about what he's doing and doesn't try to lie whenever he wants to do something. You were trying to be deceitful again, young lady. And speaking to your mother like that? It's unacceptable." Damian didn't have to raise his voice at Cassie to get his point across.

In fact, he had never raised his voice to any of them.

The only one of my mates who ever got into it with anyone was Talon and Cassie. Both stubborn and hardheaded. Yet, they were very close and had a bond the rest of us would never understand. "So, what… I'm just supposed to stay here and do nothing? Everyone is going."

"Well, you should have thought about that before you acted the way you did." Damian sighed, shaking his head. "I'm sorry, Cassie, but you're grounded. Give me your phone."

"You can't be serious!" she yelled through the tears running down her face. "This is bullshit!"

"Castor, do not raise your voice at me again. Give me your phone, now," Damian calmly snapped with his hand held out, waiting for the device to be dropped within it.

Cassie hesitated for a moment, shaking her head before taking it from her back pocket and giving it to Damian. "I can't wait to turn eighteen. Then I'll finally be able to get out of here."

Damian was used to Cassie saying ridiculous things, and as I watched him sigh, he replied. "You say that now, Cassie… but one day, you're going to miss this place. One day, it will be gone, and you will wish to have it back. In fact, you will give anything to be here again. Trust me, I know this firsthand."

Hellish Mornings

Cassie

~Two Years Later~

"Girl, I'm so glad that these stupid-ass classes are almost done," Melissa said with excitement through the other end of my phone. She and I had been friends for as long as I could remember, and though we had both been through some crazy shit, I was glad I had this girl as my best friend.

"Yeah, soon we will be on to bigger and better things."

"Don't remind me," she groaned as I continued holding up different shirts to my body in front of the long mirror in my room. "I won't be able to make it without you."

Without me? Confusion settled in before laughter escaped me at her dramatic tone. "What are you talking about? I'm not going anywhere but to college with you. Unless you plan on making it with some other girl. Which, I mean, I'm gonna need to know her name, so I know exactly who to fuck up later."

"Oh, my god, stop," she sighed. "You know what I'm talking about."

I did know what she was referring to, but it wasn't going to happen. "Nope, I'm going with you, Melissa. Stop overcomplicating it."

For the past few years, I had been excited with the notion I was going to escape my pack life to go to college with Melissa—not to mention how amazing my life had gone over the past two years—I had no intentions of doing anything my parents wanted me to do.

I had gone from being a nobody who couldn't control her shit to having almost complete control—in my eyes—as I stayed at the top of my class in all subjects preparing for an amazing life of full-ride scholarships and future college parties.

There was no way I was giving any of that up for anything.

No matter what my parents had to say.

"Yeah, right? As much as I would love that, you can't get out of your obligations. Remember what Priscilla said..."

Thinking about the woman made me roll my eyes. "She is old and crazy. She has no idea what she is talking about. Now stop complaining and get your ass ready. I'm leaving shortly, and I expect you to be there when I get to school.

"Fine, calm your tits, woman," she said. "I'll be there in thirty."

My friend was always the dramatic one out of the two of us, but without her, I wouldn't be able to move through the day like I did. "Better. Don't forget, it's your turn to grab coffee."

"Shit... well, better make it forty then. See you soon."

"See ya." Cracking a smile, I hung up the phone, shaking my head. So much had changed over the past few months, and thinking about how our last year of school was about to end, I couldn't wait to move forward with my life.

"A week left, Cass..." I muttered to myself, finally happy with the black gothic look I sported. My deep purple and pink hair was a huge contrast against the skinny black jeans and tight blank tank top I wore.

It may not have been a look my mother approved of, but it was definitely me.

Taking a deep breath, I tried to ignore the ever-growing voices hidden within the deepest depths of my mind. I had done well the last two years, learning control over my powers and many other things.

After everything that had happened between my mother and me two years ago, my father Talon changed up the punishments Pollux and I usually received and, in doing so, actually found what helped to ground me.

Fighting was the only thing I knew anymore, and while I trained with my brother and the warriors, I did it in secret. My mother didn't approve, just like the many other things she didn't approve of, but it was the one thing my father Talon stood beside adamantly.

"Cass, are you ready to go?" Pollux's voice called from my doorway, causing me to gaze at him from the long mirror I currently stood in front of.

"Yeah, I'll be there in a sec."

"Sure, whatever," he scoffed, flipping the long strands of black hair from his face before disappearing down the hallway. "Just don't take forever, otherwise, I fucking leaving you."

The sound of his voice trailing down the hallway toward my room caused me to roll my eyes. It was always the same with him anymore. The moment he got hurt playing football and was told he couldn't play anymore, he became a complete asshole.

Thank god daddy Damian was able to keep him busy preparing to take over the pack from Hale one day. Otherwise, he may have taken out his anger on everyone else around him.

Grabbing my black leather jacket, I slid on my tennis shoes and snatched my backpack on the way out of my room. Never in my life did I find myself excited to go to school until I was so close to finishing. It was the best birthday present a girl could have, finishing school two days before you turned eighteen.

The moment my feet hit the floor at the bottom of the stairs, the chaos of my family consumed me. My younger siblings ran around screaming and yelling at each other. My mother was busy making lunches in the kitchen while my father, James, finished preparing breakfast.

It was a whirlwind of chaos, but I loved it.

It reminded me I was real sometimes, and within the chaos surrounding me, I felt nothing but love. Even if the majority of them got on my nerves half the time.

"Oh, Cassie." My mother smiled as she wiped her hands on a kitchen towel. "Can you do me a huge favor on your way home today, please?"

Letting out a soft sigh, I pushed a smile onto my face. "Sure, what's up?"

"Can you just run by the pharmacy and pick up Tatum's medicine, please? It would be a huge help. He isn't having the best day today, and I don't want to take him out. Not to mention everyone else is busy..."

Tatum was the youngest of my siblings at only nine, and unfortunately, last year was diagnosed with a rare condition that quickly changed all of our lives. "Of course, Mom. No problem."

Tatum's eyes met mine as he rounded the corner into the kitchen, coughing. The dark swells under his eyes were a huge contrast to his pale white skin, and every time I saw him, I prayed I had the power to change his fate.

"Cassie." He smiled as he wrapped his arms around my waist. "Are you leaving for school?"

"Yeah, buddy. I'll be home a little early today, though, since it's only a half day. Maybe when I get home, we can climb into my bed and watch a movie. Does that sound good to you?" I asked, watching his eyes light up with excitement.

"Yes. I can't wait! We can watch the new dinosaur movie that came out."

Tatum continued to ramble, making my mom smile behind tired eyes. "Alright, sweetie. Cassie has to get going, so why don't you go eat your breakfast daddy made, and then we can get you sorted for the day."

He didn't hesitate to do what he was told, which made my mother happy because out of all her children, he was the only one who never gave her any problems. Gazing around the room at everyone who was here, I tried to imagine what it would be like once I went off to college.

I wouldn't have the continued chaos anymore. I wouldn't have dad's amazing breakfasts or even mom's homemade lunches. The thought alone made me want to change my mind, but pursuing my dreams of becoming a doctor wasn't something I was willing to give up. Even if no one knew, that's what I wanted to do.

"Cass, come on, Jesus Christ!" Pollux yelled from the front door, causing me to cringe as I rolled my eyes.

"I'm coming. Calm down," my grumbled response seemed to make him simmer, and after grabbing a piece of toast from the counter, I quickly followed him out the front door towards his charcoal gray four-door truck, lifted too high for my liking.

"I'm seriously going to start leaving you if you keep this shit up in the morning, Cass."

The moment I closed the door and the truck started down the road, I was quickly on my phone, trying to ignore his lame-ass music. "You know you won't leave me there, Pollux. I don't know why you constantly threaten it."

"Would you stop fucking calling me that?" he snapped. "It's just Lux. No one calls me Pollux but you and mom."

Glancing at him from the corner of my eyes, I scoffed with a smirk. "It's your name."

"I fucking know that, Captain Obvious, but I can't stand it, so fucking call me Lux or don't talk to me. I don't understand what's so difficult about that."

One would have thought because we were twins, we were close, but the answer to that was absolutely not. We may have been similar in many ways, but being close wasn't something we had been in a very long time.

Since the day we got our powers, actually.

"Whatever... Lux..." I replied sarcastically as I rolled my eyes and went back to scrolling through my phone. "Are you going to the party this weekend?"

"Yeah, don't I always," he sneered with irritation. "You're not going, though."

"Excuse me?" Laughter escaped me at his comment. Every time there was a party, he tried to ensure I couldn't go, and yet I always found my way there despite his efforts. "You can't tell me what to do, Pollux."

Gripping the steering wheel, he turned his gaze towards me as anger seethed in his eyes. "Cass... I'm not telling you again."

Never had I been so excited to see school as I was during this argument between him and me. The last thing I wanted was Lux ruining my morning with another lecture just because he was the future Alpha of the pack.

As soon as the truck pulled into his parking space, his many groupies flocked to the vehicle, wanting to be the first ones to greet him. And quickly, I was a ghost of a thought.

It was just how I liked it, though, and as my eyes landed on Melissa—with two cups of coffee—my excitement for school grew. "Have a fabulous day, brother dearest. Try not to catch something from these whores."

Stepping out of the truck, I ignored Lux's snappy comeback as I beelined straight for Melissa. Leggings and a hoodie were her favorites, and as I approached her messy bun, no makeup look, I couldn't help but smile. "Oh my God, you're a lifesaver right now."

Smirking, she shrugged her shoulders as she took a sip of her coffee. "I take it the morning drive was eventful?"

Eventful would be an understatement. "If you only knew."

Laughter fell between Melissa and me as we walked toward the towering brick building in front of us. The echoing sound of the school bell rang in the distance as the many voices of students rushed to class past my ears.

This place had been hell to me for many years, and now that I was done with it, I couldn't help but think of how bittersweet it really had been.

"Are you going to miss this place when we graduate?" Melissa asked, drawing me from the many thoughts which had been circulating through my mind.

"I don't know. I guess part of me will just because I made so many memories here."

"Yeah, I guess you're right," she muttered as we passed the double doors, making our way toward our lockers. "We should do something epic, though, before we go."

Glancing at her, an amused grin crossed my lips. "Epic? What do you have in mind?"

She shrugged her shoulders with a smile as we reached our lockers. "Well, for one, I think you should put Ashley in her place before the end of the year. That would definitely be the start of going out with a bang."

Ashley was the harlot who hung around my brother. The cheerleader type who was dead set on becoming the next Luna of our pack, even though she wasn't his mate. Something I was able to see the moment I met her.

In our world, you were able to find your mate when you turned eighteen, and even though none of us were eighteen, I had the gift of foresight, and she wasn't the girl I had seen my brother with.

"As much as I would love to do that, Melissa. She will be put in her place at our party. Lux will see she isn't his mate, and he will get rid of her."

"...and if he doesn't," she muttered, causing me to sigh.

"He will... he is the next Alpha, and my fathers have instilled the mate bond stuff into us since we were kids. I can't tell you how many times I heard the story of our my parents found each other."

It was a story everyone in the pack loved to tell, but so cringe-worthy, I was perfectly fine never hearing it again.

"Yeah, well, right now, he doesn't look like he cares. The two of them are headed straight for you." Turning to look over my shoulder, I noted what Melissa was talking about. Lux was making his way towards me with Ashley at his side, and considering the grim expression on his face and the ecstatic one on hers... something was up.

"Shit... and here I thought I'd enjoy my coffee in peace this morning."

Hallway Fallout

Pollux

~Fifteen minutes earlier~

I didn't understand why my sister thought she could act however she wanted. We were the future of the pack, and instead of growing up and doing what needed to be done, she continuously acted like a child. Watching her make her way toward her friend Melissa with her hot pink hair swinging behind her, I groaned.

She would be the death of me if I didn't get her under control.

"Lux! Baby, I missed you!" Ashley's high-pitched voice met my ears the moment I opened my truck door. The girl was gorgeous for sure, and in bed, she got the job done, but other than that, she honestly had nothing going for her.

"Hey, Ashley," I replied flatly, watching the disappointment on her face surface at my greeting. It didn't matter what she did, I couldn't get behind the overly affectionate shit she was into. It just wasn't me, and honestly, the last few weeks, I had been second-guessing why I even had her around in the first place.

Closing my truck door, her slender figure wrapped around my bicep, pulling me closer to her. She wasn't the only one to come flocking towards me the moment I arrived at school, but she was the only one to cling to me like a child clinging to its mother.

Something I found to be rather annoying.

"So, I was thinking about the party, and I thought maybe we can go shopping after school to pick out our matching outfits. It's going to be a very big night when the pack is introduced to their future Alpha and Luna together."

"What?" I muttered, furrowing my gaze at her with confusion. "What are you talking about?"

Giving me a dumbfounded look, she shrugged her shoulders with a small laugh. "Uh—us, being proclaimed the Luna and Alpha of the pack. Did you hit your head this morning or something?"

"No." I sighed, moving towards the school. "Just don't get overexcited when there is a chance we may not be mates."

Gripping my upper arm, she stopped me in my tracks and turned me to face her. "How could you say something like that? Mate or not, we are going to be together. We are good together, and you know it."

Disgust filled me hearing what she said. Mates were a precious thing, and I would only be with my mate in the end. Sure, Ashley and I had hooked up many times. Shit, she wasn't the only girl I had hooked up with, but at the end of the day, my Luna would be my mate, and I didn't care what Ashley or any of the others had to say about that. "Let's go. I don't want to be late for class."

With a nod of her head, we continued towards the large brick school building in front of us. Ashley and her friends talked about Cassie and my birthday party this weekend as if it was the highlight event of the year.

Which, in the past, it always had been. This year, however, felt much different.

There was something in the air that felt wrong, and the closer and closer it got to the big day, the more on edge I was with everything. Almost as if my wolf could feel something big was going to happen.

"I'm so excited. I wonder what Cassie is wearing this year." One of the girls giggled. "I'm sure something sexy for Lucas…"

Ashley quickly hushed the girl as they stifled their laughter, trying not to draw attention to themselves, but I had heard the words the girl spoke, and my sister's and Lucas' names in the same sentence wasn't something I was happy about.

"What did you just say?" I asked, spinning around to face them.

"It's nothing, Lux. Just some silly little rumor," Ashley stammered, pushing a smile on her face. "Come on, we can't be late."

"Shut up, Ashley. I want to know what she said right now."

Ashley stepped back a bit, her eyes gazing around toward her friends as she bit her bottom lip. "Well, rumor has it that Cassie has been seeing Lucas Vega and that they are... well, you know."

Lucas Vega was the area's notorious bad boy and the only person I hated in this pack. His mother was the pack's librarian, and the two came to us about seven years ago after his mother was widowed. I didn't trust the punk-ass kid as far as I could throw him, and everyone else typically stayed away from him.

Go figure my sister would be one of the ones who didn't.

"How do you know this?" I snapped at them, not caring Ashley was one of the people I was taking my anger out on.

"Seth saw Cassie talking to Lucas at the Hill party and told his sister Lauren, who you know is like my best friend—"

"Damn it, Ashley, get to the point already."

Flinching at my tone, she quickly stumbled through her response. "Seth saw Cassie and Lucas disappear into the woods together, and when Cassie came out later, she was alone and fixing her clothing."

The stammered words spoken by Ashley set my blood on fire.

How could my sister act like this, knowing what kind of people we were and who he was?

Turning, I headed straight for Cassie's locker. If she thought she was going to act like a slut, she was sadly mistaken because my sister wasn't going to whore herself out to the pack reject.

The moment I turned the corner and locked eyes on Cassie, who stood with her friend Melissa, I gritted my teeth, seething with anger. "Cassie!"

She spun around to face me, and as she did, her eyes widened. "Why do you look like someone pissed in your coffee this morning?"

"Are you fucking Lucas Vega?"

The question came out quickly as I all but yelled at her, causing her to choke on the coffee she was sipping. "What?!"

"You heard me, Cassie. Word has it you were seen fucking him at the last party."

The conversation was definitely meant for behind closed doors, and from the red tinge of her cheeks, I could see embarrassment growing inside her. Classmates of ours began to linger around, whispering to each other as they stared at us, but I didn't care.

I wanted the truth, and I wanted it now.

"Are you kidding me right now?" she whispered loudly as she stepped closer. "How dare you speak to me like that?"

"I have a right to know if my sister is whoring herself out to the pack. I'm the future Alpha, and I have to know my people, even if it's someone who lives under my roof."

Sudden laughter escaped Cassie as she stood shaking her head at me. "Are you fucking serious right now? First of all, they aren't your people yet. Second of all, we live in our parent's house so I don't know what roof you think you fucking own. Lastly, how dare you act like this toward me? I am your sister..." she hesitated for a moment as her eyes shifted towards Ashley and her friends before glaring back at me, "...you seriously choose to listen to the gossip of your dumbass girlfriend and her crowd of pink Barbies...pathetic. Get your shit together, Pollux."

The way she spoke to me in front of so many people caused collective gasps to filter through the air. Cassie had publicly embarrassed me for the last time, and if my parents weren't going to do anything about her, then I would make it my job to do so.

As Cassie turned to walk away from me, I reached out and grabbed Cassie's shoulder, spinning her around to make sure she faced me. I was going to make her realize I wasn't someone she was going to cross, whether she was my sister or not. "You're going to listen to me."

Anger blew through her eyes as they slowly began to swirl with the celestial color I knew all too well. She wasn't one to mess with, and with these stupid fucking powers, she had been nothing but a problem.

She shouldn't have been as powerful as she was.

That was supposed to have been reserved for me.

"Pollux, you know exactly what happened the last time you tried me like this. So you can either get the fuck off of me and walk away, or you and I are going to have bigger problems than what your girlfriend said."

"You need to watch your tone, Castor. You will respect me, as I deserve to be respected." I hoped she would have bowed down like I had expected any other person to do, but instead, Cassie began to laugh in a maniacal way, making me hesitate.

Before the commotion could continue any further, a voice called out, stopping us in our tracks. Our father, James, had exited a classroom somewhere nearby and was seen storming through the hallway straight for us.

Both mine and Cassie's eyes darted in the direction of where he was, and with his narrowed gaze and clenched fist, I knew we were in trouble.

"What is going on?" he demanded as Cassie quickly turned off the angry scowl she wore and put on the biggest puppy dog pout.

"Dad, I didn't do anything. I was just at my locker, and Lux came over here storming up out of control, accusing me of being seen with this guy just because his girlfriend and her Barbie friends said that somebody had seen me with him at a party."

Everybody around was listening to the conversation. It was clear Cassie was being overdramatic to try and make me look bad. Looking around the hallway, he frowned at the other students. "Don't you all have class!"

He was pissed, and as the kids who lingered around quickly disappeared. He turned his gaze to me. "The two of you in my office, now."

Our father was a very calm and kosher man. However, when things got out of control, or we misbehaved, he took it seriously. As soon as we turned down the hallway, the door to his room came into view.

"I don't know the truth behind what happened, and honestly, I don't care. The fact of the matter is I could feel your power, Cassie, from right down the hall to where I was, and that is not good for anybody," he said as he closed his office door.

"I'm sorry," she whispered, causing a smirk to cross my face.

I was glad to see Cassie getting what she deserved. Yet, when his gaze turned to me, it became even angrier. "I don't see what you think is so amusing, Pollux. You are the one that initiated this entire thing."

Standing straight with my mouth open, I shook my head. "No, I didn't. She started it by going off with Lucas at some damn party, trying to make herself look like a whore in front of the entire pack."

"Excuse me?! Did you just call your sister a fucking whore? Have you lost your goddamn mind? Do you know what Damian, or even Talon and your mother would say, hearing you talk about your own sister like this?"

Guilt filled me. Mom was everything to me. She was beautiful and graceful. Everything a boy could ever wish to have in a mother, she was the person I was the closest to out of all of them.

I knew my mother wouldn't have been pleased with how I treated Cassie today—especially invoking her powers the way that I had. "There's no need to tell her what happened. I'm sorry."

I quickly bowed to the situation, not wanting to escalate it any further, and as I apologized, Cassie turned her frown into a smile, shrugging her shoulders as she shook her head.

"Look, we will deal with this at home, but for right now, both of you get to fucking class, and don't let me hear that any kind of situation happened again. Stay away from each other," James replied, pinching the bridge of his nose in frustration.

"Wait, what?" Cassie said quickly. "He's my ride home, though, and we have to stop at the pharmacy to get the medicine mom needed."

"I'm not taking you anywhere," I interjected, refusing to be in the same vehicle with her. "Looks like you better walk or ask your friend to take you."

"That medication is for our little brother. Are you fucking kidding me?"

"Cassie, I will take you, sweetie. Just meet me here when you're done with your last class. I needed to go by the store to grab a few things for dinner anyway," James sighed, causing her to nod her head but then scowl at me.

"Fine." There was no need for any other conversation to be had, and as we both exited our father's office to go our separate ways, I couldn't help but wonder if I did fuck up in regards to this situation.

Sure, my sister pissed me off to no end, but thinking back on it now, I didn't act like an Alpha. Instead, I acted like an asshole, and the entire student body got to see me mistreating my sister over a rumor.

I wouldn't allow her to be with someone like Lucas, but as soon as I was the Alpha, I was going to make sure she was paired with someone respectable. There was no way in hell I would allow her to continue to be the loose cannon she was.

She needed a mate, and if she couldn't find hers soon... well, I'd force her to mate with someone else. That way, they could keep her ass in line.

Words of Wisdom

Cassie

I couldn't believe Pollux acted the way he did in front of everybody, making me look like a complete fool. Then to call me a whore! Who did he honestly think he was?

Rage bubbled through me as my blood boiled with anger over the entire situation. I wasn't sure who my brother thought he was, speaking to me the way that he did but thankfully, James had stepped in to stop the situation.

The moment Pollux grabbed me and forced me to stay to try and listen to him, I felt myself losing control, and that was something I didn't do often.

Walking into my English class, I spotted Melissa sitting in our usual spot, her eyes meeting mine slightly widened as the other students looked at me with curiosity. It wasn't that I wanted people to fear me, but most people at this school did.

I simply just ignored it, because after I graduated I was out of this fucking place.

Moving towards the back of the classroom, I beelined straight for my seat. Melissa had a grin on her face spread ear to ear, and I could only imagine the questions she would end up throwing my way. It wasn't the first time she witnessed one of our dads pulling us off to the side to have a sit down, and I doubted it would be the last.

Plopping down at my desk, I pulled out my notebook and opened it to where we had left off with notes for the exam notes from the day before. Final exams were Friday, and then I would be free from this prison of a school with graduation the following week.

The one thing keeping me sane every single day I woke up was knowing I would be leaving this place soon, and Melissa and I would be starting over somewhere new.

"OK, class, now that our last participant finally decided to arrive, please go ahead and open your notebooks if you haven't so I can go over everything that you're going to need to study for Friday's exam," Miss Abel said as she turned towards the board and began to write down various different things we were expected to take notes on.

She was an older woman with graying brown hair and thick-framed glasses. She had been in the pack for as long as I can remember, and even though she was nice to everyone else, she, for some reason, couldn't stand me.

"How did it go?" Melissa whispered, causing me to look at her from the corner of my eye. "Was it bad?"

"Just as you would have expected," I replied with a sigh, trying to keep my tone down low so Miss Abel wouldn't hear us having a conversation while she was trying to teach class. That pissed her off more than anything.

Interrupting students with a bad attitude. Also known as me... she hated me.

"Did your dad ground you from the party this weekend? We had plans, Cass."

Scoffing with laughter, I shook my head in amusement. "It's my party. Why would they turn around and not let me go to my own birthday party?"

"True," she said, pointedly letting out a sigh of relief. "I'd cry if that happened."

The gleam of the sun through the open window caught her just right at the moment, making her seem as if she were glowing. There was something about my friend I found extremely attractive, from the soft brown waves of her hair to the dark charcoal-colored gray of her eyes. She was beautiful, even though she didn't think she was.

Melissa wasn't just beautiful. She was extremely intelligent, and though her flat chest, stick-figured body gave her a lack of confidence she shouldn't have, I couldn't help but admire how increasingly lucky I was to have her by my side.

She had stuck by me through everything, and I was grateful. However, even though she was only my friend, every now and again, I couldn't help but wonder what it would be like to taste those plump pink lips of hers and have her as more than just my friend.

"Are you listening to me?" she whispered, pulling me out of the daze I was in. I hadn't been listening. I had been thinking of the many things we could do together and in doing so, completely embarrassed myself.

The heat of my embarrassment was upon my cheeks as I pushed a smile on my face and shrugged my shoulders. "Sorry, I was just thinking about something. What did you say?"

Rolling her eyes, she smiled. "I was asking you if what they said about you and Lucas was true."

Lucas. I couldn't help but laugh to myself, thinking about what they said. Yes, it was true. I had been seen going into the woods with him, but as far as having sex with him, absolutely not. He had bet me I couldn't beat him in a race with my wolf, and of course, I proved him wrong.

After beating his ass in the race, I left him in the dust to wander his way back to the encampment, where I turned around and took his clothes. That way, he would only be able to maneuver back through the party either naked or in his shifted form.

Lucas was incredibly sexy, and yeah, sometimes I felt the urge to want to do more with him, but that definitely wasn't going to happen anytime soon. I wasn't a virgin, but I also wasn't looking unless you count on being interested in my best friend.

I had too much to focus on worrying about stuff like that.

"No, Melissa, don't you think I would have told you had I hooked up with Lucas? You know how I feel about that stuff. I'm focusing on what's to come.

I mean, we have a future we're going to be entertaining once we get out of this place. I'm not looking to make a mistake."

The sound of Miss Abel clearing her voice loudly caught my attention, and glancing toward her, I noticed everybody in the class had turned and looked at me. "I'm sorry, ladies. Am I interrupting an important conversation? Because I could have sworn, I was teaching about the final exams you have this Friday. I'd prefer not to see you again after this year."

Ouch, that was unnecessary. "My apologies, Miss Abel. I can assure you that Melissa and I will pass your exam because we don't really want to see you anymore, either." My classmates turned into a fit of snickering, causing Miss Abel's face to go red.

"Then you won't mind spending the rest of your afternoon in detention."

"Unfortunately, as lovely as that sounds, Miss Abel, James already has plans for me after school and, therefore, I won't be able to attend," I replied, trying to make it seem like there was no way she could keep me, but instead the fucking woman went to the phone, picked it up and undoubtedly called my father.

After a few moments, she hung up the phone with a smile on her face as the hatred of her poured into my heart. "Good news. Your father told me to tell you he'll pick up the medication for you so you can stay here until four o'clock when detention is over."

"Shit," I muttered with irritation. She couldn't be fucking serious.

As I turned my gaze back to Melissa, she quickly shut her mouth, shaking her head. There was no way in hell she was going to spend detention with me, even if she was my best friend. She had shit to do, and I knew it.

By the time class was done and I finally made my way from the hell of Miss Abel, I left class with Melissa at my side in search of a vending machine. I was stressed, and a cold soda was just the amount of caffeine I needed to get through my next class.

"I can't believe that you got detention. Do you just enjoy pissing her off?" Melissa asked while digging through her purse to pull out a piece of gum.

"She's a cow," I replied, rolling my eyes. "I could breathe the wrong way, and she would try to turn it into a reason to call my parents and put me into detention."

"That may be true, but you still could have behaved for the next few days. I mean, come on, Cassie, it's the last week of school."

As our banter continued back and forth, I didn't hear the approaching footsteps and laughter of Ashley and her posse of irritating ass-kissers, but when I turned around, she stood there expectantly as if she had something to say.

"Can I help you?" I said flatly as I opened my soda and proceeded to drink from it. I only had ten minutes until my next class, and the last thing I wanted to do was entertain her.

With long blonde hair and makeup plastered onto her face, she was the spitting image of Barbie, simply missing her Malibu beach doll house. She may have been dating my brother and had been for years, but I knew that was only because she suckered him in.

The girl was a nobody, and then over the summer in seventh grade, she blossomed or did something because she came back to school in eighth grade with boobs, a tiny waist, and all sorts of other enhancements.

Then her attention was on my brother.

She stared at me for a moment, crossing her arms over her shoulders as she looked at her perfectly manicured nails. "I just wanted to remind you not to be an embarrassment this weekend. It may be your birthday too, but it's about Lux and me. We will be announced as the New Luna and Alpha of the pack."

Laughter erupted from my throat as I looked over at Melissa, who was laughing her ass off, too. I had to give it to Ashley, she was pretty damn confident and yet didn't realize how ridiculous she sounded.

"You do realize that's not how that works, right? Lux has to go into training for a year without you because you're not allowed to go and even if he didn't have to do that, my parents aren't stepping down anytime soon. He could be in his thirties before he actually becomes the Alpha and I don't even know why you think you're going to be Luna. You're not even his mate."

"You don't know that!" she snapped, stomping her foot on the ground. "I am his!"

Her frustration was entertaining, and as I looked at her friends, I could see how confused they were over what I said. "Y'all didn't actually believe she was going to be Luna, did you? My brother can barely stand to be around her anymore."

I couldn't quite understand why she was delusional enough to think she was going to be the woman he spent his life with.

My brother and I fought like cats and dogs, but I knew my brother well enough to know he would never spend his life with a woman like Ashley. He wanted someone who would support and challenge him at times. Not some idiot who thought herself a pampered princess.

Gasping with a faint heart expression, she stared at me with wide eyes. "How dare you speak to me like that? You have no right. My position with Lux gives me authority over you—"

"I'm going to stop you right there," I sighed with a smile as I cut her off mid-speech. "You have no authority over me, and you need to learn that very quickly. If you can't see how uninterested my brother has been in you lately, that's your problem. I don't blame him for sleeping with you. Why go searching for something when you can easily pick up the phone and have it delivered..."

A look of utter shock and disbelief crossed her face as I pushed past her with Melissa. She was as speechless as the girls with her, but as I continued walking, she let out a scream of anger. "You will regret this!"

I didn't bother to turn around and look at her. Instead, I waved my hand in the air before giving her the middle finger as I kept walking away. "Whatever you have to tell yourself to make yourself feel better, Ashley. Keep up the good work. Maybe being easy will pay off for you someday."

Melissa grabbed my arm, laughing as we continued walking down the hall, leaving Ashley behind us to stew over my words of wisdom. I didn't care if she cried and complained to anyone or even plotted against me.

She wasn't my problem, and if she pissed me off enough, she would simply meet a side of me that would haunt her dreams for the rest of her life.

Lucas Vega

Cassie

The moment the last bell rang, I groaned. It was time to serve out my detention, and as much as I wanted to dip and go home, I knew I couldn't. I would just get lectured by my parents and then have to do it tomorrow anyways.

Grabbing my belongings and shoving them into my bag, I sighed as I stood to my feet, walking out of my last classroom. Miss Abel's class was downstairs, and the quicker I got there to serve out detention, the faster I could leave.

However, as soon as I got to the bottom of the stairs, I spotted Miss Abel with all of her belongings walking down the hall. Had she forgotten I had detention?

"Are we not doing this today, then?" I asked flatly, curious as to where she seemed to be going in such a good mood. Turning to face me, she smiled and shook her head.

"Oh, you are. I forgot to tell you, I actually have something to do after school, so you're going to be serving out detention in the library with Mr. Danton." Judging by the smug expression on her face, she knew full well I couldn't stand the gym teacher.

Mr. Danton was enough to make me want to claw her eyes, but instead, I turned away.

Fists clenched with my irritation at an all-time high, I fixed the bag on my shoulder and made my way toward the library. If I had to endure dealing with

Mr. Danton, then so be it. At least in a few days, I would never have to see his smug face again.

The moment I got there, I instantly regretted everything I had said earlier to piss Miss Abel off because the only other fucking person in the library serving out detention was goddamn Lucas Vega.

His dark, mesmerizing eyes met mine, and as they did, a sick, sadistic smirk crossed his lips. There was an air about him that screamed mysteriousness. He had black, spiky, clean-cut hair and wore dark designer jeans and a black, tight-fitted t-shirt adorned with a black leather jacket. His look screamed walking sex machine.

"Interesting." His words pulled me back to the present, and as it did, I frowned.

Interesting? I didn't know what he found interesting about this, but as soon as Mr. Danton looked up from the desk he sat behind, a smile grew wide across his face.

"Well, well, well." Mr. Danton laughed with amusement. "It's nice to see you again, Cassie. Unfortunately, I wish it would have been on better terms."

"Yeah, sure," I replied flatly as I moved towards a table on the far side of the room. The farther away from Lucas, the better. As much as I had enjoyed making a fool of him that night, I didn't care to be around him. He was incredibly annoying, and with Pollux acting like a dick about Lucas, I didn't want to give him more reason to be on my ass.

Placing down my bag and pulling out my books, I tried to dive into the schoolwork my teachers decided I needed to complete before the end of the week. All of it I found pointless considering it was the end of the year, and with my perfect GPA, I wasn't worried about failing.

Nevertheless, I dived into it trying to ignore the stare Lucas was sending from across the room. His dark eyes bore into my head as I tried to feverishly ignore it.

It wasn't until Mr. Danton stood to his feet and moved around from the desk. I finally looked up and away from my schoolwork. "Alright, you two. I'm going to go take a break. Try not to get into trouble while I'm away."

From what I had heard from other students, when Mr. Danton took a break, he was typically gone until detention was over. I contemplated skipping the rest of it and leaving to head home, but knowing my luck, I'd get caught.

The moment the door closed and Mr. Danton disappeared, Lucas appeared in front of me on the other side of the table. "You and I need to have a little talk."

Glancing up at him, I laughed, shaking my head as I took my books and placed them back into my bag. If there was going to be an altercation, the last thing I wanted was for my shit to spread across the room in utter chaos.

"There's nothing to discuss, Vega. Leave me alone."

"No, no." He laughed, causing me to grit my teeth with irritation. "You don't get to do that. We have shit to discuss, and you're not leaving here until we do."

Leaning back in my chair with my arms crossed, I stared at him. There was no way he was going to dictate what was going to happen. "You're annoying, you know that, right?"

"I'm annoying?" He scoffed with a smile. "Says the girl who stole my clothes and made me walk naked through a party."

"You actually walked naked?" Laughter escaped me as I tried to visualize that event. It had obviously happened after I left that night, and even though Lucas irritated me, I was intrigued by the notion of seeing him naked.

"Hey, stop eye fucking me and pay attention," he snapped, causing me to roll my eyes.

"Keep dreaming. You stand no chance with me, Vega. I'd never fuck you, regardless of what people seem to want to think about what we did at that party."

"Yes, the party..." he echoed as he paced the area with a smile on his face. "So, it occurred to me that night we have something more in common than just being the outcast assholes of the pack."

Outcast? Who the hell said I was an outcast?

"I'm not—"

Holding his hand up, he cut me off, causing me to stare at him with my lips parted in disgust. "I wasn't finished, Cassie."

"I don't care if we're finished or not. Don't ever cut me off like that again."

"Or what?" he scoffed. "What are you honestly going to do besides sit there and get pissy like you always do?"

"Careful, or you might get hurt. I'm not someone you want to anger."

Usually the threat worked on people, but for some reason with Lucas Vega, he did not give a shit about what I was saying. Instead, he laughed and leaned over the table. "If you think that you can intimidate me, you're wrong, cupcake. Nothing about who you are scares me."

Shock was the only thing I felt as I stared at him, dumbfounded, trying to process the fact he wasn't scared of me. Everyone was scared of me. There was no way he wasn't. That just didn't make sense. "What?"

"Cat got your tongue, Cassie?" He laughed. "You heard what I said. You're nothing but entitled and hiding behind who your parents are.

Standing to my feet, I slammed my hands down on the table staring at him. "Don't make me fucking hurt you, Vega. Stay away from me, and don't speak. This is your last warning."

I didn't wait for him to respond as I grabbed my bag and threw it over my shoulder. I was done with detention for the day, for the rest of my life... I wasn't doing this shit with him or anyone else for that matter.

If Mr. Danton didn't like it too fucking bad.

As I moved across the room, Lucas quickly sped in front of me, blocking my way out. I wasn't sure what his problem was or why he was doing this, but it was getting on my last fucking nerve. "Would you get the fuck out of my way?"

"No," he said flatly, crossing his arms over his chest. "Not until we talk properly."

"Oh, my God. Seriously? We have nothing to fucking talk about."

It was enough to have to be stuck here with him, but having him try to keep me hostage because he wanted to speak with me was icing on the cake. No matter how much I tried to show him I didn't want anything to do with him, he was resilient in his efforts to make me talk to him.

Sagging his shoulders, he smirked. "Are you done?"

Groaning loudly in frustration, I shoved him back, watching as he stumbled laughing while I pushed past him to grab the handle of the library door, exiting into the hallway. I didn't care about Lucas nor did I care that he was currently following me down the hallway as I pushed through the double doors and welcomed the cool air.

I didn't have a car considering the Alpha, my father Hale, took my car after my late-night joy rides over a month ago. But I was never opposed to walking, and so when he took it, that's what I started doing. I walked or would simply catch a ride with Lux.

Which, of course, had come to an end after our fight this morning.

"Where are you going?" Lucas called from behind me as I made my way through the field near the school toward the treeline. It was a fifteen-minute drive from my house to the school, and walking would take close to an hour.

However, shifting into my wolf would take a lot less longer.

"Dude, are you going to just ignore me?" he called again as I got closer to the shadows within the trees, a welcoming sight as I sat my bag down and slowly stripped.

"That was the plan," I sighed as I slid off my shirt and stuffed it into my backpack before slowly unbuttoning my jeans. I didn't understand why he was so persistent, and why he continued to follow me when neither of us even liked each other.

"So you're just going to shift and run home? I have a vehicle. I can take you."

Glancing over my shoulder at him, I scoffed with a smile. "Yeah, and run the risk of my brother tripping out again. No thanks."

"You're worried about what he thinks? I didn't peg you for being one of those kinds of girls."

Sliding my pants completely down, I picked them up and shoved them into my bag as well before turning around to face him. His eyes instinctively scanned down my body, and as those sultry eyes took me in, I couldn't help but feel attracted to him in the moment. The sensation running through me quickly shut down when I realized he was Lucas Vega and I wasn't interested.

"There is a lot about me that you don't know, Vega."

Stepping closer to me, my heart quickened with every step he took. It wasn't until he was a foot in front of me I felt completely exposed, not just in physical presence but also mentally. Never had anyone made me feel this way, and Lucas Vega was the last person I would ever have expected to make me feel the way I did.

For some reason, no matter how much I tried to resist the dark gaze he gave me, and the way his close proximity set my body on fire, I couldn't. I was conflicted beyond all rationality, wanting a man I couldn't actually have.

"I'd like to know more..." he whispered, reaching up to brush a strand of hair from my face. "If you'd let me."

There were many ways this moment could have gone, but there was no way I was going to give in to the urges we both had. "There's no point in getting to know me."

Letting the turn come over me, he jumped back from where I stood until the fur of my wolf broke through me, and my enormous beast stood before him. My black coat was purer than most, and with my celestial eyes still on display, I was an intimidating sight to behold.

"Gorgeous." He smirked as I huffed in displeasure, picking up my backpack in my mouth before turning and darting off into the forest.

If Lucas Vega thought flattery would allow him to get close to me, he was sadly mistaken.

Consequences

Cassie

There was nothing like running through the forest to clear one's mind. Yet, as my home came into view through the clearing of the forest, I couldn't help but wonder why Lucas Vega suddenly had taken such an interest in me. The way he made me feel caused my heart to race with anticipation.

I shouldn't feel like this, and I definitely shouldn't be so worked up.

It was ridiculous.

As soon as I approached the treeline, I let the change come back over me. The breaking and shifting of my bones caused me to moan softly as I finally took my last step back into my human form. Growing up, no one ever expected we would have been able to shift into wolves simply because our mother hadn't been able to.

At least not like a normal shifter.

Yet, we took after our fathers... the Lycan and shifter genes running through our veins.

Searching through my backpack, I pulled out my clothes and quickly put them on. I didn't bother messing with my shoes as I stepped from the treeline, slugging my backpack over my shoulder as my bare feet touched the soft texture of the grass below.

The sun had begun to set in the horizon and with its disappearance, shadows circulated over the land, highlighting the lighting within my home through the windows.

To think, in just over a week, I would be on my way towards the coast to start my new life with Melissa. Away from the troubles this pack has brought me since the day I came into my powers. No longer would I have people staring at me like I was odd.

Instead, I would blend in and have a normal life.

"Cassie, is that you?" My mother's voice called out as I closed the door behind me.

"Yeah, sorry I'm late. I had to stay after school."

Her slim body came into view and her long, dark silvering hair pulled up into a bun on her head, she frowned while drying her hands with a tea towel. "Yes, your father told me. Go get changed, Cassie. Talon and Hale are waiting in the study for you."

Shit. Throwing my head back, I groaned inwardly, letting out a heavy sigh before nodding and heading up the stairs towards my bedroom. I already knew the lecture awaiting me, but thankfully, knowing how my parents were, I would be able to take a quick shower and change before going to face the wrath of the Sølvmåne twins.

***

As soon as I stepped from the shower, completely refreshed and feeling like myself again, I threw on a pair of shorts and a t-shirt before heading towards the study. I was prepared for the lecture that was to come, but as soon as I knocked on the door and entered, I was shocked to see the concerned looks on their faces instead of angry scowls.

"Cassie, take a seat sweetie," Hale said as he gestured towards the sofa. My eyes scanned the room, taking in the disarray of books and papers littering the area as I made myself comfortable on the gray microfiber sofa near the fire.

"What's going on?" Play innocent and stupid, and maybe they will buy it.

Talon frowned at me, shaking his head. "We heard about today, Cassie."

"That wasn't entirely my fault—"

Hale gave me a stern look, causing me to stop talking. Out of all my parental figures, these two were the only ones I refused to argue with. Just because the connection with them was different from everyone else, and, honestly, I knew the truth.

Hale and Talon were mine and Pollux's fathers.

In some weird kind of way, I tried not to think too much about it.

"Cassie, you can't keep acting the way you have been. You and Lux are the future leaders of this pack, and the fighting and arguing doesn't help. You can't work against each other, you have to work with each other," Hale said softly as he stood from where he sat and moved to sit next to me.

Tears brimmed my eyes at his words. I hated disappointing them, but at the same time, I hated Pollux treated me the way he did. "I'm sorry, but Pollux treats me like shit, so I give it right back to him. I can't let them see me weak."

"Weak? Cassie, you're not weak."

Talon wasn't pleased with my reference to being weak. He was one of the strongest men in the pack, and being a warrior and protector was everything to him. He had trained me himself, and so me being seen as weak was a reflection on him.

"Everyone seems to think that I am. Either that or they are terrified of me. They always have been, and now, with Pollux flipping his wig on me about some bullshit, they think I'm a whore too."

Anger flashed through both of my father's eyes as low growls of disapproval echoed from their throats. "What are you talking about?" Hale asked.

"James didn't tell you?" A scoff left my throat as I cast my eyes down. "Pollux' stupid girlfriend told him I supposedly was messing around with Lucas Vega, which isn't true and so he confronted me in the hallway at school and called me a whore, accusing me of sleeping around. That's what started the whole fight."

I wasn't seeking pity from my dads, but what I did want was for Pollux to receive punishment if I was going to get it. He was just as much at fault as I was, and snitches get stitches, be damned... I wasn't going to be the only one serving punishment a week before school ends.

Talon stood to his feet, pacing the room as he rubbed the back of his neck. He was who I was really worried about, because anytime some boy had approached me in the past, he was quick to make them forget I even existed.

"Cassie, I know that you're going to be eighteen this weekend and with you getting older you're going to be interested in boys and... Stuff..."

Was he really going to try and do the talk?

"Oh my god, dad, please, no. We don't have to have this conversation."

"Look, Cassie, it's just as bad for us as it is for you—" Hale's laughter cut Talon off as he stared between Hale and I, absolutely confused. "What's so funny?"

"Talon..." Hale said, taking a moment to catch his breath. "You're like two years too late."

A shocked and horrified expression crossed Talon's face as it paled, his mouth dropping open. It hurt because I had known for so long he had seen me as his little princess and he didn't want that to change.

"Is this true, Cassie?" Talon whispered. "Why didn't you tell me?"

"Dad, none of that matters, and it isn't important right now. Look, school is almost over and I only have a week left and then I will be out of here and headed off to college."

Talon and Hale looked at each other in confusion at my response. I know the old tale about us having to go to the land of the gods, but that was just a silly story. There was no way my parents would subject me to something like that.

"Cassie, you're not going off to college. You know what's happening this weekend."

Hale gave me a concerned glance as the study door opened, and my mother walked in with a glass of wine in hand. "Oh, you guys are still talking?"

"Yeah, Cassie seems to think she is leaving for college..." Hale replied to my mother, who didn't look surprised by his statement and instead sipped on her wine.

"Ivy, why does Cassie think she is okay to go to college?" It was Talon's turn to ask my mother the question and as he did, she looked between them both and sighed, rolling her eyes.

"Oh, Jesus Christ, you two. She is intelligent and has her whole life ahead of her. The only thing Cassie wants is to have a normal life. We all know this, and if that's what she wants, then she can have it. Stop acting like it's a big deal."

Disbelief washed over me upon hearing her. Never once had I ever heard her speak up for what I want and yet, here she was basically telling my fathers what was going to happen whether they approved or not.

"Ivy, you know damn well that can't happen," Hale snapped at her, causing me to flinch as he stood to his feet. "There was an agreement, and both she and Pollux have to abide by it."

"I don't care, Hale. I'm not forcing them to go."

My mother was angry, and her words were firm. The only problem was I wasn't sure if I was hearing things correctly. The tale is true, and my parents really did agree for us to go? I thought it was a joke or something... Hell; I don't know what I thought, but to know my parents agreed was horrible.

"Wait, you're telling me that you made a deal for me and Pollux to be sent away? Why would you do that? Don't we get a say in this?!"

Shaking his head, Hale sighed. "No, sweetie, you don't. There was nothing we could do about it, and honestly, they wanted to take you a long time ago, so we made it so they didn't."

This was absolute bullshit. The entire time, I thought it was a hoax. Something my parents told me so I would behave, and it was actually true. "That's fucking great."

"Cassie, language!" My mother snapped, glaring at me. "You don't need to talk like that, and you're both not going, so it doesn't matter what happened."

"Ivy, stop lying to her!" Talon roared in anger. "They are, and after today's little stunt she pulled with her powers, she isn't returning back to school. We have to be careful—"

"What?!" I exclaimed, jumping to my feet. "What do you mean I'm not going back to school?! I have only a few days left!"

All three of my parents looked between each other before glancing back at me. I didn't understand what was going on, but I didn't have a chance to say anything before Damian walked through the door and stared at me.

"You're so loud we can hear you downstairs."

"Dad, you are the one who always says schooling is important. You can't let them do this." I pleaded with Damian to agree with me, but instead he sighed, crossing his arms over his chest and shook his head.

"No, Castor. You're not going back. You will be allowed to see your friends on pack grounds if they come here to the house and to the party. However, you will not be returning back to campus. It's too much of a risk after your stunt with your brother today and therefore, James has worked out with your teachers to take the exams under his supervision here."

My life was literally falling apart in front of me. The last few days of my senior year was squashed all because of Pollux and his stupid ass girlfriend.

"Whatever. At least Pollux will feel the same way I do." I had hoped for them to agree with me, but instead the looks passing them let me know what I dreaded hearing.

It was only me receiving this punishment.

"Seriously?" I gasped, clenching my fists at my sides. "So Pollux causes all the crap that went on today, and I'm the one who gets punished. Nice to see who the favorite is in the family."

Storming past Damian and my mother, I marched towards my room and slammed the door behind me. I woke up this morning believing today was going to be an amazing day. Of course, I was fucking wrong.

If Pollux thought for one moment, I was going to let this go. He was sadly mistaken.

I wasn't going to be grounded in this house alone, and I sure as hell wasn't going to some realm. They could all kiss my ass before that happened.

Morning Complications

Pollux

After the fallout with Cassie the day before, I made sure to steer clear of my parent's watchful eyes. From what I heard, Cassie had been grounded to the pack house, and not allowed to attend school and that was the last thing I wanted to happen to me.

I had an image to uphold as the future Alpha of this pack.

I couldn't be seen being punished.

Heading downstairs, I made my way towards the kitchen just in time to spot my mother taking muffins from the pan and placing them on a plate. Her blue eyes met mine, and as they did, she smiled at me. "Good morning, my sweet boy."

"Morning, Mom. Where's Hale at? I was supposed to see him before I left this morning."

"Oh, he actually left fifteen minutes ago." She frowned as she wiped off her hands and set the towel on the counter. The house smelt of freshly baked bread, and I knew something was up because the only time mom baked was when she was stressed out.

"He left? That's weird," I muttered as I shrugged my shoulders. "No worries, just tell him I'll talk to him after school. I don't want to be late."

Kissing her cheek, I stuffed a muffin into my mouth and grabbed my truck keys. With only a few days left in the school year, I was looking forward to spending the last few days with the boys on the football team, even if I couldn't play anymore.

The moment I walked outside, the cool air from spring hit my face, causing me to smile, my feet crunching across the gravel as I walked towards my truck. Only a few more days were left and though I was looking to the quickly ending year so I could begin my training, the last thing I expected when I turned the corner towards the garage was to see three flat tires on my truck.

"What the fuck!" I screamed loudly as I quickly ran towards my truck, running around admiring only three of the tires had actually been slashed and one had been left untouched.

The scream that left my throat caused my brother Dillon to come running from out the front door. He usually caught the bus to school, but he hadn't been feeling well the last few days and so mom had let him skip. More than likely trying to play hooky because he didn't want to take his final exams.

"What's wrong? Why are you screaming?" he said with a panic expression that turned to shock as his eyes laid upon the completely flat tires of my truck .

"Who the fuck did this?" I roared in anger. "Who in the hell slashed my tires?"

With all the commotion and yelling I was doing, it attracted the attention of my mother and even my father Talon, who came running from the woods. As his eyes landed upon what I had seen, his expression turned to one of anger.

"What in the hell happened to your truck? Did you run over something?"

I stared at him in disbelief, in shock. Did he honestly think I ran over something and it only popped three of the tires? "Seriously. Only crazy bitches slash three tires."

My mother, who stood next to me with her arms crossed over her chest, furrowed her brows in confusion at my comment. "What are you talking about? Why would a girl only slash three in all four?"

"Because the insurance won't cover it if only three of the tires have been slashed."

It was Cassie's voice which triggered me, and instantly I realized she must have had something to do with what happened. Turning around to face her, I watched as she stood leaning against the side of the house with her arms crossed over her chest in nothing but a tank top and shorts, with her hair a complete disarray.

Of course, she would have been the one to do it.

"You're such a bitter bitch. You did this, didn't you? You slashed my fucking tires because they told you, you couldn't go to school. What kind of sadistic whore are you?"

I had forgotten my father and mother were both standing here as I spoke to her, the anger trickling out of me. Her eyes went wide, her mouth parted as she looked at Talon. "See what I mean? He constantly blames me for everything. I was literally inside. I just came out here."

"Lux, it is absolutely unacceptable you would speak to your sister like that and blame her for something when she was literally inside. I checked in on her this morning and she was sleeping." My mother gasped as she stared at me, absolutely mortified I would speak to Cassie that way.

"Oh, come on. You and I both know that she did this. She's fucking pissed because you won't let her go to school and you're forcing her to go through with the agreement. I heard the entire conversation last night. Do you really think she's going to be okay with me being able to go and her having to stay here and miss out on everything?"

It didn't make any sense why my sister would lash out like this, and for a brief moment, I started to doubt whether I had assumed wrong.

"Look, son. You need to apologize to your sister. As for the truck, take one of your other rides. You have your motorcycle," Talon replied, obviously angry, but trying to keep himself together.

With a groan of protest, I tossed my keys to my truck on the ground and opened the garage. The problem was, as soon as the garage door opened, it was clear I wouldn't be taking my motorcycle either, because the front tire on that had been slashed as well.

As a roar of frustration and anger escaped me. I spun to Cassie once more. However, I didn't make it a step further as Hale stepped out from the house and quickly snatched me by the back of my neck, stopping me in my tracks. "What the fuck is going on?"

His Alpha aura radiated around me and even though I was his son and the next alpha in line, I had to submit to him when he was telling me to stop. "I'm calm," I snapped as he gently let go of my neck

"Tell me what happened," he replied, staring down at me with nothing but anger in his eyes. I hated it when he was pissed at me, but I did start my morning off in the wrong way. Not that it was my fault.

"Someone slashed three of the tires on my truck and I know it was Cassie. However, Mom and Talon seemed to think it wasn't. I was going to take my bike, which is in the garage, and I opened the door to find one of those tires slashed. It's not a coincidence. Someone in this house did it, and she's the only one with motive."

Again, my sister stood there looking at everybody who had turned to look at her. "Are you fucking kidding me right now? You honestly think I did this out of everybody else that lives in this house? I'm always the fucking culprit."

With a sigh of disgust, she turned on her heels and marched inside. Cassie may have claimed she didn't do it, and part of me was starting to believe she didn't. But this was completely her M.O. so the conflict of the situation just pissed me off even more.

"Son, I don't know who did this and I will find out, but for now, take your mother's car and go to school. When you're done, I want you to come directly back here because you and I need to have a conversation about how we treat our family and our pack members, because it's obvious you don't know how to rein in your temper."

Hale handed me my mother's car keys after he spoke, causing me to nod in understanding. I had disappointed him, and that was something that didn't sit well with me.

Gritting my teeth, I turned and made my way to my mother's car sitting at the end of the driveway. I didn't mind driving her vehicle. She had a beautiful Lexus and it was better than having to walk or have one of my parents drop me off.

Putting the car into drive, I backed out of the driveway and started heading down the road. Everything that had been going on was complete bullshit and I was sick and tired of my sister going at it with me as if she had some type of objective to win.

Everything was perfect at one point in time and then it seemed like a few years ago she changed her personality and became this rebellious bitch who solely sought to make my life a living hell.

We were supposed to be close. She was my fucking twin. Yet, it didn't matter what I said or did, she never had my back. I tried so many times to help her and all she did was turn her aggression and anger towards me.

Maybe she was jealous of me, who knows.

The moment I pulled into the school parking lot, I saw Ashley standing there. She knew my mother's vehicle and, with a furrowing brow of confusion, she walked towards the car as soon as I stepped out. "Where's your truck?"

"In the shop," I replied flatly, deciding not to tell her the truth. It was honestly none of her business and I was in a bad mood. The last thing I even wanted to do was speak to her.

"Okay, so then why didn't you bring your bike? Why would you bring your mother's car? It's so—not cool."

Stopping in my tracks, I turned to face her. I couldn't believe how petty she actually was and this, honestly, was the last straw. "Ashley, I don't know what it is that you expect to have out of being with me, but I can tell you right now this relationship needs to end. You and I are done. I don't have time to deal with whatever grievances you have. I don't care about matching outfits. I don't care about what vehicle I drive. I'm the future Alpha of this pack, and I actually have more important things to worry about than how good you look."

She stared at me in shock, her eyes brimming with tears as her mouth hung open. "I'm going to be your future wife. You can't do this," she whispered, trying to keep her voice down as she looked around at everybody around her.

"No, you're not. Nobody knows who my mate is going to be, and I will only marry my mate, Ashley. You need to realize that and accept it." The cold response was not what she wanted, and I didn't care anymore. I was tired of her petty bullshit, and I was tired of my sister, too.

Before I turned to try and walk away from her, she spoke again and her words stopped me in my tracks. "You're such a fool if you think that this is going to be the end. Your sister is playing her fucking games and messing with your head. She wants the title too, and if you think you're the only one who can have it, you're wrong. She's your twin, and by law, she can lay claim."

I had no idea what she was talking about, and had never heard that law. However, honestly, the more I started overthinking things, the more her behavior made sense.

Perhaps she did want the title.

Maybe everything she has been claiming to want all these years has been a lie.

Maybe she's waiting for the right moment to strip it all away from me.

Birthday Surprises

Cassie

Days passed and when Saturday finally came, I was prepared to have the night of my life, considering I had been unable to see Melissa for the last few days. Cooped up in the house was absolutely aggravating. I finished my final exams Thursday, a day ahead of schedule thanks to James and I was ready to be done with that part of my life and look forward to finding a way to leave this God awful pack and make a new life with Melissa on the West Coast.

Standing in front of my mirror, I tried on multiple different outfits, trying to figure a way to make myself look absolutely irresistible tonight, and ended up settling for a short black miniskirt and a black crop top that shimmered every time I moved.

It was gorgeous, and I felt absolutely gorgeous in it. I fluffed my purple, pink hair behind my back, smiling at the overall effect the entire outfit and my makeup had on me.

"Damn girl, you look absolutely delicious," Melissa chuckled from my door, causing me to look over my shoulder at her. I knew she had been on her way, but I hadn't realized that she had already arrived.

"Thank you. It took me a few days to decide what I was going to actually wear, but I think I'm pretty pleased with the overall outfit."

Turning from the mirror, I walked over towards her and wrapped my arms around her. She looked super cute in her dark skinny jeans and yellow tank top. She wasn't a girly girl per se, like I could typically be, but she did do a very good job at making herself look absolutely ravishing.

The last few days I had thought more and more about the future I was going to have, and regardless of what my parents had thought and what other people thought I was going to end up doing, I had made the choice I would make my future what I wanted it to be.

Which included me telling Melissa tonight I wanted to be more than just friends with her. I wasn't sure how she was going to react to that, but I had hoped everything would go the way I had dreamt it.

"It's already starting to get dark, and I saw your dad's out there going ahead and lighting the bonfire. If you're done, why don't we go ahead and head down?"

I couldn't agree with her more. I was ready for the clock to strike 8:00 PM, which was the hour we were born the moment my mother had given birth during the battle. It would be the moment I would be able to finally find out if Melissa could be my mate, and even if she wasn't... Well, I still wanted to be with her.

I never really gave thought to mates, and I didn't particularly take advantage of it like my brother did. But the idea of being able to have someone to spend my life with, to love and care for me, no matter what kind of person I was, was enticing.

Even if it was someone who I wanted mated to.

Looping my arm into hers, we quickly made our way from my bedroom, heading down the stairs to mingle with the rest of the guests still arriving as time ticked by. There had to have been at least fifty people meandering around my house.

My mother was in the kitchen with her friends as my dad's wandered around the house, coming in and out, lighting the grill, preparing the bonfire, the same as they did every single year. The only difference being this year Lux and I were finally adults.

No more being forced to do things we didn't want to do.

No more curfews, and having to stay in the pack. I was going to be free, and I was excited about it. My entire life had been caged, and now I would be an adult. I could do what I wanted.

The moment Melissa and I made our way outside, music and chaos consumed me. Everybody was dancing, laughing, having a good time, and for some reason, the turn out this year was larger than it ever had been.

My eyes quickly found my brother Pollocks, and as he stared at me, his gaze narrowed and he frowned. He obviously wasn't pleased with my outfit, but considering the attitude he had towards me since the day his truck tires got slashed, I could honestly give two fucks.

It wasn't even me that had done it, but yet he and even my parents thought it was.

Go figure. I'm the rebellious teenager, the one who doesn't ever listen and beats to her own tunes, so of course, I'm the one who did it. Fucking stereotyping assholes, if you ask me.

"So what do you wanna do first? Shall we get a drink?"

Taking a moment to think about Melissa's offer, a grin slid across my face. "Sure. But if we're going to get a drink, we're going to get a real drink."

Her eyes widened in surprise as she giggled and looked around to see if anybody had heard. "Aren't your parents going to notice?"

Shrugging my shoulders, I tipped my head to the side and gestured for her to follow me. "Who cares if they notice I'm eighteen now? Well, at least I will be in two hours, so I can make my own choices. Plus, a friend owed me a favor and this happened to be it."

Melissa was still seventeen and would be for another month, but that was okay. Her birthday being at the start of summer just meant when she did turn eighteen and we had our apartment on the West Coast, we would be able to have a lot more fun than we currently were having.

As we walked around the bonfire, heading for my secret spot that sat off to the side, I stepped around the bushes, revealing a dark navy blue cooler with a white top, I quickly popped open. Inside of it was a bag of ice, a couple cans of soda, and a very large bottle of whiskey.

It didn't take me but a second to make Melissa and I a drink, and as we chug down our first glass, we quickly prepared for a second. "Shall we go find trouble?" I asked her with a mischievous smile, she nodded.

"Shit, trouble is your middle name."

Wandering around, the last person I expected to see at my party was Lucas Vega, but there he stood on the other side of the bonfire, watching me. The flickering light of the fire cast shadows across his face as the moon rose high in the sky.

I didn't think he was going to come, and I hadn't seen him since that day after school. But it was obvious Melissa had seen I had noticed him, and as she nudged me, I glanced over towards her. She smiled and gestured with her head for me to go speak to him. "What are you waiting for?"

"Dude, absolutely not. Lucas Vega is completely off limits. Not to mention Lux would fucking kill us both if anything happened. He isn't even my type."

"Not your type?" she laughed hysterically. "Oh, come on. I have known you for years. He is SOOOO your type, Cassie."

"Well... still, I can't. It's just asking for drama."

Rolling her eyes, she smiled at me. "Cassie, you deserve to be happy. You can't keep putting off everything because of what Lux may say. He isn't going to have anything to do with your life once we leave, so don't miss out on opportunities like this. Lucas Vega may be a bad boy, but he's completely fucking hot."

Something about the way she spoke about Lucas made my heart ache. She was right. I did need to make a move, but the move I currently wanted to make was not on him, it was on her.

"Melissa, actually, I was wondering if I could talk to you about something."

She gazed at me with a waiting glance, but the moment I opened my mouth, the crowds began to sing happy birthday and my attention was taken from Melissa towards my parents, who were bringing out a very large birthday cake.

Realizing duty called, I gave her a sympathetic look and quickly walked over to where my parents were waiting so Lux and I could blow out our candles together.

The time had finally come. We were about to be eighteen and as the moment struck, I would be sent into a frenzy if my mate was near or at least that's what I was told.

I just hoped whoever it was wouldn't be disappointed when I told them my heart belonged to somebody else. That even though Melissa was my best friend, I had to have her in my life as well.

"Happy birthday, guys," My mother cooed as she stared at us with misty eyes, my father Damian wrapping his arm around her shoulder as James came up behind her and snuggled in close.

I couldn't help but admire the love my parents had, and hoped one day I would have that, too. No matter how much they pissed me off, they had a bond that couldn't be matched and I secretly longed for the day to understand what they felt about each other.

I longed for the day to have my mate look at me the way my fathers looked at my mom.

With a one...two... three... Lux and I blew out our candles and, as we did, I felt an unfamiliar shiver run across my spine. I wasn't sure what it was, but as Lux turned to me, furrowing his brows in confusion, my nose went up into the air and I inhaled deeply.

The smell was erotic and intoxicating. Almost like fresh rain on a summer day.

It was hard to explain what I was feeling, considering it wasn't really a scent per se that attracted me, but almost like a pull to follow this invisible rope connecting me with somebody else.

My mother must have sensed what was going on, because as I looked at her, hope filled her eyes and she nodded her head as if encouraging me to follow it.

My father's each glanced between them, seemingly uncertain if they were ready for this moment and, as for Lux, he held nothing but disappointment in his gaze.

As if he did not feel what I was feeling, but I already knew he wouldn't. I had seen his mate, and she didn't belong to this pack. Even though I had hoped by this point, she would have moved here.

Unable to control the pull, I turned and walked, following this invisible tether pulling me in a direction towards my future.

Towards someone who I was meant to be with.

As I passed around by the bonfire. I came to a halt for a moment at the place where I had last seen Melissa and my heart swelled. It was her. She was my mate, and with excitement. I pressed forward quicker. My movements took me towards the treeline where she must have been waiting for me.

Step by step. I was enveloped in darkness until a small clearing up a head caught my gaze and I spotted a figure that stood there, waiting. The only problem was when I stepped through the clearing, it was obvious it wasn't Melissa who was waiting there.

Instead, it was a familiar figure I would never forget.

One that had made me feel complicated in more ways than one.

As Lucas Vega turned to face me, his eyes flashed gold with recognition. He was my mate, and if he knew, that meant he had known for months.

Because if memory serves me right, he turned eighteen four months ago.

And the prick never said a fucking thing.

Mated to a Lycan

Mouth parted, I stood in utter disbelief, staring at Lucas Vega. His eyes flecked with gold as he stared upon my figure, moving from the shadows out into the moonlight. How is it that this man, a man I had detested because of his cocky personality, was the man I was supposed to be mated to?

So many questions ran through my mind, and as I got closer to him, flutters of nervousness flowed through my stomach. "You are my mate?"

It was a question, but it was also more of a statement. I couldn't believe the Fates had paired me with Lucas Vega, the notorious bad boy who wanted nothing more than to make my brother's life a living hell.

"Yes, I am. I waited so long for you to realize I was your mate, so I didn't have to be away from you any longer." Lucas stepped closer towards me, and as he did, I felt myself become completely uneasy.

I shouldn't have felt this way around my mate, and yet I couldn't help it.

"You turned eighteen four fucking months ago and you couldn't bother to tell me back then I was your mate? What the fuck is wrong with you?"

My explosion was the first thing to come out of my mouth after realizing he knew. I wasn't actually thinking when I had spoken, but now I had said what I did, I didn't regret it. Four months he had known I was his mate and never once did he bother to tell me who in the hell does something like that?

"I didn't want to tell you because I wanted you to figure it out on your own. It would have been unfair of me to come to you and tell you I was your mate before you even turn eighteen. You deserved to enjoy the moment of finding me."

So he was thinking about me. I found the notion sweet, but I couldn't be clouded.

No matter how badly I wanted those gold-flecked eyes to stare down at me as his plump, thick lips kissed me, I couldn't let my emotions take control. This was Lucas Vega. The same Lucas Vega who had tried countless times to piss me off, tease me, taunt me, and do everything in his power to come between my brother and I since the school year started.

The moment he stood only a foot in front of me, shivers of pleasure spilled down my spine. His warm, fresh rain scent wrapped around me, trying to comfort me, but all the while my stubborn mind couldn't get past the fact he had lied and hid this from me for four months.

Perhaps I was being ridiculous. Hell, maybe my stubborn mind was taking control, but at the end of the day I was Cassie, the Alpha's daughter. No way in hell was I going to let some bad boy come into my life and try to ruin things.

The moment he reached out and ran his hand down my arm, I was pulled from my thoughts and jumped back from his touch. The recoil caused him to growl as his eyes narrowed in my direction. "Don't do that."

"Don't do what? Move away from you?" I sneered. "If I wanted to touch you, I would have allowed it."

Even with his eyes narrowed, a grin crossed the corner of his lips, turning up as he watched me. "I knew from the moment I met you that you were going to be feisty, and even when I found out you were my mate, I watched you from the shadows. I couldn't help but wonder if you were going to act like this."

That didn't sound stalkerish at all. I internally groaned. "Look, it's obvious that the moon goddess made a mistake. There's no way we can be mated."

He sneered at my comment, an utter look of disgust crossing his face. "Are you rejecting me?"

Was I rejecting him? I wasn't quite sure. Honestly, I didn't know how I felt. I had waited for this moment for so long, and though I didn't quite believe in mates, because I wanted Melissa, I found myself conflicted.

"I don't know what I'm doing," I replied softly. The honest answer I gave him was enough for him to quickly clear the space between us and wrap his arm around my waist, pulling me close to his body.

"Don't reject me. Give me a chance to show you I can be good to you, that I can give you a life that you want." As much as I wanted to believe him, there was a darkness that surrounded him which made me wary.

A darkness that called my name, wanting me to give in.

I wasn't the kind of girl who could easily love. With all of the power that radiated inside me, I was constantly cautious. Worried someone would try to take advantage of me, worried someone would try to use me to hurt the ones I loved.

Melissa was the only one outside of my family I trusted.

The only one I could ever let in.

She was everything to me, and nothing would change that.

Past had proved I couldn't trust men. One time, I tried to let a man in and that failed. Even the one-night stands I had to try and relieve the built up tension in my body proved to be nothing but a waste of time from men who thought they could get in good with my family. Fucking assholes, all of them.

"Lucas—" The moment I said his name, I hadn't been thinking. For forever I'd always called him by his last name, and as I said his first name, his lips descended upon mine and took my breath away in the most passionate and heated kiss I'd ever had. His tongue fought for dominance over mine, flicking and tasting me, a deep rumble erupted from his chest.

Every ounce of my body screamed for the desire to have more, but I couldn't. I was so conflicted about how I felt, I wanted to cry. I was honestly overthinking it more than I probably should have.

So, after he parted his lips from mine, I quickly placed my hand against his chest and stepped back, trying to catch my breath. Glancing at him, wide eyed in shock, I turned and ran.

I wasn't sure why I was running, hell wasn't sure what I was doing at all. But the moment I cleared the woods and my eyes landed on Lux, I knew bad things were about to happen. "Lux, please. It's not what you think."

My brother narrowed his gaze at me with a disgusted look in his eyes. "Not what I think. What the fuck are you doing with him?"

"I'm her mate. I have a right to be with her." Lucas's voice caused shivers once more to cross over my skin, and as I looked over my shoulder at him, I watched him step from the shadows with his arms crossed over his chest in a defensive manner.

"He's your mate?! Are you fucking kidding me? This piece of shit is the man you're meant to be with?" Pollux was being completely unreasonable and I was slightly offended he would even talk about Lucas like that.

"Lux, you-you're being unreasonable," I stammered. "Can we not do this tonight? Let's just take tonight to finish enjoying the party and then tomorrow we can talk about this."

I saw the look in my brother's eye I had only seen a handful of times before. He was angry, far past angry, and with the power flowing through him, he was slowly spiraling out of control. I wasn't so sure why he hated Lucas so much, but it was obvious whatever was going to happen was not going to be good.

"I should have fucking killed you a long time ago," he growled as he glared at Lucas. "You will never have her. I told you before to stay away and you just couldn't fucking do it, could you?"

What the hell did he mean, he told him before? Does this mean my own brother knew that Lucas was my mate, and he never told me?

"Did you know?" I asked him in shock as I slapped my hand across his chest, watching his eyes dart to me, his teeth bared and a slow shift coming over him. "Did you know that he was my mate and you didn't say anything?"

"Of course I fucking knew. He came snooping around the day he turned eighteen looking for you. I didn't approve of him from the beginning, and if you thought for a second I would ever approve of a man like him being with my sister, then you're sadly mistaken."

"Pollux, that isn't for you to decide!" I screamed in frustration.

"It is my right as your brother, and the future Alpha of this pack, Cassie. When are you going to learn that what you want doesn't fucking matter!"

"Go fuck yourself, Pollux. You're just jealous I actually have a mate!" I snapped back, and as I did, he raised his hand to slap me but stopped when a deep, evil growl resonated from Lucas. Lucas was daring him to do it, and Pollux better reconsider.

"Your fucking mutt thinks he's going to do something..." Pollux laughed in an egotistical way as he glanced around the area. I couldn't understand why he was acting like this, and with embarrassment and ever raging hormones, I felt the tears fill my eyes. I refused to let them fall.

"Are you crying?" Pollux gasped with laughter. "You have no one to blame but yourself."

Narrowing my gaze at him, I let a surge of power flow through me. "Shut your fucking mouth."

Pollux seemed concerned for a moment, and then the concern washed away. "What are you going to do, Cassie? Are you going to fucking hurt me like you did before? Maybe it will be one of your other siblings this time instead... you're fucking pathetic, Cassie. Always with the enemy."

"He isn't Marcus, Lux. Don't compare them," I whispered, watching as my brother's eyes softened for a moment before turning hard once more. "You always preach about how mates are so important, and yet you're acting like this? I don't get it."

He had been cruel to me more than once, but I just didn't understand why he would be cruel to me about something like this.

The chaos happening between the three of us had started to draw the attention of others, and as they looked on, I realized if I didn't get control of this, something bad was going to happen. "Lux, you have to stop."

"Don't tell me what to do. I will not listen to a girl who whores herself out to the enemy." His words were triggering Lucas, and I could feel the tension between the three of us growing slowly out of control.

"Look, stop. We need to take the night to think this over and tomorrow we can... we can do something about it then... just for tonight, Lux... Please."

Panicking, I watched my brother step forward, ignoring my words, and as I looked towards Lucas, he too was standing prepared for whatever my brother had to throw at him.

I didn't understand why Lucas could remain so quiet through this whole conversation, but it was as if he was trying to allow me to handle this without him interjecting, which I respected and was slightly shocked by. "Don't do this, Lux. It's only going to end badly for the both of us."

"Don't you dare tell me what I should and shouldn't do in my own pack. You're fucking nothing but a goddamn pain in my ass," Lux growled as he clenched his fist at his side, stepping forward.

"I said enough, Lux." I screamed at him as I used my hands to push him back. However, I should have known it would be useless, because in one swoop, he shoved me, tossing me aside to the ground.

A roar unlike anything I had ever heard escaped Lucas' lips, and as I turned to look at him, I watched as the shift came over causing me to realize he too was half-breed.

Natural werewolves were not able to partially shift. They either shifted into a wolf or they were human, but here before me, Lucas stood with fangs protruding over his lips, his eyes completely golden with black swirling masses, and his hands had razor-sharp claws.

Oh, my god. Lucas was a fucking Lycan.

Saying Goodbye

They say when you lose something you love the most, your world stops spinning and nothing makes sense anymore. I never thought much about what my life would be like without the people closest to me. But the moment my life was faced with hard choices and bad decisions, I realized there was no turning back.

"How dare you touch what's mine?" The roared comment that came from Lucas echoed throughout the area. Panic consumed those around us as they watched the scene before them unfold. People went running, screaming for help, and I knew somewhere close by, my parents were trying desperately to find out what was causing the chaos.

The chaos centered around me.

"Stop!" I screamed as the two guys went at it with each other. Claws flying through the air, slashes being made upon skin, howls of pain, roars of anger. It was all too much for me, and as I jumped to my feet, I tried desperately to find a way I could stop at all.

There was one way, but using my magic was forbidden by my parents and the pack. I wasn't allowed to do that, but as I tried to see another way around it, I couldn't.

I didn't shift into my Lycan form for a reason because I was more uncontrollable than my brother. But I so desperately didn't want either Lux or Lucas to get hurt.

With panic setting into my racing heart, anger bubbled inside me, mixed with confusion, hatred and love. I didn't know what I was doing, but before I knew it, I allowed myself to change.

The only problem was it wasn't the change I was expecting. The change that ended up consuming me was of power and darkness. A rage boiling inside of me that finally exploded with a screaming yell for them to stop.

The power bursted from my hands, my body and my soul was unlike anything I had ever felt before. There were those who had made it away in time from where we had been consumed in chaos, but those that did not were thrown back hundreds of feet, landing on the ground, pleading for the chaos to stop.

"Cassie, no!" My mother screamed as my parents tried to get to me in time. Both Lucas and Lux both turned to me in shock as the power radiated off my body in green waves.

All I wanted tonight was to enjoy the time with my family I had before I left for college. To enjoy my birthday and possibly meet my mate even though Lucas was not the mate I was hoping for.

Yet that didn't happen. Instead, hell broke loose all because I was paired with a man my brother hated.

As both of them turned to me, they slowly transformed back into their normal forms, their clothes completely shredded, their half-naked bodies bared before me.

"Cassie, you have to stop," Lux pleaded with me as he held his hands up as a sign of defense. "You can't do this. Look, we're not fighting anymore. Please, you have to calm down."

It didn't matter if I wanted to stop or not, at the moment I was unable to, it was as if I had taken a back seat in my mind, and the forefront of power which controlled me currently was driving this ride.

"Why is it that every time I find something in my life that could possibly make me happy, you try to stop it?" I bellowed at him. "I'm your sister. Why can't you be happy for me?"

"I am happy for you, Cassie, please, you have to stop. You're scaring people, and if you're not careful, you will not be able to redeem yourself for whatever you do when you completely lose it."

He was trying to reason with me, that was obvious, but he was doing so in a very poor manner. I didn't understand why he couldn't just let me be happy, let me figure my own shit out. He always thought he had to control me, tell me what I needed to do.

He was my brother, not my keeper, and he didn't seem to want to understand that.

"Cassie—" Melissa's soft words caught me off my guard for a moment, and glancing at her, a part of me calmed at her presence. However, that was quickly ruined when Pollux took note of Melissa, stepping closer and decided to open his mouth.

"Look, Cassie, even Melissa is scared of you."

Narrowing my eyes, a low growl echoed from my throat. "Don't you dare say her name."

"...Or what? If you keep this up, there is no redemption for you, Cassie. Someone is going to get hurt all because you don't know how to keep your shit together."

"You're such a fucking liar. You are not happy for me. You never have been and you never will be. You have been nothing but jealous of me since the day we came into our powers and you blame me for every moment of your life, not being exactly how you want it."

The words I spoke were me, but then again, they weren't. It was as if my subconscious was tired of the bullshit and finally spoke of everything that had rolled through my mind over the years.

It seemed to hit my brother hard with what I said, but he tried to distract me. Something I wasn't prepared for.

I hadn't been paying attention to Lucas, who had calmly been circling behind me. I wasn't sure what he was trying to do, but the moment his arms wrapped around my waist, my brother tried to tackle me down.

The problem was they didn't realize how much power I was on the verge of using until it was too late and flew from me in a frenzy, seeking to hit any target in its path.

I hadn't meant for anybody to get hurt.

I had it meant for things to go sideways and had they just let me be to calm down on my own, perhaps things would have been fine.

My mother's scream echoed around me. I looked up from the ground over towards the fire. I spotted Melissa laying there unmoving, and my heart absolutely broke.

As if a combustion inside me had finally let go, I screamed in frustration and pain. My eyes wide with fear as tears rolled down my cheeks. The power within me exploding, tossing Lucas and Lux from my body as I quickly climbed to my hands and knees and scrambled over to where Melissa layed.

"No. Please No." I never meant for anybody to get hurt and yet the one person I had loved and trusted my entire life was now gone. She lay there, her eyes wide open, her hair sprawled around her.

There was nothing I could do now, but I wanted to. Goddess, I wanted to.

Pulling her body up onto my lap, I kissed the top of her head, my hand running over her cheek as tears fell down my face landing onto her own. "It's going to be okay, Melissa. Don't let go. I can bring you back. I'll find some way to bring you back."

I had never lost control like this. I had never allowed myself to lose control like this and the one time I did, in order to try to stop two men I cared about from killing each other, the one person I cared more about than anything in this world was taken from me.

"Cassie, sweetie... What did you do?" My mother's voice brought me to the forefront of what had actually happened and as I let my eyes slide up to hers, I couldn't hold back the sob that escaped me.

"I didn't mean to... I just wanted them to stop fighting, Mama, I didn't mean to."

I broke in half and as I did, she broke in half with me falling to her knees, because Melissa had been like a daughter to her all these years as well. She cried with me holding both me and Melissa. "I know you didn't. I'm so sorry."

"We can bring her back. I can bring her back, Mama. I can do it."

My mom once had the power to bring my father, Damien, back, and if she could do it, I could do it too. There was a way for it to work. There had to be.

"Cassie, you have to let her go." To my left Damien stood with Talon. They both stared at me tight, lipped with sad expressions on their faces as Damien shook his head.

"You can't bring her back, sweetie. She's gone. What your mother did for me isn't the same thing. It took all of them to bring me back and the only way that was able to happen was because of the Lycan gene and because of the celestial blood. Melissa isn't one of us."

I knew what they were saying was true. She wasn't one of us, at least not by blood. But she was mine, and I loved her. I loved her more than anything and now she was gone.

"No, that can't be it. We had plans. We were going to go to college..." I whispered softly. "I never got the chance to tell her. Daddy, I never got to tell her the truth."

"You didn't, sweetheart and losing somebody you love hurts. But right now you have to let her go and come with me." Damien's words were not the words I wanted to hear and even as I glanced at Lux and also Lucas, I could see how remorseful they were.

Had they not tried picking this stupid fight if this would have happened?

Melissa would still be alive, and I wouldn't be a murderer.

Seeing I wasn't going to move, my mother had my father's help pull me away from Melissa's body, and as they did, a part of me died with her.

How was I ever going to be able to go on without her?

She had been with me my entire life? She had been my rock, my anchor to this world since the day my powers came into play and now she was gone.

A swirling mass of wind and a crack of thunder in the distance brought all of us to attention and as it had happened once before, a void opened within space and through it I came face to face with someone I hadn't seen since I was a child.

Kara, my grandfather's Valkyrie.

"It seems that the party is over and things didn't turn out the way they should have."

Anger flashed through me at her comment. It wasn't needed and even though I wanted more than anything to put her in her place, I couldn't. "Go fuck yourself, Kara."

A chuckle escaped the woman as she looked at Melissa's body and then turned to look over her shoulder. I wasn't sure what to expect, but before I knew it, a large, burly figure of a man with a white beard stepped through the portal.

The white robes he wore screamed hierarchy and I realized this himself was Odin, the man my father Hale had told me about often.

He wasn't pleased by the sight before him and everyone, including my parents, seemed to quake under his gaze. All except me.

As silver eyes stared at me, he shook his head. "I should have known that this would have happened, and it is my fault that it did. A young life was lost because I thought my daughter could keep my grandchildren in check."

"Excuse me, how dare you say something like that?" My mother snapped, standing to her feet as she came to stand in front of me. "Get out of here now. You're not welcome."

"Child, you no longer may say anything. We had a deal, and I gave you till their eighteenth birthday. Now I was going to be nice enough to give him a bit of extra time to say goodbye to their family and friends, but after this? There's no way that I can allow that to happen."

The tone of his voice echoed through the air, and as it did, the surge of power and authority echoed with it. He was right, though. I should have gone a long time ago. I was dangerous and because of my inability to control myself, Melissa got killed.

Glancing at my parents, I could see they were willing to fight to keep me here and there was no way in hell I was going to allow that to happen.

I couldn't allow someone else to get hurt because of me and honestly, disappearing from this place sounded a lot better than staying put. "I'll go."

"What?" My mother gasped as she looked over her shoulder at me. "Don't say that. No, you're not. I've worked too hard for too many years to protect you guys. You're not going. You're my children."

"Mom...I–I just killed my best friend..." I stammered, trying to make sense of what had happened. "Do you really think that I can stay here after that? Do you really think that I.. I could risk somebody else getting killed because of me? Because I can't control myself?"

She was speechless at my comment, and there was nothing she could say. I was a risk to everybody around me in the state I was, and until I learned how to handle this, nobody was safe.

"Cassie, you can't go. You belong here with me." Lucas' soft words only irked my nerves even further. I knew he was my mate, but I couldn't even think about that right now.

Turning to him, I tried to hold back further tears, but instead they just continued like a river down my face. "Why would you want somebody like me? I'm a murderer. You're free to be with whoever you want."

A chuckle escaped my grandfather at this point and as I looked at him, his eyes were focused on Lucas. "Interesting. How in the world did I not notice you before?"

Lucas' entire demeanor shifted, and he became fearful as he tried to step away from the entire situation. "I don't know what you're talking about."

"Oh, I think you do, little celestial Lycan." Gasps echoed around the area, and as Odin looked at each of us, an amused smile hinted within the depths of his eyes. "I suppose instead of two, I'll be taking three."

Welcome to Asgard

Pollux

Everything had happened with Cassie was like a movie playing in slow motion while I stood by unable to do anything. I had tried to tackle her, to stop her from hurting anybody, and even Lucas tried to calm her down.

Yet, her powers bounced back and Melissa, her best friend, ended up getting killed.

Never in my life did I think something like this would have happened. Of course, I hated my sister for some of the shit she did, but I never meant for this situation to get out of hand. It broke my heart seeing her shed tears for a girl I had watched her grow up with. A girl who had been her only real true friend.

I lost myself the moment I saw her step out of the woods with Lucas and because I did, it started the trickling rollercoaster of events that played out. So in a way, I was responsible for Melissa's death as well, and that was something I would never be able to forget.

How was I supposed to be the future Alpha if I couldn't even rationally control myself.

"It's time to go," Kara, Odin's Valkyrie said as she stood before me with her wings flexing behind her back and an eerie gaze in her eyes. She was a mysterious woman, one I had frequently seen over the years when she came to check in with her family, and as I gazed at my mother, I realized this was it.

Tears streamed down her cheeks as my fathers stood at her side. She had been so adamant for years this situation was never going to happen, and between her and our fathers, they had tried so hard to help prepare us, to control the uncontrollable.

I was prepared to go though. Priscilla had told me it would be inevitable and honestly, I had been excited. The idea of learning from the gods, and then being an Alpha who far surpassed the training of normal wolves, it was a calling I desired regardless if it meant I would have to remain away for an entire year.

With a heavy sigh, I walked towards my mother and wrapped my arms around her. The woman who had given birth to me and been my rock for my entire life. I would miss her when I was gone, but I knew one day I would return.

"It's okay, mom. Everything is going to be okay."

"How can you say that you're both leaving me?" she replied tearfully. "How can you say it's going to be okay?

"Because it will be." I smiled gently as I wiped a tear from her eye. "It's only going to be a year, and if you think about it, that's the same length of time it would have taken me to go through the Alpha academy."

Taking a deep breath, my mother sighed, nodding her head. It was going to be hard for her, as it would be for any parent, but she still had four of my siblings at home to look after, and I knew that would keep her focus.

"Make sure you look after your sister," Damian said firmly as he clasped a hand upon my shoulder. "I know you both haven't been close for a long time, but you have to overcome this."

"What about Melissa, what will happen?" I asked, letting my gaze fall to Melissa's body being tended to by the pack doctors.

"Don't worry about that. I'm taking care of it," Hale's words echoed through my ears and as I looked at him, I knew he would. Being an Alpha wasn't an easy thing, and this was something I would have to learn eventually.

"I won't let you guys down," I told them with confidence as I squared my shoulders and held my head high. "I'll come back as the man I need to be."

"I know you will." Damian chuckled. "Just take care of Cassie. She... she's going to need you more than you realize."

Nodding my head, I finished my goodbyes, and as I turned, expecting my sister to be waiting for me, I was shocked to find she wasn't. Instead, I watched as Odin gave her a small smile placing his hand on the top of her back as she proceeded to step through the portal without so much as looking back to say goodbye.

She was a hollow shell of herself, and with every moment she was away, I prayed the gods would be able to fix her. That by some miracle she would become who she was meant to be, because I couldn't be expected to look after her forever.

I was honestly surprised to see Lucas was going along so willingly. He didn't seem like the kind of person who would, and looking at how he was a Lycan as well, I could only imagine why.

Stepping forward, Kara waited for Lucas and I, and as we stepped through the portal, I knew there was no turning back, and honestly I was excited.

As a blinding white light filled my vision, I felt myself being twisted and pulled until peace flowed over my body like a warm blanket. Gasping, I looked around and found myself lost and alone but something in front of me called me forward.

With one foot in front of the other, I made my way through the white clouds of mist encircling my body until a small, green clearing came into view and I took in the sweet smell of fresh air and bright blue skies.

"Welcome to Asgard." Odin grinned as he held his hands up into the air, spinning slowly to show us the magical realm we were entering. I honestly wasn't sure what I was expecting, but I can promise it definitely wasn't this.

Tall white pillars loomed around us, holding up large white marble roofs seemingly cascading far off into the distance. An as I stepped forward, I realized among this pantheon-styled buildings laid mountains decorated in green forests and waterfalls. There had to been a thousand buildings all built into the mountain sides, and turning to Odin, I frowned in confusion.

I had expected something far darker or perhaps more isolate, but instead, I was in a city.

"Where is Asgard?" Lucas asked, causing me to turn and face him. He was just as confused as I was, and I was glad he asked the question instead of me.

There was no way I was going to make myself look like an idiot.

"In time you will learn," Odin replied in a booming voice deep and distinct it made your soul shake when he spoke and there was amusement in his tone. He headed towards the large white steps of the massive marble building in front of us. I couldn't help but be wary of the man he was. "Follow me this way, and I will have Freya show you to your rooms. You can settle for tonight, and tomorrow you start school."

"School?" Both Cassie and I said at the same time as we looked at each other in confusion and then looked back to Odin. We had just graduated school. The last thing we wanted to do right now was go back to school.

"Yes, school. You didn't think you were just going to come here, pick up an axe or throw in some fighting skills and we would let you on your merry way, did you?"

"Well, yeah," I muttered to myself as a giggle caught my attention and I took notice of a beautiful woman walking towards Odin.

She was beautiful, more beautiful than I could ever have imagined. It was clear she far surpassed my mother in age, her long golden strands were perfectly braided down her back as a crown sat upon her head.

"It's lovely to see you all," she said with a soft almost sing-song voice. Her eyes scanned the three of us before falling onto my sister. "Castor, sweetheart. I have been waiting for this day since you were born."

What the hell? She was only interested in my sister. What kind of bullshit was that?

"Sorry, I don't know who you are," Cassie said softly, her eyes darting to me with confusion as she shrugged her shoulders.

"That's Freya. The motherly goddess who looks over us all." Lucas belted out as he crossed his arms over his shoulders, a content gaze on his face as he glanced over at me and smirked.

"That would be correct. I am Freya, and you must be Lucas the celestial Lycan we hadn't been expecting... no worries, though. I will figure out who you came from in time."

Lucas scoffed with annoyance as he rolled his eyes. "I'm no one, and there's nothing to know."

Freya and Odin shared a knowing glance between each other at his comment before she clapped her hands together. "Let's get you to your rooms. That way you can get freshened up before dinner."

Not bothering to ask any questions, I remained quiet as I followed behind Cassie and Lucas. It didn't please me to know, once again, my sister was the center of attention. I got she was unique, but for once, I had hoped the spotlight wouldn't shine on her.

The moment we stepped into the halls, I took note of how more extravagant the inside of this building was to the outside. White walls decorated with ornate objects, and paintings of historical scenes littered the area. It was cool, but with how fast Freya was moving, I didn't have time to take in it all.

It was brilliant to think, in a place like this, they had created something with such beauty. Who knew with everything these people had, they could create something so much closer to nature than the world I was used to growing up in.

The moment we turned down another hallway, I quickly realized this must have been the residential area. Doors of various designs lined the walls for what seemed miles and upon every door was a name.

The first door we came to was Lucas' room, his name engraved with silver upon the wooden door. I didn't realize that this place would be so name specific, and as Freya opened the door, we were met with black and red decor, that reminded me of a sex den I had once seen on a porn movie. "Uh—nice decor," I chuckled, watching as Lucas rolled his eyes.

"Yes, all of these rooms were decorated based on your personalities and the way you lived in the human realm." Her words caught me off guard, and instantly I worried about what mine would look like.

"Come on, Cassie." Lucas looked to Cassie expectedly, and as he did, Cassie crossed her arms over her chest and raised a brow in his direction.

"Uh–no."

"No?" He furrowed his brows. "What do you mean, no? I'm your mate."

A small snicker came from Freya as she clasped her hands in front of her and smiled. I wasn't sure what she found funny, but maybe it was the same thing I found funny. My sister was out right refusing to go stay in Lucas' room.

"Lucas, Cassie may be your mate, but that doesn't mean she has to stay with you. She has her own room, and you have no claim over her, I'm afraid." Freya's comment didn't seem to sit well with him and walking into his room, he quickly slammed the door.

"I guess he didn't like that," I muttered as Freya held her tongue and quickly turned, continuing down the hallway.

"Your room is right here, Pollux." As she went to grab the handle, I quickly beat her to it and smiled.

"I got it. Thanks again for this. I'll see you guys at dinner."

The last thing I wanted was for my sister to see the things I was into. I wasn't sure if that was the shit in the room, but there was no way I was going to risk being mocked by her if my room looked anything like Lucas' room.

With a shrug of her shoulders, I watched Freya and Cassie disappear further down the hallway, and as they did, a sigh of relief escaped me before I took a deep breath. With a fleeting glance at my name engraved across the door, I turned the handle and stepped into my room.

I wasn't sure what I had expected, but blue walls and modern style decor definitely wasn't it. I felt like I was staring at a more mature version of my bedroom back home, and with it, I found myself slightly annoyed. Lucas had gotten a sex room, or at least that's what the glimpse reminded me of.

Instead, I was faced with blues, whites, and silver. A ship's captain style room with a large golden anchor on the far wall. I was a wolf, not a sea captain, and even though the room was really nice, I felt slightly let down.

Part of me was hoping for something dark and dangerous, but I wasn't going to complain. Instead, I would pay less attention to the minor details of my stay and look forward to what was to come.

Taking the time to walk around and admire everything, my eyes took in everything from the large king-size bed with a dark navy blue comforter. To the small sofa and a desk near a large floor to ceiling bookcase. It was the typical shit you would see in a room, but on a larger scale.

"Guess this is as good as it gets," I muttered to myself as I jumped onto the bed and closed my eyes. This was the start of something better for us all, and if I had to be here for the next year, I was just gonna have to make the most of it.

Meeting Trixie

Cassie

The moment we appeared in the realm of the gods, I found myself taken aback by the sights in front me. Rolling green hills and high mountains lined the vicinity. The white marble cathedral styled buildings and architecture were breathtaking. The one thing, though, which struck me the most, was how kind Freya was. I had never met her in person, but I had heard stories my mother had told me of the kind of woman she was.

How she was kind and caring. How she was a mother figure to all that were around her. I wasn't looking to get close to anyone, but something about her made me want to trust her. Something about her was familiar.

The moment she guided me down the hall, I found myself in a void of tunnel vision unable to take in the marvels of the area. As much as someone may have been excited to take in the new place we were going to be residing, I couldn't.

The only thing playing through my mind was Melissa was gone, and I had killed her. How was I supposed to be excited or even interested in being here when I had done one of the worst things someone could have possibly done?

Every now and again, she turned to glance at me as if checking if I was okay, and when we stopped at Lucas' room and he expected me to follow him, it honestly made me despise him even more.

The audacity of him to expect me to be okay with everything that happened, and jump at the opportunity to be his mate, was fucking ridiculous. I was glad Freya came to my rescue. She made it clear I was able to choose my own path and it gave me more confidence in the whole mate situation.

"Here we are." Her voice pulled me out of my thoughts as we stopped before a large black wooden door with a black steel handle. From the outside, someone would have thought it was a dungeon door, and part of me expected it to be, but when she opened the door, I was surprised by the site in front of me.

The room was large, far larger than the guys had been, and on the farthest wall sat billowing black sheer curtains leading to an open door with a balcony. Glancing at Freya, she gestured for me to enter, and as I did, I took a hesitant step.

Dark oak floors were decorated with white, black, and gray fur rugs. In the center of the room, sat against the longest of the walls, was a massive black four poster bed with the same sheer curtains hanging from the railings that hung by the open balcony doorway.

It was more than I could have asked for, and turning to Freya I frowned in confusion.

"Why is my room bigger than theirs?"

She paused for a moment, opening and closing her mouth before shrugging her shoulders. "We figured you could use more space. Plus, you have a small living room set off to the side here, and even an art station to continue your work—"

"I doubt I will be able to paint again," I murmured, casting my eyes from the paint station they had set up for me, towards the balcony that called my name.

Stepping through the billowing black curtains, I let the cool air of the afternoon sun greet me. From the looks of it, their time was different from ours back home, but the sun was slowly setting and as it touched the tops of the mountains, I wondered if I would lose control here just like I did back home.

"Cassie, I know that you're upset and I'm sorry you lost your friend, but you can't let that stop you from controlling the life you have ahead of you."

Sneering in disgust at the thought, I shook my head. "How can I possibly think of a life ahead of me when I killed the person I loved?"

Turning to her, she gave me a sad smile and sighed. "I wish I could bring her back for you, but I can't. Everything happens for a reason, and because she had a pure soul, I can promise you she will be reborn one day."

"Reborn?" I asked, pausing at the idea. "What do you mean?"

"You don't honestly think that when you die that's just it?" The laughter that escaped her I didn't find amusing. I wasn't asking for her to laugh at me. I didn't know how things worked. My parents only ever told me what I was supposed to know and nothing else.

"I don't see what's so amusing."

Taking a moment, she cleared her throat and sighed. "When you die, you're reborn, or at least most of you are. Melissa, like some of the others who are pure-hearted, are given this opportunity."

Hearing this made me feel slightly better, but it didn't stop the ache in my heart from the loss of my friend. "Oh. So am I going to be when I die?"

Freya hesitated a moment, before opening and closing her mouth again before simply smiling.

"That's a conversation for another day, but don't worry, it's nothing for you to bother with right now. All I want you to do is to get situated in your new room."

Before I could reply a soft voice called out from inside my room. "Knock knock!"

Stepping towards the open door, I peered through the sheer black curtains and frowned. A girl stood there about my age with bright electric blue hair that sat in two buns on the top of her head, her eyes a hypnotically glowing green.

"Who are you?" I asked before glancing back at Freya.

"This is your assistant for your entire time here. She will tell you anything you need to know and be here to help you get situated. I have a feeling you both will get along very well." Freya replied before quickly making her way towards the door.

Running after her, I grabbed her wrist before she could leave my room, and watched as she turned to me with the kindest eyes I had ever seen. "Cassie—"

"Tell me that I'm not making a mistake being here... Tell me you can fix me."

Freya's eyes glanced up towards the young woman in the room. "Help her get ready for dinner."

She refused to answer my question and as my grip on her slipped, I watched her disappear down the hallway, out of sight. The silence of my question was almost an answer on its own, and with every bit of hope slipping from me, I quickly realized there was a chance I would never leave this place.

"So—" the girl said cheerfully. "I hope you like the room. It took forever to get things right, but I did manage to get most of your stuff—"

Spinning to face her, I frowned in confusion. "Most of my stuff?"

"Uh–yep." She nodded. "I couldn't bring everything from your room, of course, but your mother helped me pack everything she thought you would want."

"You saw my mother... And she helped you pack my stuff?"

The girl raised a brow with a smirk on her lips as she scoffed with laughter. "That's what I said... Did you hit your head on the way here?"

Did I hit my head? Was she being serious right now?

"No. I just didn't know some random girl was going to go through my stuff."

"Oh, I didn't." She laughed. "Well, not most of it, anyway. Your mom picked it out, and I snapped my fingers and brought it here."

This girl was overly excited about what she did, and I could tell she was being as nice as she could be but something about her was off. From her perky personality to her hippy style clothing. I couldn't help but wonder if she was one of those peace, love, and freedom kind of people.

"What's your name?" I asked with a sigh as I tried to make the most of my situation.

"Trixie," she replied confidently, her green eyes locked onto me as I slowly moved towards the bathroom. I couldn't say I had ever heard someone with the name Trixie before, but it definitely fit her.

"Cute name." The moment I stepped in front of the mirror, shock crossed my face. I didn't recognize the woman looking back at me. Dried blood and cuts lined my skin as mud caked parts of my hair and small leaves nestled inside.

No wonder Freya wanted to let me get refreshed before dinner.

"Yeah, you kind of look like shit." Trixie's comment caused me to glare at her and as I did, she simply shrugged her shoulders. "Hey, would you rather me lie to you?"

The comment was something Melissa used to say to me all the time, and hearing Trixie say it triggered the pain in my chest to radiate again as I tried to push it down. Seeing I was obviously upset, she stepped closer to me and stared at me in the mirror.

"Hey, it's okay. We can get you cleaned up, and looking like you in no time. Come on, let me show you the most amazing part of this entire room."

I wasn't sure what she considered to be amazing, but as she walked past me towards another door in the bathroom, she opened it and quickly disappeared from sight. Furrowing my brows, I followed, and when I stepped towards the open door, my mouth dropped. It was a closet, and the damn thing was the size of my room back home.

"Holy shit."

"I know right." Trixie laughed, looking around. "I stocked it with your clothes from home, of course, but there was still so much room, so I went shopping and filled the rest. Everything is exactly your size, and since you didn't have much in the way of jewelry—"

Watching Trixie skip towards a huge cabinet near a lit up vanity mirror, she pressed buttons and the cabinet opened to reveal a massive jewelry box adorned with more sparkling jewels than I had ever seen. "What in the hell..."

"I know it's amazing, right!" Trixie laughed. "I couldn't resist myself when it came to shopping, and your grandfather said to get whatever."

Pulling back from admiring the jewelry, I raised a brow and shook my head. "Do me a favor, Trixie. Never call him that again. I don't care if we share DNA. He isn't my grandfather."

"Oh, hostility... No worries. I'll just use first names then."

This girl was something else, and as I looked through the clothing in the room, I picked out what I would change into after my shower. "So what are you, anyway?"

"What do you mean?" She tried on some of the jewelry in the cabinet. Her obliviousness to my question causing me to stop in my tracks and stare at her as if she was stupid.

"I mean—" Gesturing towards her ears and overall appearance. My question seemed to click, and she began to laugh hysterically.

"Oh! You mean like what am I... Well, I'm a Pixie."

She had to be joking. "Trixie the Pixie?" I snorted, watching as she rolled her eyes.

"Yes, yes. I know." Shrugging though, my comment didn't seem to bother her. "My parents are hippies, and I kind of am, too. Regardless, they weren't very original and with them being free spirits, they decided to keep it easy."

"No kidding..."

With a heavy sigh, I grabbed my underwear and made my way towards the shower. I was expected to attend dinner, and if I didn't get moving now, I was never going to be ready. Stopping at the door to the closet, I looked at Trixie, waiting for her to disperse.

"Oh–" She grinned as she stood to her feet, seeing I was patiently waiting. "I'll go ahead and check on some things. I'll be back in like thirty minutes?"

Nodding my head, I watched as she sheepishly backed out of the bathroom and disappeared from sight. The sound of my bedroom door closing causing me to finally let out a small laugh.

She was something else, and perhaps someone I could get along with.

She'd never be Melissa, though.

Dinner with Odin

Thirty minutes later, I was freshly cleaned and out of the shower, drying my hair. I had never thought a hot shower could feel as amazing as it did, but the moment I finally turned off the water and stepped from it, a sigh of relief escaped my lips.

Yes, I had been through hell, but I couldn't allow my sorrow over losing Melissa to keep weighing on me. I cried for twenty minutes in the shower to the point I couldn't breathe, and wanted the world to destroy me. I was lost without her, and I hated myself for what I did, but I couldn't let it destroy me.

I had to get better for her. I had to.

When a soft knock came at the door, I knew my time was up. Trixie had made a point letting me know she would be back as soon as I was done getting ready so she could take me down to dinner. Odin, my so-called grandfather, wanted us all to join him—even though I had no interest.

Taking a deep breath, I pushed off from the bathroom countertop, putting a smile on my face as I made my way towards the bedroom door. This was a new place, and with it, I could be different. I would do what I needed to and in the end, I would become someone people could trust, someone they could look up to.

Or at least, that's what I hoped.

The moment I opened the door, Trixie's glowing green eyes met mine, and quickly she scanned them up and down my body. "What are you wearing?"

"Huh?" I glanced down at my black leggings and white oversized t-shirt. "Clothes?"

"Well, yeah, I see that." She scoffed, causing me to meet her gaze once more, crossing my arms over my chest with a frown.

"What's wrong with my clothes?"

"I literally got you all kinds of cute shit, and that's what you chose to present yourself to Odin and his table? Brave soul." Laughter escaped her, causing me to shrug.

"I don't fucking care what they think. I'm not wearing some fancy dress, crown, and shit. That's not who I am, and if they don't like it, oh well."

Nodding in agreement, she looped her arm through mine and closed the door behind me. "Fair enough. I love this rebellious nature of yours. It's definitely going to provide for an entertaining evening."

The simple touch of her looping her arm through mine brought me once again back to Melissa, and with every ounce of energy I had left, I pushed the thoughts to the back of my mind. "So what's for dinner?"

A few moments later, we arrived at the grand hall. The large vaulted ceilings and arched walkways of dark wood were a contrast to the white marble of the rest of the building. I had half expected statues of gods to line the way, but instead, I found more animal skins and a roaring fire.

In the center of the room was a grand dining table made of the same dark wood that lined the archways, and upon it were platters and platters of food from a roasted pig, and chickens to heaping piles of vegetables and bread.

"They sure do know how to eat dinner, don't they?" I muttered to Trixie as we walked towards the table.

"You guys don't eat like this back home?"

Meeting her curious gaze, I shook my head no with a smile. "I'm sure my siblings would love it if we did, but no, my mother makes sure to keep them eating right, and not over indulging."

"That's odd… Oh, look, here is your seat." She smiled cheerfully as I took my place. "I will see you after dinner."

She was leaving?! No way in hell. "Wait, where are you going? You're not eating?"

"I'm not invited to eat at Odin's table, Cassie. But I'll see you when you get done."

Shaking my head, I grabbed her wrist and pushed her into the chair next to me. "No way in fucking hell are you leaving me here to deal with these people? If I'm stuck here, so are you, 'caretaker'."

Trixie's eyes widened at my actions, and looking around, she seemed to pale. "This is your brother's seat. I can't. Plus, I have to have a formal invitation."

"Fuck my brother!" I exclaimed with a smirk. "I extend a formal invitation to you, Trixie. Will you eat with me?"

Her mouth opened and closed as she glanced around the room at those who entered, taking their places. A sigh escaped her before she quietly nodded in agreement. "It would be rude to refuse royalty," she whispered, causing me to glance at her in confusion.

"What royalty?" Before she could answer me, I thought my brother's voice sounded from behind us, and I glanced over my shoulder to look at him.

"Who is this in my seat—" Pollux's words were cut off as Trixie turned to look at him. He became speechless and with confusion I glanced at her as she looked at me as if asking what his problem was.

"Dude, go find somewhere else to sit. Trixie is joining me."

Usually, my brother would have argued. Hell, he would have demanded she be removed from the chair, but instead he moved towards the farthest end of the table without so much as a word from his mouth, which I found completely odd considering he was usually a dick.

"What was that all about?" she murmured, pulling my gaze from where my brother had gone to sit. His eyes cast down, and a frown marred his lips, as if he was troubled in some way.

"I don't have the slightest fucking clue, honestly."

"Good evening, everyone!" Odin's voice bellowed throughout the hall as he entered with his arms open and a smile on his face. "Tonight is a very special night."

Watching the white bearded man, who proclaimed himself to be my grandfather, enter the hall like the king he was, was indeed admirable, but something about him made my inner self want to claw its way out.

I was angry, and honestly, I wasn't sure why. But the moment he took his seat, and spoke softly to two other men I wasn't familiar with, I tried to dive into conversation with Trixie.

"Everyone, as you know, my grandchildren Pollux and Castor, have made it to our realm after many years of waiting." Cheers and calls of excitement came from the various figures around the table. They were excited by it, and just when I didn't think it could get any weirder, silence fell over the hall and, with all eyes turned towards the main entryway, I turned and caught Lucas' gaze.

His dark cool eyes stared at me with a look I had never had anyone give me before. It was as if he was trying to look into my soul, and stepping forward, heading in my direction, he was quickly intercepted by a young woman with blonde braids.

She muttered to him and gestured towards a seat across from where Pollux had sat. Personally, I didn't think it was a good idea to have the two men sitting next to each other, but as soon as the connected gaze was broken between Lucas and I, I tried to pay attention to anything but him.

If I wasn't careful, I'd get distracted by whatever it was he wanted with me and I couldn't allow that to happen. "Cassie, tell me how you're finding your room."

My gaze drifted from the other up to Odin, "It's okay. I only just got here."

His smile fell a bit as Freya whispered something to him, to which he nodded his head. "I suppose you're right, Cassie. No mind, there are big things coming from you—"

"How do you know?" I asked, cutting him off mid-sentence.

It obviously wasn't something people were used to seeing because the shocked expressions on their face made me smirk as I stared at Odin waiting for a response.

"What do you mean? How do I know? You have my blood in you, as does your brother—"

"Yeah, about that," I replied, watching him slightly get annoyed with my continued interruptions. "How is it that you're my mother's father? I mean, my grandmother was adamant she only slept with Zane. So it doesn't make sense."

If looks could kill, I'd be dead because Odin wasn't pleased with the bratty tone I took. Not that I gave two shits. He forced me to come here, and he was going to get every bit of me.

"I figured at your age that kind of talk would have been done already." He chuckled, trying to make it seem like I was naïve. Of course, though, the soft choking from Pollux coming from the end of the table made Odin's eyes drift for a moment, only to replace his amusement with slight concern.

Was it a concern for my brother? Who knows. However, I had a feeling he was worried if my brothers choking was a warning of sorts.

"Hate to break it to you, but I haven't been a virgin for a long fucking time. So tell me how you tricked my grandmother into fucking you and then making sure she couldn't remember." Crossing my arms over my chest, I leaned back into my seat, staring down Odin as he stared at me with an irritated expression.

"They were right when they said you had fire, Cassie."

A scoff escaped me as I rolled my eyes. "People don't know shit about me."

"So you think."

Laughing, I stared at him in disbelief. "So I know, Odin. Now why are you deflecting the question? Do you not have an answer the rest of us would care to hear?"

Freya stood to her feet as her eyes looked to me with disappointment, but before she could move, Odin grabbed her wrist gently and stopped her. "She wants to know so I'll tell her."

With a heavy sigh, Freya took her seat at the same time Odin snapped his fingers as a nearby servant brought a pitcher of amber liquid to which they poured into his horn. "I spent time on earth, but not long. While I was down there, I spotted a beautiful woman with beautiful eyes. I wanted her, but I saw she was with another and so I took his form and made love to her—"

Was he being fucking serious?! He basically lied and deceived my grandmother without her consent. What the fuck!

"Are you fucking kidding me?!" Cutting him off this time, he slammed his hand down upon the table causing it to shake.

"That's enough, Cassie! You will not disrespect me at my own table!"

"No, I will because what you did was tricked and deceived my grandmother for your own pleasure. She had no idea it was you and not Zane, and because of that, she gave herself to you. That's fucking horrible—" I was disgusted with this man, and I didn't care if he was the big man in charge here, that was wrong.

Pushing the chair back, I stood to my feet, throwing my napkin down on the table proceeding to leave. However, Odin had other plans and before I knew it, he was grabbing my arm forcing me to stop in my tracks.

"You will obey me while you're here in my realm, Castor."

Narrowing my gaze, I ripped my arm from his grasp. "I didn't ask to be here, and in fact, it's your fault I'm here at all. If it hadn't been for these stupid powers you passed down to me then I wouldn't have did what I did and there would never had been a problem."

The entire room was silent, and as Odin stared down at me with an angry scowl he said nothing. It was, in fact, my brother who spoke up. "Cassie, that's enough."

Spinning around to glare at him, I laughed. "You don't have a right to speak to me, Pollux. It's your fault I lost control trying to stop you and fucking Lucas from killing each other and in the end, Melissa died while I was trying to do the right thing. Some kind of Alpha you're going to be. You can't even keep your anger in check."

I may have gone overboard on both of them, but I had a right to be angry.

Yes, I was the one who pulled the metaphorical trigger in the end but that was only because I was trying to do the right thing, and as ironic as my life was,

I should have known no good would come from the powers Odin's wild night passed down to me.

Fuck them if they thought I was going to follow directions.

I'd burn Asgard to the ground before that happened.

After dinner Confessions

Pollux

The moment Cassie left the room became extremely silent. Odin stood where Cassie had once been, his fists clenched at his sides as he stared towards the empty archway that led to the dining room. I wasn't sure what he was going to do, but the powerful aura radiating off him right now was enough to make my wolf cower in fear.

"Odin, please come sit," Freya said as she stood from her seat.

For a moment, I thought he was going to agree, but as he stood there, he growled with what seemed frustration. "Everyone get out! Dinner is over."

He didn't have to tell me or anyone else twice as we all scattered, including the blue-haired beauty who had once been sitting with Cassie.

I wasn't sure who the girl was, but something about her I found completely intoxicating. The soft strands of electric blue hair framed her face perfectly, highlighting those mesmerizing green eyes, and when she moved, it was almost like she glided across the floor, her long purple dress flowing behind her.

Everything in my body told me to go after her, but the moment I stepped from the dining hall, she had disappeared and I didn't have the slightest clue as to where she had gone.

"She's the one, isn't she?" Lucas' voice taunted from behind me, causing me to groan. The last thing I wanted to do was entertain him, but no matter how much I tried to avoid this asshole, he always seemed to be around at the worst of times.

Turning to face him, I narrowed my eyes and glared in his direction. "What the hell are you talking about?"

"Are you seriously going to play that card?" He laughed before heading down the hallways towards the dorms. "Of all the people, I thought you would have been excited."

"Again, what the hell are you talking about, Vega?"

Lucas stopped in his tracks, glancing over his shoulder at me with nothing but amusement lingering in his eyes. "Aren't you the one who was always determined to find your soul mate, Lux? Yet, you can't even see her when your given the chance."

Soul mate? He thought that girl was my mate?

It was my turn to laugh and as I did, I passed where he stood. "She isn't my mate."

For him to even think the girl was my mate was amusing. Yeah, she was gorgeous, but she was no shifter and my mate had to be a shifter. Honestly, was Lucas not aware of our culture at all? I wasn't sure where he had been educated by pack life at all.

"Whatever you have to tell yourself, Lux. Anyone in that room could see the tension between you and her. Not to mention you couldn't keep your eyes off her the entire time we were in there, minus when Cassie went off on Odin…"

Reaching my door, I turned to look at him from down the hall once more. "You know, for someone who can't even be with his mate because she despises him, you have a lot of shit to say, don't you?"

Lucas gave a low growl as his canines protruded. "Watch yourself, Lux, the last thing you want to do is piss me off. You have no idea who I really am."

Not wasting time for me to reply, Lucas entered his room and slammed the door behind him, leaving me staring at the space he had once occupied. Anger wasn't the only thing I was feeling at that moment, and as much as I wanted to ignore what he said, I couldn't.

No one really knew who Lucas was, and that was unsettling. If he was going to be mated to my sister, I needed to know. In the end, I had no doubt about his ability to end up taming my sister. After seeing how she looked at him when they were near it was obvious to anyone who took notice that she wanted him.

Just as much as he wanted her.

Cassie

The nerve of that man. To think, once upon a time, I looked at Odin as an all powerful being. One who could fix all of our problems, and instead, he was a complete fucking asshole. "Cassie, are you okay?"

Trixie's voice called out to me from my bedroom door, and as I stormed around my room, I turned to her, watching her close the door quietly before walking further in with caution on her face.

"Can you believe what he said in there!" I yelled, shaking my head in anger. "He is a complete dick."

"Cassie—" Trixie quickly said, looking around as if someone could hear us right now. "You can't say things like that. He is the man in charge, and trust me, you don't want to get on his bad side."

His bad side?

I wasn't worried about getting on this man's bad side. What I was worried about was trying to find a way to get back home. There was no way I was staying here under the care of a man who had basically used my grandmother the way he did.

"Trixie, do you honestly think what he did was okay? I mean, that's horrible how he tricked my grandmother like that—"

"Cassie, you didn't even let him finish. For all you know, he did tell her afterwards, but instead of listening, you freaked out on him and caused a scene. There are always multiple sides to a story."

Raising a brow, I stared at her in shock. How she spoke to me reminded me so much of Melissa, and with a heavy sigh, I nodded.

Maybe she was right, maybe I did freak out on her for no reason.

"Whatever–" I muttered before plopping down on my bed staring up at the ceiling. "First night in Asgard, and I created a shit show."

Laughter escaped Trixie as she made her way towards me and laid upon the bed beside me. "Don't worry, you're not the first one to have a crazy first day. But I will admit you're the first one who has ever gone off on Odin like that. It was entertaining."

Glancing at Trixie, I stared blankly before we both burst into a fit of laughter. Thinking back to the moment when I went off on Odin, I did remember briefly seeing a look of shock on his face as his lips parted, obviously having not expected me to flip out like I did. I didn't mean to be disrespectful, but I was angry at time.

"So, they said I was going to be attending some school or something." I finally groaned after the silence that had fallen between us. It was clear Trixie didn't plan on leaving anytime soon, and if she wasn't, I might as well make conversation.

Shooting up from the bed, she turned and looked at me with the brightest smile I had ever seen on anyone. "Oh my god, yes. You're going to love it, it's amazing."

"I don't know about love it... but I don't really have a choice but to go."

Trixie didn't seem to notice my sarcasm over the idea of going to this school as she launched into a conversation about what extracurricular classes they offered and how amazing the cafeteria was. Not to mention the green house and gardens where her parents worked from what she explained.

"I'm telling you, Cassie. There are so many different people that go there. Shifters of all kinds and the best part... They are all like you."

"Like me?" What the hell did she mean they were like me?

Furrowing her raised brows, she giggled, nodding her head. "Yeah, they all have celestial blood in them, too. There's about a hundred, I think."

Taking a moment to take this information in, I realized quite quickly what she was insinuating. "You mean to tell me that all of these kids here are the results of the gods of Asgard getting their fuck on in the human realm?"

Rolling her eyes, she frowned at me. "Well, when you say it like that it makes it sound bad."

"Because it is." I scoffed with a chuckle. "At least I'm not the only one here."

"Well—" she muttered, letting her sentence trail off as if she wasn't sure she should tell me whatever it was that was on her mind.

I wasn't a person who liked secrets, at least not secrets kept from me.

"Trixie, what are you not telling me?"

A heavy sigh escaped her as she shrugged her shoulders again and began to fiddle with her hands placed on her lap. "Well, you and your brother are the only ones that came from Odin."

There was no way that was possible. After hearing the stories of who Odin was, and what he used to do in legends, there was no way I could believe that.

"No way, there is no way he only produced my mother through his time of fucking women on earth. I can't believe that." Standing from the bed, I made my way towards the balcony, admiring the dark shadows dancing upon the realm welcomed by the darkness that consumed us.

It was crazy to think how in the dark, this realm and my own could look so similar. The land completely enveloped and every flaw or imperfection hidden away from the sight of those who could potentially judge it.

"There were others, Cassie." Trixie said softly, causing me to sigh. "But none of them lived to make it here."

Turning quickly, I stared at her, unsure if I had heard her correctly. "What?"

"They died, Cassie. Why do you think everyone is excited about you and your brother being here? It's never happened before."

Trixie gave me a meek smile before turning and walking towards my bedroom door. I hadn't ever thought there were people like Pollux and I who existed, and hearing now there were, but we were the only one descended from Odin, was shocking.

"Thanks for coming to hang out with me," I called out to her, not wanting to seem ungrateful for her company. No matter how much of a cow I had been since I had come here, she had been nothing but kind to me.

Looking over her shoulder, a small hit of a smile played at the corner of her lips. "Don't worry about it. Just promise me tomorrow you will be properly dressed."

She really did hate my choice of clothing tonight, but nodding my head, I sighed. "Yeah, okay and I'll make sure my brother and I are on good behavior tomorrow... or I will try, at least."

The moment I mentioned Pollux, curiosity seemed to pass her gaze as if she was thinking about something. "Yeah, about him. He is strange, isn't he?"

Trixie was calling my brother strange?

"Yeah, I guess." She was the oddest person I had ever met, but perhaps to her we were the oddest people she had ever met. It made me worry about what I was walking into tomorrow at this supposed school.

"Well, I'm off. I need to get some stuff done before class tomorrow. I'll swing by in the morning and grab you," she suddenly said cheerfully as she opened the bedroom door. "Remember, dress to impress or I will dress you myself."

With the close of my bedroom door, I was once again left alone, and turning I cast my eyes once again out over the dark horizon, looking for anything that would tell me I wasn't alone in this place.

Just because I had come with my brother and Lucas didn't mean they were on my side, and honestly, the thought of Lucas right now was something I didn't want to dwell on too long. My body called out to him, wanting him because he was my mate.

At the same time, though, I was terrified to get close to him.

The last thing I wanted was for history to repeat itself.

First day of school

Cassie

When Trixie said she was going to be at my room early, I had no idea it was going to be before the sun even rose. I tried my hardest to ignore her persistent knocking, but in the end, she let herself into my room and forced me from bed.

"Remind me again why we are up so early," I groaned as I took my brush to my hair, trying to tame the wavy locks which seemed to have a mind of their own.

Trixie laughed at my comment as she stood from my bed and walked towards the open bathroom doorway. She had been insistent on waiting for me to finish in the shower and get dressed. Proclaiming I would go back to sleep if left alone.

"Because breakfast is in thirty minutes, and our first class is in an hour. Now stop messing around. You're lucky I'm agreeing to you wearing jeans."

Glancing out the bathroom door, I stared at her before rolling my eyes. "I don't even eat breakfast." The grumbled response caused Trixie to groan.

"Stop, just brush your damn teeth so we can go."

My mouth dropped open upon hearing Trixie's annoyance. I hadn't known her for long, but in that time, I had never heard her get annoyed like she was now. Cocking a brow, I stared at her as a slow smile spread across my face. "Was that annoyance?"

She stared blankly, her eyes unmoving before a snort of laughter escaped her. "Oh, my God. Just come on already. I want coffee—"

"Wait, you guys have coffee here?" I asked, cutting her off, more than excited about getting coffee and perhaps using it to survive the day. My question seemed to shock her as she stared at me as if I had grown a second head.

"Uh–yeah. Don't you guys have that in the human realm?"

Opening and closing my mouth, I placed the brush upon the counter and nodded. "Yeah, we do. Sorry, I guess part of me just thought this place would be super different."

Glancing back at Trixie as I moved from the bathroom, I headed towards my bed where my small backpack sat waiting patiently for me to collect. I contemplated what else I would uncover here that was similar to my old home.

"So about this coffee, there wouldn't happen to be donuts too, would there?"

Slinging my bag over my shoulder, Trixie grabbed her stuff as we made our way out of my bedroom. A wide smile spread across her face as she gave me a knowing glance which all but answered my question. "What's your favorite flavor?"

I wasn't sure what I had expected going to this school, but it definitely wasn't to walk up to a massive gothic building amongst the white marbled structures that surrounded it and be hit with the feelings of overwhelming chaos. It was beautiful with it's stained glass windows and high arches which swirled with elegant mason work raising the roof high into the heavens.

My breath was taken away, and as I let my eyes take in the area, I was truly taken aback by the lush green gardens, peaked tops of a large glass greenhouse in the distance, and mass amounts of decorated ponds with waterfalls. The place reminded me so much of a high fantasy castle the only thing missing as the flying dragon and damsel in distress.

"Cassie, are you coming?" Trixie called out from ahead of me, snapping me back to the present. I had stopped walking and stood in shock staring at the surrounding area I hadn't even paid attention to her continuing without me.

"Yeah, sorry. I was just—taking it all in."

She let her glowing green eyes gaze around the area, taking in everything I myself was admiring, but as she did a puzzled look crossed her face before she turned back to me. "I guess I can see why you would find it pretty. I'm so used to looking at it I don't even notice it like that anymore."

Moving towards her, I felt nothing but shock in her words.

How could she not want to admire this place all the time? It's beautiful.

"You're crazy. I'd admire this place every moment of the day."

Letting a small smirk of amusement escape her, she shrugged her shoulders. "Maybe, but without coffee? I don't think so."

Coffee... It was my best friend and comfort to survive anything.

Something my mother and I had in common. "Lead the way... I need like four cups."

"Four cups?" Trixie laughed. "Why do you need so many?"

Staring at her with my mouth parting, I shook my head. "To get through today. How else do you expect me to be nice to anyone? It's better to caffeinate me to make me cheerful otherwise I'm likely to bring this whole place down."

"Yeah, okay let's not do that." She smirked as we passed through the large burnt red and black wooden doors accented with black iron that went from the ground high up above me. The door had to have been at least twenty feet high, a little excessive in my opinion but to think about how they made that was pretty amazing.

The moment we passed the doors, I was stopped in my tracks once more. Outside there hadn't been many people wandering around, but the moment I stepped inside, the building people were everywhere. It reminded me of the college my parent's went to I had toured my senior year of high school.

There was no rhyme or reason to the chaos, but one distinct difference between them all was they didn't look quite like the people I had known in the human realm. Most looked human-like which was nice, but others had brightly colored hair, gold shimmering accents, and most of all—wings.

"Trixie... that pink-haired girl has wings."

They weren't the glittering wings someone would have initially thought of when you say wings, and they weren't exactly feathered either. They were red and white and though there were scattered feathers throughout, they were also almost fur-like. An odd look for someone who was supposed to fly.

"Oh, her?" Trixie replied with a sigh. "Yeah, that's Cersei. She has Griffin in her, and honestly, I don't see how but don't get too close to that one. She is a bit... unstable."

Trixie wasn't someone who typically said bad things about anyone, and hearing her say this girl was unstable, and I was best to basically stay clear from her was shocking. "Noted."

Pulling me along behind her, Trixie took me down various hallways lined with photos, and floral decor, dark wood floors lining wall to wall. Every inch of the place I admired until we approached the dining hall as she explained and I was taken back by how many people actually filled it.

Tables upon tables littered the massive hall adorned with black, white, and red table clothes. Floral centerpieces with strange flowers I had never seen before, not to mention the awesome black steel candle hanging candle chandelier sitting massively in the center of the room.

As soon as I entered the room with Trixie all eyes fell upon me.

Being put on the spot like wasn't something I enjoyed. And as I followed Trixie past the vast amount of people lingering about their tables eating breakfast and drinking coffee, among other things, I took note of the brightly colored hair, eyes, and even tails which adorned some of the figures.

Even though they were different from the type of people I was used to, I could see couples, best friends, and what appeared to be siblings.

"You keep staring like you have been, Cassie, and someone is likely to think you, weird."

Weird... I was weird. I had been called weird and dangerous my entire life and though I played it out by acting like I didn't care, truth be told, deep down I really did. I just was very good at not letting people see my emotions.

Hiding was something I did well.

"I'm not worried about what people think," I replied with a grin as I nudged her with my shoulder. "Now, where's this coffee? As pretty as it is here, I need coffee before anyone else comes to speak to me."

As the giggle escaped her, we made our way towards a small bar area in the far back right corner of the hall where a pretty brunette with golden eyes stood handing out cups of drinks to students in line. The entire place seemed like an upscale resort with the way staff seemed to maintain everything, at least from what I had seen so far.

"What can I get you ladies today?" The brunette woman said with a razor sharp smile. Her fanged teeth caught me off guard as my eyes widened in surprise by the sight of them. I hadn't meant to stare, but when she frowned at me I quickly realized I was.

"I'm sorry... I just—I'll take a coffee with cream, no sugar, please."

The woman's smile was shy, but she gave me a knowing look which had nothing but amusement dancing within her eyes. "It's okay. You must be Cassie, the new girl."

Surprised she knew who I was, I nodded slowly, and glanced at Trixie who shrugged her shoulders. "I am." As she handed my coffee I continued down the line with Trixie towards where the spread of food sat upon platters. Heaps of meat, fruit, and breads. Enjoy food to feed an army, but instead simply feed a bunch of shifters.

"Cassie, you're awfully quiet for someone who wouldn't stop talking yesterday."

Glancing up at Trixie once more, I sighed, shrugging my shoulders. "It's not that I mean to be quiet, I'm just taking all of this in... It's a little—"

"Overwhelming?" she replied finishing my sentence.

"Yeah, something like that." I nodded as we turned and made our way towards an empty table. I didn't want to seem awkward, but shit... this place was more than overwhelming and honestly, I just wanted to go back to bed.

"Trixie!" an annoyingly sweet voice said with a slight bit of amusement. I watched Trixie's shoulders tense for a moment before we both turned and took in the overly prideful figure of a girl with golden blonde hair and fiery golden red eyes. "Is this her?"

"Am I the new girl?" I asked, causing the girl's eyes to widen as a smile spread across her face. She didn't seem to expect my outburst but frankly I didn't care.

I had only just arrived here and currently I felt like an animal at the zoo with how everyone kept looking at me.

"This is Cassie," Trixie replied quickly, giving me a wide eyed look to stop talking.

"Cassie—" the girl purred with a grin. "Well, Cassie, I'm Ambrozia but everyone calls me Zia. If you ever need anything don't hesitate to ask. I'd love it if we could be friends."

It was more than obvious this girl was only acting the way she was because she wanted something, and if there was one thing I hated more than being stared at—was fake ass people with secret agendas.

"Thanks," I replied, trying to tame the disgust brewing at the bottom of my stomach. "But I think Trixie has everything covered."

"Excuse me?" Zia scoffed, placing her hands on her hips. "That's a bit rude."

I nodded my head in agreement with a smile before crossing my arms over my chest. She wasn't wrong. It was rude, but it was intended to be. "So is being fake just to make yourself look better."

I hadn't planned to come here and start problems but it seemed like this girl thought to highly of herself. "You're going to regret that decision."

"Perhaps." I laughed while taking a seat at the table. "I guess we will wait and see."

It didn't take Zia long to get the hint and disappear and as she did, Trixie sat next to me with her mouth wide open in complete shock over what I had just done. "No one talks to her like that."

"Maybe no.. But she won't get me with her fake shit."

Inanna

Pollux

I hadn't bothered setting an alarm for classes, expecting I would get up early, just like I had done so many times before. The problem was though, today of all days ended up not being a day why I got up early. The moment the sun hit me in the face, I had opened my eyes and realized I only had forty minutes to get ready for class and make my way there.

Lucas could have been nice enough to tell me it was time to go, but as I passed his room in a rush, it was clear he had left long ago by the empty look to his room from the cracked door he had left open.

"Fucking asshole," I muttered under my breath as I followed the route I was explained when I had first arrived. The letter had been vague, but I could see the peaks of the school from the window in my room.

Rushing through the gardens, I headed down the cobbled streets of the town, making my way towards the dark peaks of the school ahead. The entire argument from the previous night with Cassie and Odin rolled through my mind, but trying not to let it bother me, I pushed through until the large doors of the school came into view.

Did I know where these damn classes were? No.

But I was going to have to figure it out because I didn't have another choice.

The moment I passed the threshold of the building, I came face to face with a dark-skinned boy with blue eyes and black curly clean cut hair. He leaned against the pillar just inside the entryway, a white t-shirt clinging to his muscles, and blue jeans tight around his legs. I wasn't sure exactly who he was, but when his eyes met mine, he laughed.

"Pollux, right?" His voice was cool and collected tone. He glanced down at his watch and pushed off from the wall, walking towards me.

"Yeah... who are you?" I wasn't trying to be rude, but honestly, I had no idea who this dude was and yet he knew my name, obviously. He must have been waiting for me.

Chuckling again, he rested his arms across his chest as he looked me up and down. "My name's Bronn, Bronn Straton. I'm your tour guide for the first day, but I will admit we were supposed to have started forty-five minutes ago."

"Yeah, I overslept," I replied, rubbing the back of my neck in a sheepish way. "I take it class already started?"

"Yeah, you could say that." He chuckled as he turned and gestured with his hand for me to follow him. "However, they will make exceptions because you're new. Just don't make it a habit."

The way he said not to make it a habit had me rolling my eyes behind his back. I had just graduated high school and the last thing I wanted to do was go back to school again. I had no interest in going to college. I was supposed to be training to be the best Alpha my world had ever seen, and instead, I was dealing with more bullshit than I wanted.

I suppose the training grounds here will suffice to strengthen me.

I just didn't want to do anymore book work.

The moment the thought crossed my mind, I instantly groaned because Bronn led me to a door that said Magic Basics 101. "What's this?"

Glancing over his shoulder at me, he quirked his brow and frowned. "Your first class."

"My first class? I don't remember this on my schedule." I said, pulling the paper out of my pocket listing four classes, and most of them were sparring and training.

"Oh, yeah." Bronn chuckled. "Your schedule was changed this morning. Here I was given this list."

Bronn pulled out a piece of paper from his own pocket and handed it to me. The class list on it was far from anything that I wanted. Basic Magic 101, History of Celestials, Art of Self Defense, Leadership, and then Training. My eyes gazed over the paper he handed me and slowly my irritation rose.

"No way. This has to be a mistake. I don't need any of this shit."

Bronn found amusement in my anger and simply shrugged his shoulders gesturing for me to enter the class. "Sorry, but I don't make the rules. I just follow them."

"Who do I need to speak to about this? There is no way I'm doing any of this." I was firm in my response and unwilling to negotiate. I wasn't going to be stuck doing shit I didn't need. None of it was going to benefit me apart from the training.

Hell, I was a natural born leader! An Alpha with every right to my throne.

Bronn didn't seem impressed by my attitude and with a sigh, he shook his head. "You know... I get that you don't want to do this crap, but honestly, all of it would benefit you whether you think it would or not. So instead of giving me shit about something that was handed to me... go to fucking class, man."

I understood he was just trying to do what he was told to do, but that didn't mean I had to comply. If I was going to be the best Alpha I needed to be then I had to strengthen myself. I had to be the strongest fighter the universe has known, and none of that I would learn within books.

"Just tell me who I need to talk to."

Shaking his head again, he looked off down the hall for a moment as if lost in thought and then laughed. "You want to meet her... okay? Let's go."

Continuing further down the hallway, he came to another staircase and heading up it we walked two flights before coming to the landing his destination was on. I didn't know who it was I was going to speak to, but the moment we came into a small lounge, I noted the large brown double doors in front of me and hesitated.

The power radiating from behind the door made me want to submit, but also find solace in whomever it was. Not wasting any more time, Bronn pushed open the door and there in front of me behind a large white wooden desk with her head buried in a file of papers was a red-haired woman on a mission.

"Inanna, do you have a moment?" Bronn replied with nothing but respect. His body completely straightened and his legs spread slightly with his hands clasped behind his back as if he was a guard stationed outside of an important building.

Her deep sea-green eyes glanced up towards us, and as soon as she saw me, a small smile crept across her lips before she placed down her pen. "Bronn, is something wrong with our new resident?"

"No ma'am, but it does seem something is wrong with his schedule. He wanted to come see you."

"I see." Gesturing with her hand, she urged me forward, and with haste I approached. "Pollux, what seems to be the problem?"

"The schedule I was given last night by Freyja doesn't match the one Bronn handed me. I was hoping to get this clarified," I replied, trying to show her that this was a serious matter that I wanted handled.

However, as she stared at me, she strummed her nails against her desk and sighed. "Unfortunately, Pollux, your schedule was changed for a reason. You need more help in those categories and that's why it was changed."

"More help?" Scoffing, I rolled my eyes, crossing my arms over my chest. "I don't need more help unless it's training to become even better than I am now. I'm the future Alpha of my pack. It's my birthright to lead. No one can tell me otherwise."

Inanna leaned back in her chair with a smirk on her face as she watched me. "You know the fact you think that shows you need help. Just because it's supposed to be yours doesn't mean it will be, and in fact..."

She quickly ruffled through the documents on her desk, leaving me speechless and in shock at what she was saying. This woman obviously had no clue who I was, and if she didn't, someone desperately needed to tell her.

Finding whatever she had been looking for, she scanned over the paperwork with a smile. "Ah, yes—you have a sister, don't you? A twin?"

Realizing where she was going with this conversation, I jumped to my feet, fists white as I clenched them together. If she thought for one moment I was going to allow my chaotic sister to become Alpha of our pack, she was wrong.

"It is mine!" I roared at her with anger. "My sister will never hold that title. She is too much of a risk, and if she isn't careful will end up killing someone again."

At my words, Inanna's brows rose in surprise, and it was obvious she didn't know that little fact about Cassie. Which shocked me because I would have assumed Odin would have let them know that small bit of information.

"Tell me more about what your sister did..." Inanna replied, leaning forward, her elbows resting on the desk and her hands clasped in front of her mouth. There was intrigue in her eyes that made me slightly uncomfortable, and swallowing, I contemplated what to tell her, suddenly worried about my outburst.

"It was an accident, but she lost control and her best friend died."

The admission of what happened to her friend Melissa struck an empty pain in my chest I hadn't expected to be there. I didn't want to believe it was my fault what happened to her, but at the same time, I knew I was responsible as well.

"I see," She muttered softly. "You saw this happen, I take it?"

Nodding slowly, I sighed. "Yes, as did the rest of our pack." The vague memory of their horrified expressions was something that would be forever imprinted in my mind.

"Why didn't you stop her from losing control? You said you're the future Alpha. Surely there was something you could have done to stop her... Unless you were part of it."

Narrowing my gaze at her, I squared my shoulders with a tight-lipped expression. "It wasn't that easy. Cassie isn't—" Pausing in my thoughts, I tried to find the right words, and as Inanna's brows raised with interest to what I was going to say I shook my head.

"Cassie's what?"

"Nothing, she's my sister and everyone makes mistakes," I replied firmly, unwilling to make anymore comments on who my sister was. It wasn't anyone's business and I shouldn't have opened my mouth to begin with.

"I understand, but considering that I don't see the proof of why you don't need these classes. I'm afraid you're going to have to take them. Give me one semester, and if you can show me after that semester you don't need them, then I will change your schedule. Does that sound like a deal to you?"

With no point in arguing further, the hollow sensation of defeat grew in my chest. "Understood. Thank you for seeing me."

Turning, I marched from Inanna's office more upset than I had been when I went in. I wasn't sure what it was about the entire situation that irritated me the most, but Bronn seemed to get I was pleased and so he walked behind me without saying a word.

If she wanted proof I deserved my title, then I would give her proof.

I would be the Alpha everyone would remember.

Proving a point

Cassie

Class after class, I was introduced to so many people. I found my mind swirling with the amount of names I was supposed to remember, and I was happy to see the end of the day come quickly. The entire day I hadn't seen my brother, and wondered whether he had actually come to class at all.

Following a few other students I didn't know, I headed out to what they said were the training grounds, prepared to see if that was where Pollux had gone. Leaving the large vast buildings of the school, I followed down the cobbled paths and covered breezeways until the path led me through grassy fields with the site of a massive golden arena in the distance.

The voices of the warriors grunting, groaning, and yelling commands to one another coil be heard before even stepping foot into the arena, and I had no doubt this was where my brother had gone.

I hoped Trixie would have been able to go with me, but I found it unfortunate she was preoccupied by some task she had to do with her parents, so instead, I ventured out here alone.

As the building grew closer, I noted how the high walls of the area stood taller than the school itself, reminding me of the colosseum in Rome. A place where gladiators used to fight for the entertainment of their people. The same people who were ruthless and desired to see the blood and gore that made a lot of men lose their lives.

It didn't surprise me once I stepped in and took notice of the men sparing that they would have something set up like this. Odin may not have been what people called a "Greek" god, but according to legend, the gods all were the same in the eyes of their believers, no matter the culture they came from. And here in these walls, it was obvious to see fighting was a sport all took seriously.

Stepping forth down the stone steps of the arena, the littered sounds of students sitting and watching as they yelled for their favorite people took me by shock. I didn't find this kind of thing entertaining. I knew training was important, but the way they were acting was barbaric in a way, at least to me.

"Hey, your name's Cassie, right?" A voice called from my left. Glancing over my shoulder, I took in the brown hair and golden eyes of a dark-skinned girl who was in my second period advanced magic class.

"Yeah it is. You're Sansa, the witch."

Small laughter escaped her as she nodded her head, "Yeah I am. Well, I'm a hybrid like everyone else here. Celestial blood and all of that. Come sit with me. There's no point in watching alone."

Hesitating for a moment, I gave a tight-lipped smile and nodded as I watched her slide over so I could sit down. "Thanks, I'm not really here to watch. Just see if my brother actually showed up today."

Her eyes lit up when I spoke of my brother and, with an eager smile, she nodded. "Oh girl, he did."

"Why did you say it like that..." I mumbled with a sigh. A million and one thoughts ran through my head at her comment, and as she pointed in the direction of the field, I followed her finger and caught sight of my brother heaving up and down with golden eyes and protruding fangs as he stared down at his opponent, who laid upon the ground.

"He has been killing them out there... metaphorically, of course. Bronn was our strongest fighter, and as you can tell, he dominated Bronn in no time. Which I'm not sure if that's going to be a good thing or a bad thing."

Glancing at her quickly, I raised my brow in question. "Why do you say that?"

"Well, Bronn is my half-brother, unfortunately. Only by our father, of course, celestial blood. His mother was a werewolf, and friends with my mother–a witch. From what my mother said... Our dad enjoyed poly relationships."

Sansa spoke about the situation as if it wasn't a big deal, and whereas I was only Odin's granddaughter, they were direct children of a god. How was it my brother was stronger than a direct child? It made little sense.

"That's crazy... who was your dad?" The question made her laugh and looking to me she shook her head.

"Who knows... there were speculations on who he was, but no one dares to claim their heritage. Odin, Freya, and Frigg just try to clean up their mess."

"That's not cool. I mean you should at least know," I replied, feeling slightly bad for her that she didn't know who her father was.

"It's okay, I'm not too bothered," she added before cheering for the people on the field. As I looked back towards my brother, I watched him walk towards the sidelines where a group of girls were flirting. His signature smile came on display causing me to cringe as I watched him "work his magic" or so he liked to call it.

"God, can he be anymore annoying..." I muttered with disgust, rolling my eyes as I admired the others. It was then when my eyes met Lucas', I noticed he was staring right at me. Those same damn mesmerizing eyes catching me off guard as a slow smirk slid onto the corner of his lips.

"Oh, snap... does he belong to you?" Sansa asked, causing me to scoff.

"He kinda does, but she won't admit to it."

Trixie's overly cheerful voice appeared behind me and gave me a heart attack and as I jumped, I placed my hand upon my chest to turn and glare at her from over my shoulder. "Jesus Christ, woman... you about gave me a heart attack. You can't go sneaking up on people like that."

Both Sansa and Trixie laughed at my reaction as I grumbled my unhappiness under my breath. "Don't change the subject," Sansa added. "I need the juicy details."

I wasn't sure what it was about Sansa, but between her and Trixie, I felt like we had been old friends who had known each other our entire lives. "It's complicated."

"Everything is always complicated with you." Trixie smirked. "He is hot, though, just like your brother. I'm not sure why you're opposed to him, but if you're not careful, one of the other girls will try to snag him up."

The thought of one of the other girls touching Lucas did bother me, and I didn't like that it did. Yet, no matter the fact he was supposed to be my mate, I couldn't get past the shit he had done. To hide being my mate, and then act like an asshole all these months.

He confused me, like an internal war brewing in my mind that just won't let up.

"He is an ass—" I mumbled, trying to look away from him and not let him see how much he was bothering me.

"Looks like someone else likes his ass—" Quickly darting my gaze back to Lucas, I watched Zia walk to him with a smile on her face and anger flared through me. A swirling mass of chaos slowly started to build inside me, and as if he knew, his eyes met mine and he smiled.

"Oh, that's how he wants to play is it?" I replied in a sinister tone as I glanced towards Sansa and Trixie. "Two can play at this game.."

Trixie's normally happy expression turned to one of concern as I stood to my feet. "Cassie, what are you doing?"

Sliding my jacket off, I grabbed my hair band and quickly pulled my long purplish-pink hair up into a messy bun, and continued down the steps of the arena. I knew very well people were watching me, but right now I didn't care. The swirling chaos in my heart was calling me to play with him.

"Hey, coach!" I called out letting my gaze slide from Lucas to the extremely tall older shifter who stood on the sidelines watching my brother and another kid spar. My brother of course dominating the kid with ease. "Let me have a round with him."

Laughter escaped the man as he shook his head no. "No way. You will get your ass hurt, and I'm not being responsible for it."

"I wasn't asking for your permission," I said through clenched teeth as I ran, leaping over the figures of the three men who had been in my way. I was far more skilled than my brother was. With perfect timing, I landing on the ground in front of the kid, my eyes locked onto Lux with a wicked glance.

His blow to the kid stopped in it's tracks as I caught his wrist when I landed. "What the fuck, Cassie!"

"Get that girl off the field!" The coach yelled from a short distance away as murmur's and gasps echoed around the stadium.

"Oh, come on Pollux. Let's give them something to really get them excited."

My brothers eyes narrowed as he sneered. "No fucking way. You're not supposed to be out here."

"Are you worried about losing to me again?" I asked him in a teasing tone as I stepped closer to him. "Come on—brother. You never refused to TRY and beat me before... do you not want them to see who really is the best out of us?"

"You let it out, didn't you... Talon told you about that—" Laughter escaped me at his response. Yes, Talon had said a lot of things but he wasn't here.

"Fight or die, Pollux. Your choice."

I wouldn't really kill my brother, and he knew that. It was simply something we had done as kids. The first one to land a potentially deadly blow was the winner of the fight, but the problem was where he did like to fight he didn't train as often as me because his ego over being the "future Alpha" made him believe he didn't need to.

I however... I thrived for the battle. A secret I held deep inside me.

The desire to watch blood flow like rivers upon the ground.

Standing his ground, he took his stance with an angry glare. A glare I lived to see, because honestly, he and Talon were the only ones who ever gave me a run for my money when it came to battling and the adrenaline was a drug I craved.

Taking the same stance as my brother, I heard the murmured words of the coach. "Lux, are you sure about this..."

"Yeah, I am. Start the fucking match. If she wants to get what they had, that's on her."

So cocky and foolish.

A voice inside me spoke softly in the darkness, and as it did, I hesitated for a moment. One single moment, and during that moment, Pollux made his move catching me in the side of face. I paused for just a moment, the tangy metallic taste in my mouth causing something in me to smirk with satisfaction.

"Oh, brother—is that all you have?" Making my move, I launched myself into attack. Swing after swing, hit after hit, we battled and our movements matched like that of an elegant dance between partners. We were evenly matched in our current state, but there was a side of me he would never be able to touch.

With a sudden blow, we both landed on the ground knocked back by each other's hits, and landing on the ground, I wiped the blood from my mouth one more. Just to realize Zia was standing near me. "Aww, did you fall?"

"Go fuck yourself, Barbie," I spat at her. The distraction gave enough time for my brother to grab me by my hair and throw me to the ground once more. The stupid bitch distracted me on purpose, and knowing she did pissed me off.

Slowly the burning fire inside me grew, and as I gazed at Lux, who stood in front of where Zia and Lucas stood, their eyes growing wide with realization of how pissed I truly was. Lux had no choice but to face me, and as he charged, I spun and kicked him, landing a hit to his chest which sent him flying through the air until he hit the ground with a thud.

"Using a girl, Lux!" I yelled at him with a maniacal laugh. "That's cheating."

"Cassie, that's enough." The coach yelled, but his words fell on deaf ears as I stalked towards my brother.

"Do you submit, Lux?" I asked as I watched him struggle to stand. "Just submit, and this will all be over."

"Go fuck yourself, Cassie," he snapped as he struggled to his feet. "I'll never submit to you."

Placing my hand on my chest, I smirked, shaking my head. "Pity... So I guess you want to continue then. Well, come on... I'm waiting."

"I said enough!" The coach yelled again as he came to stand between Pollux and I. "I don't know how you did things back home, but that isn't how shit works here. When I say enough, that means to stop. Do you hear me?"

Looking up at the man, I smiled, seeing the irritation and anger swirling behind the depths of his golden eyes. "Sure thing, coach. It was just fun and games anyways. May I suggest picking your best fighters another way? Clearly some of your men aren't up to the challenge."

Turning on my heels, I didn't bother to wait to hear what the man was going to say. Instead, I passed him and headed out of the circle towards where I had once been sitting. Hopefully, everyone now knew I was more than just some new girl.

I was hell, and they would remember me forever.

Sexual Tension & a Party

Cassie

Who says you can't be classy and sassy at the same time? The moment I put my egotistical brother in his place and showed everyone what kind of person I was, I felt better than I ever have. Lucas wanted to gain the attention of the surrounding woman, and I had no doubt many other men there noticed me at that moment as someone who was... Attainable.

Grabbing my jacket, I made my way back through the tunnel entrance of the colosseum, ready to get back to my room to relax. It may have been my first day, but the teachers here were unforgiving when it came to homework... The sound of that word was disgusting on my tongue but needed, regardless.

As the shadows of the tunnel enveloped me from the sun, a firm grip caught me, and as I was spun, I came face to face with Lucas' deep enchanting gaze, matched with a frown. "What the fuck was that out there, Cassie?"

Laughter bubbled in my throat as I ripped my arm from his grasp. "Don't fucking touch me, Lucas. I was having fun, and I know you enjoyed it."

"Fun?" He scoffed with irritation. "You and Lux both went too fucking far and you know it. What do you think you have to be badass and show the school who you are? I didn't take you for being the center of attention kind of girl."

With my mouth open, I glared at him as I gripped my jacket in my hand tightly. "Who the hell are you to tell me what kind of girl I am? I can be whomever I want to be, and it's none of your concern, Lucas."

Turning, I continued to storm down the path, but was only able to make it a few feet before I was grabbed again and this time pinned against the cold brick wall of the colosseum. My heart raced in my chest as he pressed his body against me. His thigh was in between my legs as my wrists were held above my chest.

"You're my fucking mate. It's my job to be concerned."

"Get the fuck off me," I all but spat at him as I struggled within his grasp, unable to break free. He was stronger than he looked, and even though my body was on full alert, wanting him to devour me as that delicious fresh rain scent wrapped around me, I had to stay alert. I couldn't allow myself to get distracted by him.

"No. You're going to listen—"

"Go fuck yourself, Lucas. I'm not listening to shit you have to say. Why don't you go back to the whores, you were entertaining and leave me the fuck alone. This between us is never going to happen," I snapped, causing his eyes to go wide before a small smirk crossed his lips.

I had expected him to lash out because of my comment. To tell me he hated me or that he never wanted a mate like me, but instead, he stood there holding me in place with a shit-eating grin on his face. "You're jealous."

"What—no." I scoffed, rolling my eyes. "Why would I be jealous of them? They are beneath me."

"Beneath you, huh?" He chuckled as he leaned closer, our lips only inches apart, causing my breath to hitch at the proximity. "Seems like right now I'm the one technically beneath you... in between you—" The whispered response as he brushed his lips against mine caused me to gasp before he leaned in towards my ear.

"I can make you feel things you never have before, princess."

Part of me hesitated when Lucas spoke, but the other part of me begged for him to show me. Yet, the part that controls my mouth was asking to be punished. "So can any other guy at this school. What makes you so special?"

There was not a moment of hesitation on his side as his lips captured mine and his tongue invaded my mouth. The taste of him on my tongue was pure heaven and as I moaned into the way he possessed me, a low growl escaped his throat, pushing him to become rougher and more dominating with every passing second.

Roaming hands and heated moments were things I wasn't accustomed to. I had always preferred one-night stands and quick satisfaction, so this was beyond mind blowing, and caught up in the moment, I seemed to forget completely about what was going on around us, including where I was.

"Whoa, so much for not liking him." A voice called out, stopping Lucas and me in our tracks.

There before me were Sansa and Trixie, staring at the compromising position Lucas and I were in. Pushing against him, the interrupted moment caused him to loosen up his grip and, with my push, he let go and stumbled back with a smile.

"Geez, no need to get aggressive, Cassie," he muttered as I quickly adjusted myself, embarrassed by being caught.

"Go fuck yourself, Lucas." The grumbled response caused Sansa to snort with laughter as she looked everywhere but at me.

Stepping close again, he brushed his fingers down my arm, leaving a trail of erotic sensations running through my body. "Don't act like you didn't enjoy that."

"Oh, I hope you did," I replied teasingly before letting my smile fall. "Because it will never happen again. Stay away from me... I'm not the girl you want."

Pushing past him, I made my way towards Sansa and Trixie, gesturing for them to follow me. The last thing I wanted was for him to tell them anything, but no matter how I tried to tell myself that once again, the shared kiss with him was nothing—I couldn't.

"So—" Trixie started to say before I quickly glared at her. "Nevermind..."

It took twenty minutes to get back to the place where I was staying, and the entire time we walked, I listened to Sansa and Trixie talking about the party that was supposed to be happening this evening. Some back to school thing that excited them.

"I think this season is going to be more chaotic than usual with how everyone is already acting," Sansa commented, causing Trixie to laugh.

"No kidding. Especially with our two new pupils." Looking at me as she spoke, a mischievous grin crossed her lips. "You're coming tonight, right?"

"Coming to what?"

"That party?" Sansa replied. "Were you listening to anything that we said?"

Shaking my head, I gave them a sheepish grin. I had been too preoccupied thinking about Lucas and the fight with Pollux to think about anything else. Now that my "badass" mood was gone, I felt embarrassed for acting out the way I did.

I didn't like being the center of attention, and I had literally just painted a target on my back in a good and bad way. "No, sorry guys, I just have a lot on my mind."

"You mean like Lucas?" Sansa grinned as Trixie playfully elbowed her.

"No, other things." The response was meant to be vague, but it didn't work. They knew I was lying by the way they busted out laughing. "I'm serious..."

"Sure you are. Regardless, you're coming tonight," Trixie said pointedly as she looped her arm through mine and pulled me down the hallway towards my room. "Come on, there is a lot to do before dark."

"Guys, I can't... I have homework—"

Never in my life had I used homework as an excuse to get out of a party, and now here I was, doing just that. All because I didn't want to face anyone who had seen me act crazy today out in the arena. "Don't be silly, Cassie. You're going and I'm going to make you look hot, so stop worrying."

The two women didn't give me much room to protest as they quickly dragged me into my bedroom and plopped me down on the round vanity chair that sat in front of a large lighted mirror. I wore makeup and made myself look good on occasions.

However, I wasn't the kind of girl that obsessed over it.

Not like Trixie and Sansa seemed to be.

"Trixie, you tackle hair and makeup and I will look for the perfect outfit." Sansa directed as Trixie nodded and quickly got to work.

"Guys, seriously, I don't want to go—"

"You're going," they both replied in unison, causing me to groan as I rolled my eyes.

There was no way out of this, and honestly, I was fine with that. If they wanted to dress me up then so be it. I could play the part, for once, instead of always trying to control a situation because I didn't want to do something others did for a chance.

Watching Trixie work her magic with makeup, I found myself entranced by every swirl of the brush that played against my skin like a canvas being painted by an artist. She didn't go super heavy, and she didn't dive too much into the bright colors I assumed she would have, considering she loved everything bright and cheerful.

Instead, she went with a dark purple lipstick and cool black smokey eye that matched my flawless skin, and when she curled my hair, she left every strand in a perfect spiral that fell down my back in waves.

If there was one thing I loved about myself, it was my hair, and seeing how she took such care with it touched me for some odd reason. It was as if she knew I was particular about this part of myself, and when she finished and laid down the curling iron, I stared at a version of me I almost didn't recognize.

"Do you like it?" she asked softly, causing me to turn to her with a smile.

"Trixie, I love it. You really have a talent for this stuff."

Shrugging her shoulders and giving a meek smile, we both broke out into laughter just as Sansa reappeared from my closet. "Okay, I think I have the perfect outfit—damn girl, you look good!"

Her exclamation to my appearance caused me to laugh again as I stood from the small vanity seat, making my way towards the closet. I didn't know Sansa very well but from the little I did know; she was quite the character.

Her fun loving and very blunt personality almost matched my own. But she also was very artistic and had Trixie's bright, happy persona. It was as if someone had decided to blend Trixie and I together and come out with a third to our quickly growing friendship circle.

The moment I stepped into the closet, I was shocked.

I half expected something bright and outstanding, but instead, that was far from the truth. Sansa also seemed to know my style, and the black skin tight dress she picked out for me was to die for.

"Look, I know you love black, so I kept it simple. However, I expect you to be in those killer ass shoes." I had no idea what shoes she was talking about until I turned towards where she was pointing and spotted the bright red and black dagger designed heels. The silver of the blade glistened in the light, screaming nothing but danger.

Of course, there was a bottom to the heel tip, but the designer was able to implant the danger into the heel, giving it a terrifying look I was in love with.

"Where in the hell did those shoes come from?" I gasped as I quickly picked them up. "I don't remember those being in here."

Gazing back up to Sansa from the shoes, she shrugged with a smile as she turned towards Trixie, who remained laughing. A part of me knowing they planned this somehow. That all of it was part of their plan to make me go wild tonight.

Something I wasn't sure about doing. Seeing as parties and I only end in regrets and bad decisions. "Stop over thinking it, Cassie." Sansa said jokingly. "Get dressed."

She was right, I was overthinking it. At least, I think she is right.

Taking a moment, I mustered the courage I needed and took the dress into the bathroom to change. If I was going to prove I could be someone who was competition, then I had to stop second guessing things and take initiative.

Interrupted Conversations

Cassie

Blaring music, drinks, and wild dancing were what awaited me when Sansa, Trixie, and I finished getting ready and made our way towards where this party was supposed to be located. I was still trying to wrap my mind around how this place worked, but for the most part, it wasn't too much different from the home I had left.

Feeling confident in my outfit, I walked into the school with my head held high. The last thing I was going to do was let my little stunt from earlier prevent me from enjoying myself. Perhaps I had made a spectacle of myself, and maybe I did make out with Lucas.

But that wasn't too bad, and now I'd be prepared. Right?

"Oh, wow!" a tall lavender-haired girl said with sparkling blue eyes. "Trixie, you guys look amazing."

I didn't have the slightest clue who this girl was, but as Trixie leaned in, giving her a hug, I figured they knew each other well so didn't bother to say anything. "Hey Prim, I didn't think Mom was going to let you come."

Prim shrugged her shoulders with a smile. "She changed her mind."

"You mean you snuck out?" Trixie replied with laughter before both girl's gazes turned towards me. "This is my friend Cassie."

Prim's eyes gazed over my body, taking in what I was wearing. She looked quite young, much younger than I and Trixie. "Hey."

After a few more moments and a quiet smile, she quickly turned and disappeared into the crowd, her head bobbing up and down as she moved to the beat of the music, following in with all of the dancing taking place. When Trixie looked back at me from where her sister had once just disappeared, she seemed amused by the entire situation.

"My sister is so dead. Mom's going to freak," Trixie mumbled with laughter before taking my hand. The three of us made our way toward the bar, where I noticed top-shelf booze. I won't lie. I was impressed.

Somewhere through the night, I lost track of Sansa and Trixie, both of my friends venturing off to dance with men I didn't know. I, however, was currently happy doing exactly what I was doing. Which was absolutely nothing as I reclined back in the massive hammock that hung between two enormous trees out in the garden.

Multiple empty bottles of beer scattered the ground below me while a half-empty one relaxed within my grip. I had met a couple of interesting people tonight, but for the most part, I kept to myself. Heads did turn and people did make comments about how gorgeous I looked, but it didn't matter.

The last thing I wanted to do was entertain those people, and the only reason why I came was because my friends made me.

Stretching my arms out over my head, I let my gaze fall to the sky, where the two beautiful, large iridescent moons circled one another, taking my breath every time I saw them. One thing I loved about this place was how beautiful the nature was. It was so intoxicating and so different from what I had been used to back home.

With my eyes captivated by the celestial orb above me, I didn't take notice of the slow movements coming up from the left side of me. "What's a gorgeous girl like you doing out here all alone?"

Startled by the deep, intoxicating voice, I quickly sat up in the hammock and turned to face a man I had never seen before in my life. He was incredibly sexy, with dark chocolate brown hair, penetrating bluish green eyes and a white smile that literally felt like it had its own spotlight. Even his body was toned to perfection, his chest on display with the four top buttons of his shirt completely open. I was ogling him, of course, and the dark patterns of tattoos that crossed over his left pec made me bite my bottom lip with wonder.

"Gorgeous?" I chuckle to myself. "Why is it that someone like you is out here worrying about someone like me?"

Yes, I was being vague, but I wanted to know who he was. After all, he could be someone to have fun with. I know I wouldn't mind having fun with him.

"Changing the subject, I see," he replied with a smirk as he stepped closer. His eyes gazing down at me, making my heart race with every single step he made in my direction. "I came out here to get some fresh air. The girls inside tend to be overwhelming."

"They want to fuck you and you are not interested. I find that hard to believe."

My blunt response caused him to laugh even more as he nodded his head. "I don't want a girl who's going to be easy. I want a girl who's going to challenge me. And there's not a single woman in that room in there who can do that."

"I see. So you just decided to come out here and find one instead?"

Again, I was being forward and, honestly, I didn't care what he thought about me. I found this whole interaction amusing. Climbing out of the hammock, I moved toward the sidewalk with my beer in hand, leaving behind the complete mess I had made. I noticed he followed close behind me.

"Where are you going? It's not safe for someone like you to be out here all alone."

Stopping in my tracks, I turned to look over my shoulder at him. Was he being serious right now? Me, of all people, wasn't safe walking alone at night. "You're joking, right?"

"No, I'm being serious. There's all kinds of weirdos out here," he chuckled, shrugging his shoulders.

"I hate to break it to you, Mr, but I am a weirdo." I had heard the line so many times while sitting there watching movies and going through social media, I couldn't resist the opportunity to be able to use it.

He blanked for a moment, obviously not expecting what I had said. It seemed to have dawned on him, and he broke out into a fit of laughter. "Touché. You said that with a straight face."

There was something about this guy I just couldn't get over. He was mysterious and yet sarcastic, and I enjoyed every moment of it, quite different from how Lucas was, or even my brother, for that matter. "What's your name?"

He rubbed the back of his neck as he stared at me, his smile growing just a little bit wider. "My name is Silas, and you're Cassie."

"Oh, so you have heard me?" I replied with a small smile as I watched him nod.

"After your little stunt today, everybody in school knows who you are. You really did put your brother to shame out there. Not cool. But I mean, I could understand being your brother. He probably pissed you off and deserved it."

Staring at Silas, I shrugged my shoulders. "It's complicated."

It wasn't actually as complicated as I led on, but that wasn't something he needed to know. Instead, I'd rather have Silas be curious about what the issues were. Keeping them living in suspense was always so much more interesting.

The way his eyes watched me while I moved was as if he was the hunter and I was his prey. I wasn't sure if he was trying to determine his next move with me or if perhaps he was simply trying to figure me out.

Regardless, I was slightly drunk and perhaps a little in need of something much more sustainable. Something physical I had been lacking for quite some time.

"What's running through your mind right now, Cassie?" The chuckled murmur of his question made me smile as I reached out, wrapping my hand around a nearby light post, swinging my body around it slowly as I watched him.

"There is a lot on my mind, but the one thing that stands out is why you're out here wasting your time with me."

Shifting from foot to foot, he laughed, rubbing the back of his neck. "I just came out for fresh air—"

Laughter escaped me as I shook my head, cutting him off mid-sentence. "See, I don't think that's true. In fact, I think you came out here for something more."

With raised eyebrows, a smirk crossed his face as he took two steps closer towards me.

"Is that right?"

"Mhmm–" I nodded, glancing up at his towering figure. The smoothness of the alcohol ran through my veins, calming my nerves that would usually be present. "What is it that you want, Silas?"

The moment his name rolled off my tongue, I could have sworn I heard a low growl of satisfaction leave the belly of his throat. Only a foot of space laid between us as he wrapped his arm around my waist and pulled me against him. "Perhaps I want you."

Perhaps he wanted me? The internal amusement of his comment made me warm, and as I contemplated the idea of telling him no, the lust driven desires coursing through me wanted so much more. "Perhaps then you should prove it?"

Using his freehand to brush back a piece of hair from my face, he bent down to kiss me. Yet, before his lips could even brush mine, his body was ripped away and a thundering roar echoed about the air. Shaken up and unsure of what the hell had just happened, I looked up at the figure of a man standing between Silas and I.

It was Lucas, and with heaving shoulders moving up and down, I could tell he was pissed. "Lucas—"

"Shut up, Cassie," he growled without even looking in my direction. "I'll deal with you in a minute."

Silas stood to his feet quickly and spun to face Lucas with brilliant fiery red eyes and a snarl on his lips that spoke of nothing but the anger that must have been coursing through him. "Who the fuck do you think you are touching me?"

"The man who will fucking rip you apart if you touch what belongs to me again."

Lucas' warning was not to be toyed with, and as much as he got on my nerves, I prayed Silas would just walk away. The last thing I wanted was something else to draw negative attention to us being here.

But honestly, what was I to do?

It wasn't like I knew Silas well enough to save his ass, even though he was absolutely sexy. "Oh, come on... can we not do this tonight?" I asked them with a sigh as I brushed myself off.

Lucas glared at me from over his shoulder with a look of disgust. "You're my mate."

"Wait, what?" Silas replied, his demeanor calming down as he looked between Lucas' and I with confusion. "That's not possible—"

"Are you calling me a liar, dragon?" Lucas snapped as his fangs protruded from beneath his top lip. He was slowly losing control, and moving to stand in front of him, I placed my hands upon his chest to calm his quickly rising temper.

"Lucas, enough," I muttered softly before turning to face Silas. "Silas, I think you should go."

He scoffed, running his hand through his hair before shrugging his shoulders. "Yeah, sure. I'll catch you later."

Lucas moved to charge after him, but I quickly stopped him in his tracks, watching as Silas disappeared from sight before I let him go. "That was uncalled for, Lucas."

"Uncalled for?" he snapped at me as I rolled my eyes and moved to walk away. "Where do you think you're going?"

Snatching my arm, he pulled me back to him, spinning me so my eyes stared into his. The touch of him set my body alive, and as I looked up into those angry, deep, swirling masses, I found my breath hitch.

"Let me go."

"No!" he yelled, "I'm your mate. How could you entertain that fucking dragon?"

I hadn't meant for him to get upset like he was, and part of me felt guilty. But the fact of the matter was he had entertained and flirted with girls at the arena, so why shouldn't I have fun?

"Mate? Last time I checked, we weren't bonded, Lucas."

Gripping me tighter, he pulled me flush against his chest. "That's because you keep denying what we should be, Cassie."

He wasn't wrong, but at the same time, I wasn't going to give in to him so easily. I wouldn't just allow him to claim me because he thought it was his right. That wasn't the kind of relationship I wanted. "You have to earn my trust, Lucas. I won't just give it away because the gods deemed us compatible."

"See, it's comments like that Cassie… that make me think you're simply scared of me."

Tight against him, his breath fanned across the side of my face. I couldn't let myself fall into the desires he created within me. However, the longer I remained wrapped in his scent, the harder it became to resist the urges brewing inside me.

I had thought I would be able to resist the urge to let him take me, but no matter how hard I tried to deny the inevitable, it kept pulling me in.

"Let me go, Lucas," I whispered as I turned my gaze to his once more. "Now…"

A chuckle of amusement glinted from the corner of his eyes as he smiled. "Never."

The moment his lips brushed against mine in a savage and passionate kiss, I moaned in satisfaction, wanting more.

God, I wanted so much fucking more.

Sexual Prowl

Cassie

Since the moment he had kissed me the night of my birthday, I tried to avoid the feelings I had for him, but once again, I was wrapped within his arms and taken over by the lust our bond created. I wanted more than I knew how to handle.

With a rush of desire, our hands went wild and, as his skin brushed against mine, a moan escaped my lips. It was like my body was on fire, and the only thing that could quench it was Lucas.

As his hands reached down behind the backs of my thighs, he quickly lifted me up, pressing me against the lamppost as he continued to kiss me with feverish intent. I wanted him, and I wasn't sure why the desire was so hard to resist.

Breaking the kiss, I tried to speak, but his lips just trailed down over my jawline towards my neck. "Lucas—" I gasped. "We can't... not here."

His eyes met mine, and as they did, a small smirk crested the corners of his lips. "Okay."

"Okay?" I whispered as I stared into the dark abyss of his eyes.

"Cassie, I want you and I will have you whatever way I can. So you can either have me now and right here... or we can go somewhere else. That is, unless you would prefer the company of others' tonight?"

His statement was daring, and there was no mistaking the meaning behind his words. He had been jealous Silas was out here talking to me, and I felt slightly guilty I flirted back with him. Especially because Lucas was my mate.

No matter how much he irritated and pissed me off.

Taking a moment to think about what I was going to say, I leaned forward and brushed my lips ever so gently against his. "I want a bed."

He didn't think twice when he placed my feet on the ground and took my hand in his. A slight pull towards the path and I realized he was leading me towards the building we were staying in. Soft giggles left my lips as I tripped over a rock in the path. The alcohol I had been drinking flooded my mind.

"Shit!" I spat out, causing him to glance over his shoulder at me as he laughed and shook his head.

"If you're any louder, someone is going to catch us."

"So, we're adults. Who cares?" My reply seemed to make sense in his mind because before I knew it, I was tossed over his shoulder and taken through doorways and down halls until finally we entered a room and I was placed on my feet once more.

He could have picked his room. The dark and sultry air of it seemed to fit the current mood of sexual tension between us, but instead, he went to mine.

With my gaze locked onto his, I watched him take steps towards me as I slowly moved backwards. A wicked side to him emerged as he pulled his black shirt over his head and dropped it to the floor.

The tan, toned curves of his muscles rippled in the dim lighting as he approached me like a predator on the hunt. Every bit of him was sculpted in a way that made my mouth water, and when he stared at me, I couldn't help but feel a wave of anticipated pleasure was over me.

The way Lucas looked right now stalking towards me had me biting my lip as I took in his bad boy persona. The air about him screamed danger, and everything about me wanted it.

"Come here," he said. The command sending shivers down my spine I hadn't expected to enjoy.

Yet, remaining in my spot, I cocked an eyebrow and smiled. "Make me."

Never had I thought those two words could hold as much power as they did the moment I said them. As if a switch had been flipped, he snatched me by the ankle and drug me to the end of the bed. The weight of his body was held up by his arms as he hovered over me.

"Are you sure you want to go with that answer?"

Was I sure? Hell yes, if it meant he would punish me. "You heard me."

Lacing his fingers through my hair, he yanked my head towards his and pressed his lips against mine. My own hands grasped at his arms as his tongue dove into my mouth, the taste of him dancing within, causing me to moan in satisfaction.

"I'm going to make you scream for me, princess," he murmured as he broke the kiss for a moment. His hold on my hair released as he shifted his hand, trailing a single claw down over the curves of my breast until it slipped under the thin material of my dress, ripping it all the way down the front of me.

I liked that dress and destroying it was rather irritating. However, the moment that claw danced along my skin between my thighs, I gasped out in pleasure. He was doing things to me no other man had, and I loved it.

"You talk a lot of talk for someone who hasn't made a move yet, unless you count kissing." He was going to make me eat those words the moment he tore the black panties from between my legs, grasped the backs of my thighs, and raised my hips up to allow his mouth to devour my core.

Diving in like a man who hadn't eaten in days, he sucked against my clit before diving his tongue deep inside me, causing my back to arch as my eyes rolled into the back of my head. "Sweet Jesus—" I moaned as the knot in my stomach slowly built from the very quickly approaching climax.

Every stroke of his tongue against me had my hands gripping at the blankets on the bed, begging like a bitch in heat for the passion he provided. It was crazy to think he was able to do this, that a man I had been against for so long was able to make me feel the way he did. When I thought I couldn't take anymore, he had me screaming in pleasure as he tipped me over the edge.

My eyes connected with his the moment he came up licking his lips.

"You taste divine." The low growl that emitted from his throat had me biting my bottom lip as I smiled. He stripped out of his pants, his thick, rigid cock standing at attention. It was huge, far larger than the other guys I had been with in the past, and I had no doubt it would punish me in every way I wanted to be punished.

The moment he pulled me to the edge of the bed, no words were said, and honestly, that was okay. He slid the head of his cock against my soaking wet core. There was no going back.

Not that I would want to.

Gently, his hand slid behind my neck, and in doing so, he sat me up, bringing my lips to his. The kiss started off slowly but quickly grew more feverish as he slowly slid every inch of his long, thick cock deep inside me. My breath hitched at his size as he filled me to a point I hadn't expected. He was definitely bigger than anyone I had been with before, and with every inch of him invading my tight cunt, the pressure in my stomach grew until he completely hilted inside me with a low growl.

"You have no idea how long I have waited for this moment," he whispered, my heart racing as he stared down into my eyes. "You're mine, Cassie."

The carnal hunger of our lust drove us both towards a desire I denied for too long. The moment those words left his mouth, his lips captured mine again. No longer was it soft and gentle. It was hurried, rough, and completely erotic. My back hit the soft comforts of the blankets as his hips thrusted deep inside me.

As if his Lycan side had taken control, he punished me with pain and pleasure. Nails scrapped at my skin as his hand slid to my throat, fucking me harder than I could have imagined. My cries of pleasure echoed around the room as I bounced under him.

"Oh, fuck yes–" I moaned, wanting more. "Harder, please harder."

With a maniacal laugh, he pulled out quickly and flipped me over onto my stomach. His hands gripped my hips as he pulled my ass up and shoved a pillow underneath my stomach. "You have no idea what you just asked for."

Suddenly nervous, I hesitated for a moment before the head of his cock thrust back inside me. At this angle, every bit of him hit deeper and with the new sensation of his rigid member deep inside of me hitting all the right places, I gasped. "Oh, fucking hell—"

A deep chuckle left his throat as he reached up, grabbing my hair. "Hold on…"

The thrusting force behind his movements caused me to cry out as I took what he offered. I wanted it, every inch of the pain and pleasure he could bring me and as I took it like a bitch in heat. I spiraled out of control, coming undone over and over again until my throat hurt from screaming out.

"Let me mark you," he growled as he reached down, gripping my throat. "You have no idea how bad I want to sink my fangs into your pretty little throat."

For a split moment, part of me wanted to say yes so I could feel the rush of euphoria, so many of the mated people I knew talked about, but at the same time, I wasn't ready for that. I wasn't ready to be completely mated to him, and as his cock got harder and harder, I pushed back against him, trying to make him cum.

"Not yet—" I cried out as he thrusted harder, obviously unhappy with my response by the sound of the growl that left his lips. The movement tipped me over the edge as I came, my core clenching around his cock, begging to milk every last drop from him.

But instead of cumming inside of me, he quickly pulled out and spilled himself into his hand. I didn't know why he pulled out, but I was pleased. The last thing I wanted was to get pregnant, and glancing over my shoulder at him, I saw the confliction on his face.

His brows knitted together before going lax, and without glancing at me, he stood to his feet and made his way towards the bathroom. I wasn't sure what had just happened, but the drunken feeling I had before was long gone after the sexual pleasure he had pushed through me.

Falling back onto the soft white pillows of my bed, I pulled the blankets around me, staring at the ceiling and trying to think why he would suddenly act the way he did. I wasn't sure if it was because I said no to marking me, or perhaps I had done something wrong during sex.

If it was the marking, I hadn't meant to upset him. I just wasn't ready to take the mate mark and start bearing children yet. I was only eighteen, and being a mother at this age wasn't something I wanted. Not to mention, I didn't want some mate mark telling me who I loved. I wanted to feel that love and connection without a mark.

The moment he came back, I propped my head up on my hand and stared at him.

"What's wrong?" My question seemed to stop him in his tracks as he stood before me completely naked, looking like a ripped Tilly's model waiting to go on deck.

Shrugging his shoulders, he grabbed his pants and began to get dressed. "Nothing. Why would something be wrong?"

I wasn't stupid, and the fact he literally responded the way he did made me wonder if he thought I was. "I'm sorry I said no..."

Lucas scoffed at my comment as he shook his head. "Do you really think that bothered me? I'm not bothered you said no. Honestly, it's best you did."

"What?" Shock filled me as I listened to him. "What do you mean, it's best?"

He didn't bother giving me an answer as he pulled his shirt over his head and covered up the gorgeous muscles of his body. His dark hair was disheveled, standing up on end and clearly just-fucked. It was clear he was leaving, and as he turned, I couldn't help but feel disgusted with myself in a way.

"Are you going to refuse to answer me?" The snapped remark was unexpected, but he paused and a deep breath escaped his lips before he turned to me once more.

"I don't have to say anything, Cassie. Have you not realized you're no longer a pampered princess here? We are exactly the same, and as great as the sex just was... we don't have time for things like relationships. Isn't that right?"

I had never said I didn't have time for a relationship, but I had said I would never have sex with Lucas—and it happened anyways.

Gripping the sheets around me, I stood to my feet and stormed towards him.

"You're acting like an asshole right now, and all I'm trying to do is see what's the matter with you. You went from loving and passionate to not giving a fuck at all."

Lucas didn't seem the least bit bothered by what I had to say, and even though I was looking for something to tell me what was on his mind, he just stared at me with complete indifference.

"It was fun, Cassie. But I do have to go," he said firmly as he glared at me, "perhaps if you're ever in need, we can do this again. If not, well, that's fine too."

I wasn't sure what the hell just happened, but as he closed the door behind him, I stood there mouth wide open with what I was sure would be nothing but shock written all across my face. "What a complete asshole!"

Questions & Hangovers

Lucas

The moment I stepped out of Cassie's room, my heart sank into my stomach. For a moment, I had actually thought our bond was blossoming, but instead I was a fool to think I was anything more than a quick lay for her. Mate or not, she was adamant to keep me away at every turn.

So of course, I showed her how much of an asshole I could be.

It wasn't hard to hear her scream once I left her room. I had stayed for a moment trying to decide if I wanted to go back in and apologize. Goddess knows every part of me wanted too, but my Lycan... he wasn't pleased.

She doesn't deserve our mark...

The dark, stormy whispers within my mind were loud, and as hard as I tried to shrug them off, they had gotten louder since I came to this realm. I needed something, anything to quiet them, and as much as I wanted to sleep, I didn't see it happening anytime soon.

Step by step, I stormed down the hallway with my room in sight, but even the thought of going there right now didn't seem comforting. The last thing I needed was to get into trouble with all of these people lingering around, but at the same time, all I really wanted was a drink.

A drink to clear my mind and perhaps the company of a woman who was actually worth talking to. Not that I could actually do that. I had just laid with my mate, my fated chosen by the gods themselves, and in a way, I was rejected—even if she didn't say it.

Passing the threshold of my door, I exited the same way I had come in with Cassie and ventured outside into the garden. The cool night air blew gently against my skin, and inhaling deeply, I tried to ignore the scent of my beautiful mate still lingering around the area.

She was everything I wanted in a mate, and yet pissed me off more than anything. How was I supposed to complete a bond when she refused my mark? It was in our nature to want to be bonded—at least, that was what I was told.

Could I honestly have been wrong?

Was this not how the mate bond worked?

"Are you okay?" The sound of a woman's voice caught my attention, and looking to my down the shadowed path that led towards the school, a red-haired woman with glowing eyes stepped forth into my view.

I wasn't sure who she was, but I remembered seeing her around campus. Her long red hair blew against the breeze as the glowing greenish-blue eyes she had stared into the darkness like a cat stalking its prey.

I wasn't sure why she was out here or, better yet, near the dorms but shaking my head, I brushed her off and turned my attention back towards the moons above. "Yeah, I'm fine. Just getting some air."

Turning away from the woman, I closed my eyes, and hoped she would take the hint to walk away, but instead, she stepped closer to me, causing my body to stand on edge.

"You look like you could use a friend—" she said softly as if she was trying not to alert me in any way. "You're Lucas, aren't you?"

Snapping my gaze to where she was now, only standing feet away from me, I had the opportunity to really take her appearance into account. Red hair, glowing eyes and a wicked smile on her face spoke of the trouble this woman was. She was older, much older than me, but something about the look of her seemed so familiar.

"Who are you?" The snipped question caused her brows to raise impressively.

"The dean of your school for one," she replied, causing a knot to form in my stomach due to my rude stupidity. "But also someone who knows how to find something you want."

Confusion filled my mind as my brows knitted together. "What do you mean, something that I want? I don't want anything, and I don't have time for riddles, lady, no offense."

A soft chuckle escaped her lips as the corners of her eyes crinkled in amusement. She may have been the dean of students, but something about her seemed completely off. "Tell you what... you answer a few of my questions and I will take you to him. Does that sound fair enough to you?"

"Take me to him?" Laughter escaped me as I shook my head. "There is nothing that you can tell me, and I don't have time for the games. I'm sure there are other students around here drunk that you can harass."

The moment I tried to walk past her, she gripped my arm firmly and stopped me in my tracks. Shocked and irritated that she would touch me, I ripped my arm from her hand and stared down at her.

"Please refrain from touching me."

She wasn't in the slightest phased by the Lycan aura surrounding me. In fact, she seemed almost thrilled she was able to bring forth this part of me as if she was almost hoping she could. "My apologies. I simply wanted to help you."

"As I said, I don't have time for this. No please leave me alone." My reply was short, but when I turned away from her once more, her words stopped me.

"Even if it's about your father and those remarkable gifts you have?"

Stunned in silence, I turned once more to face her. I wasn't sure if she was messing with me. Yet staring at her, she showed no signs of deception.

I didn't know my father, and as far as I was told, he abandoned my mother and I when I was two. Part of me wanted to tell her to fuck off, because honestly, I didn't want to know the piece of shit who left me. The ache it brought my mother was something unbearable, and when she died two months ago, I hated him more for leaving.

The other part of me, though... was intrigued.

"What about him?"

Cassie

"Dude, you look like crap. Hungover from last night?" Sansa's question caused me to roll my eyes as I grumbled underneath my breath. I had hardly slept after what happened with Lucas, and actually had been searching for him all morning to see where he had gone.

I wanted to confront him, ask him what the hell his problem was. Yet, everywhere I looked, he wasn't there. Even his bed had looked untouched as if he hadn't even slept there last night.

"No, just slept like shit," I finally replied as I grabbed a cup of coffee from the barista and turned, heading towards our usual table on the far left wall of the room. I hadn't seen Trixie at all this morning, and while I had expected her to come bounding towards me with endless amounts of rainbows and sunshine, I was pleased she hadn't.

There was too much confusion in my mind right now to deal with another one of her many lectures on my appearances and also what we were supposed to be doing in magic class. Not that I needed it. Most of the students there could barely use their magic.

Yet the teacher told me it's about me being able to control it... and I could, mostly.

"So, are you going to just act like you didn't sneak off with Lucas last night?" Sansa stated in a matter-of-factly. My eyes quickly darted to where she sat as I tried to understand how she even knew that.

"I don't know what you're talking about."

Rolling her eyes, she opened her mouth to speak, but a smooth, sultry voice perked my ears to attention instead. "Hey gorgeous, still dancing this morning, I see?"

It was Silas, and god, did he look absolutely delicious. "Silas."

Running his hand through his dark chocolate brown hair, he gave me that signature white smile, flexing his arms as he leaned over the table. The conversation with him from the night before had been enchanting, to say the least, but of course, it quickly died when Lucas made an appearance and went all high and mighty.

"You don't look too happy to see me," he replied, his smile forming into a playful frown.

"I'm tired and have a headache," I mumbled, trying not to seem as annoyed as I was. It wasn't that he was annoying me. I simply just had no interest in that particular moment to be entertained by him. Even if he was absolutely delicious to look at.

There was a twinkle in his eyes as his smile grew again. "Hangovers are never any fun."

"I'm not hungover—"

"Yes, you are," Sansa replied, causing me to shoot her a daggered glare that made her smile. "Don't look at me like that, it's the truth."

Maybe I was slightly hungover, but I didn't need people pointing it out. Turning my gaze back to Silas, I sighed. "Did you need something, Silas?"

Hesitation twinkled behind gaze. He did want something, and the fact he did made me nervous. He didn't seem like the kind of man who calmly asked for things. At least not to someone like me.

"Actually, I wanted to see if you would have dinner with me."

Sansa went into a coughing fit, drawing both mine and Silas' attention as well as a few people sitting near us. Patting on her chest, her eyes wide she quickly took a sip of her drink and gave me a sheepish grin. "Sorry, that went down wrong."

I wasn't stupid. The only reason why she choked was because Silas asked me out, and looking at him now, I could see he was dead serious with his question. "Didn't last night warn you about being around me?"

Laughter left him as he shook his head. "You mean the overgrown dog with a territory issue? I'm not worried about him."

It was my turn to laugh as I thought of Lucas as an overgrown dog. I couldn't get upset at Silas cracking a joke. Lucas did act a little crazy last night, but it didn't make accepting Silas' offer easier. "Can I think about it? Right now, my head is killing me."

Silas seemed genuinely taken back by my question of whether or not I could think about going out with him. Which meant he more or less was used to people accepting right away. Too bad for him, I wasn't easily swayed, and as he went to open his mouth, Pollux decided to join in on our conversation.

His egotistical smirk bounded up right next to my table as he clasped a hand on Silas' shoulder with a smile. "Hey, we're getting ready to head out... are you coming?"

Not surprised by the fact Pollux had made friends with Silas or any of the other Alpha males around this place, I rolled my eyes and laughed. "Looks like you better get going. My brother has plans with you."

"Am I missing something?" Pollux snapped as he glared at me.

"Nope, nothing at all." My reply was more than sarcastic, and my brother knew it. He stared at me for a moment longer before Silas straightened himself and turned. The tension in the air was strong, and as Silas said a few whispered words to my brother, I watched them both quickly disappear.

Whatever it was Silas said was enough to make my brother ease up, but I knew the conversation wasn't over. At least not for now. Pollux had a way of making things difficult, and if he knew I slept with Lucas or that Silas was asking me out, well, we can just say he would flip his shit.

Because no matter the issues we had, he was damn sure not happy about me having a mate before him—let alone a friend with benefits.

Pixies & Karma

Pollux

The moment I saw Silas near my sister, I knew he was up to something. She was never one to really put herself out there, even though it seemed she was. She was rebellious, yes, and had a wicked side when she wanted to but to be an attention whore... no way.

Yet since the moment we had gotten here, she had become different from the way I knew her. She was no longer the sister I had grown up with. She was more confident and determined to establish herself in this place. Normally, that wouldn't have been a bad thing, but the way she was going about it felt wrong.

As if coming here had done something to her that couldn't be undone.

Staring off across the green training fields, I thought to the day I battled with her. I was used to having sparred with Cassie growing up, but something about her that day was so much different from before.

Almost as she thrived for the blood she spilled.

A warrior that had no fill until death presented itself.

Letting a sigh escape me, I watched the men who had the late sparring class take their stance and wished I could get back on the field with them. At least it would keep my mind preoccupied so I wasn't busy thinking about my sister. It wasn't like I was her keeper or anything.

She had to learn to take care of her own affairs and do so quietly.

"Hey Lux!" Destin, another wolf shifter, called from across the field as he came jogging up. "Are you all done for the day?"

"Yeah, I finished about twenty minutes ago. Ready to head out."

Destin laughed as he tossed me a football. "You kicked ass out there on the field today, man. You up for a few rounds?"

As much as I wanted to say yes, I just didn't have it in me. "Not today, man. As much as I'd love to, if I don't get that paper done for Stuckey he's going to kick my ass."

The comment made us both laugh, and as I tossed the ball back to him, I stood from where I had been sitting on the bench. "Hey, before you go, there's a small bonfire this weekend. You should come, man. I can tell Zai has a thing for you."

Thinking of Zai made me roll my eyes. Yes, she was fucking gorgeous, but her pride and ego were what made her unattractive in my eyes. The last thing I wanted to do was get involved with someone like her.

Especially when there was one girl in particular here I couldn't stop thinking about.

"Honestly, Destin, I'm not interested in her."

Shock registered on his face as his mouth made an 'O' shape. "Whoa, really?"

It was obvious most men wouldn't dare turn down the opportunity with Zai, and that, of course, made me question if I was making the right choice. "Yeah, for real. She's a little too... dramatic for me."

"Oh, come on. You don't have to go be with her. Just have fun and claim the right." That was typical fuck boy shit, and once upon a time, I would have done just that. But I wasn't like that anymore. I didn't want meaningless sex.

Not when my mate was out there somewhere.

Shrugging my shoulders, I grabbed my bag and tossed it over my shoulder. "Honestly man, I'm good. But I expect a full report from you on how wild it is though."

Taking my time, I walked across the field towards the tunnel that led out of the training arena and toward the school. All I wanted to do was get a hot shower and something to eat, but the moment I walked into the locker room, I knew something was off.

Eyes fell on me from various guys in there as if they knew something I didn't. Trying to ignore the rush of emotions running through me, I quickly opened my locker and shoved my things inside, grabbing my stuff for my shower to try and relax.

The amazing feeling of the hot water rushing over my skin was a welcoming moment. Even though I was a shifter didn't mean I didn't get sore, and today, I worked out harder than I normally have in the past.

With a sigh of relief, I washed away the things that had been bothering me and listened to the pelting of water against the tile flooring.

"Dude, what's up with you and the new girl," a voice called out, catching my attention. I wasn't sure who they were talking about, but I suspected it was my sister.

"I don't know what you're talking about," Silas' voice registered in my ears, and the moment I heard him chuckle, I knew full well they were talking about Cassie. My blood boiled at the realization as I stayed quiet, listening to what was being said.

"I know something is up. Would have thought for sure you would have got some of that ass the other night—"

"Hey, don't talk about her like that," Silas growled in response to the other guy's words, "she ain't that kind of girl."

"Whatever," the kid replied. "She ended up hooking up with that Lucas guy right after you left her."

She hooked up with Lucas?!

I knew the guy was her mate and expected eventually for them to be together, but for my sister to entertain Silas and then sleep with Lucas was completely fucked up. I had thought my sister was more reserved than that, but perhaps I was wrong.

Turning off the water, I grabbed my towel and wrapped it around me as I exited the shower. Both Silas and the dumbass he was talking to stared at me with wide eyes as I narrowed my own in their direction. "Got something else to fucking say?"

"It's-it's not what you think," Silas replied, stuttering over his words.

Not wanting to hear any more of what Silas had to say, I growled at him, my nails sharpening as fangs protruded. "Stay the fuck away from my sister."

The warning was clear, and deciding to handle this with her myself, I didn't bother to hear what Silas had to say. Instead, I strode to my locker, threw on my clothes, and decided to hunt. The only problem was this hunt wasn't like the others, instead, I was hunting my twin.

I was hunting Cassie.

Thirty minutes later and after much searching, her scent grew stronger the moment I turned into the main foyer of the school. The large vaulted ceilings overhead made it look like a cathedral, and as my eyes scanned the surrounding area, they fell upon Cassie, who stood with two girls laughing.

One of the girls ended up being the electric blue-haired beauty I remembered seeing at the dinner Odin had thrown for us. Even now, staring at her, I found myself frozen in my steps, not wanting to approach Cassie. But at the same time, my anger over what Cassie was doing grew stronger and stronger with every passing second.

Pushing aside my doubts about the entire situation, I narrowed my gaze on Cassie and stormed forward with my fist clenched at my sides. Cassie had crossed the line more times than I could even count, and where she thought there was no big issue, she didn't realize the repercussions of what she did.

"Cassie!" I yelled from across the hall, catching her attention and the girls she was with and anybody else nearby. "You and I need to talk."

Her eyes widened in surprise a little bit as if she didn't have a single clue as to why I was in such a rut, but she quickly narrowed them in my direction as she realized I was obviously coming to her with an issue.

"I don't know what your problem is but if you're going to sit here and run your mouth at me, you need to do so somewhere else because I don't have the time for it."

The sarcastic and snippy way she responded to me ticked me off even more and as I stepped in front of her, snarling down at my sister's, whose eyes glanced up at me with a blue hue I was all too familiar with, I didn't know whether I wanted to slap her for her insubordination or punish her in other ways.

"You're going to listen to what I have to say," I snapped at her. "After the conversation I just heard some of the guys having in the locker room about you, it makes me wonder what kind of person you've become since you came here."

Cassie's eyes widened in shock as her lips parted. "What the fuck are you talking about?"

"Don't play stupid. First, you reject your mate and then decide that sleeping and toying with him is fun and games. And then, on top of that, you're flirting and trying to hook up with every other male on this campus. You really have lowered yourself to being a whore, haven't you?"

The anger that quickly swept over my sister was unlike anything I could have ever expected. Her eyes glowed blue as she snarled at me, fangs over her lips, stepping forward, ready to lash out at me in any way that she could.

"I don't know who the fuck you think you're talking to, but you have no clue what the hell has been going on. And maybe if you tried being more my brother instead of the egotistical prick that you are because I am better than you, maybe you would have some type of insight into what's going on in my life."

Collective gasps were heard all around. Before I could bring my hand back to slap the crap out of her for what she said, the electric blue-haired girl stepped in between us. Her eyes narrowed at me as she placed her hands against my chest and shoved me back as hard as she could.

I hadn't expected someone as small as her to be able to shove me as she did. I flew back three feet, falling onto the ground, my eyes wide as I stared at her, the electric current of her touch still running through my skin.

The first time I met her, I knew there was something about her, something that drove my inner beast crazy. But I didn't want to admit there was a possibility she was my mate, even though she smelled more heavenly than I could have ever imagined. Yet the moment she touched me, even though it was to shove me to the ground for speaking to my sister the way that I did, I knew for a fact this girl was my mate.

"Trixie!" the darker girl said standing near Cassie. "What are you doing?"

"I'm handling a problem. He may be her brother, but that doesn't give him the right to speak to her like that!" she snapped as she crossed her arms over her chest, looking down at me with disapproval. Disapproval that hurt me more than I was willing to admit.

"Trixie, it's okay," Cassie said before Trixie held up her hand, cutting Cassie off. The tension of the situation quickly dissipated as we tried to wrap our heads around what just happened.

Everyone around seemed just as shocked as I was that this small, petite girl could do what she did, but there was no denying the anger in her eyes as she looked at me.

Shaking her head, Trixie gave me a sad look and sighed. "I understand that you're her brother, Lux, but honestly, that was uncalled for. I had such higher hopes for you."

When those words left Trixie's mouth, I wanted to break down and beg for her forgiveness. I had waited for a mate for so long, and even though I had hoped for a shifter, I couldn't deny the draw I had to this girl.

"I think you've registered him speechless," the dark-skinned girl said as she crossed her arms over her chest with a smirk. Everybody in the entire hall was staring at me as if waiting for me to respond.

However, I wasn't able to speak because I didn't know what to say.

Looking at my sister, I watched her brows furrow in confusion as she looked from me to Trixie and then back. Her brows lifted as her mouth parted in shock.

"Holy shit!" She laughed, making both Trixie and the other girl glance at her in confusion. "This shit just got a lot more interesting, guess karma's a bitch, isn't it."

Mistakes with a Mate

Cassie

Staring at my brother, I was completely pissed by the way he had approached me in the hallway, as if he was my keeper and had a say in everything I did. One, he didn't have a single clue what had happened that night with Silas or Lucas, and two, I was an adult. If I wanted to fuck three men in a night—which I didn't—that wasn't his place for him to say I couldn't.

The last thing I had expected as I stood there trying to decide how badly I was going to beat my brother for talking to me the way he was in front of all these people was for Trixie—sweet, kind Trixie—to jump in and defend me.

She stood fiercely in front of me, looking down at Pollux, who lay on the ground, staring up at her in shock, just as the rest of us were.

Had anyone else done this, he would have shifted and caused all kinds of torment, but with her, he didn't. It took me a minute to process what was going on, but as I watched him staring at her in utter disbelief with his eyes wide and his mouth parted, it suddenly dawned on me the reason why he hadn't jumped up.

Trixie was mated to my brother, and she had no idea.

Part of me had suspected something was up after the dinner we had with Odin where he quickly backed down once his eyes landed upon Trixie, but I had just cut it to him not wanting to start shit in Odin's dining hall.

Laughter filled me as Trixie turned, glancing over her shoulder in my direction. "What are you talking about? What is karma?"

Quickly knocked from the trance he was in, Pollux jumped to his feet and brushed himself off. "Keep your fucking hands off me."

His comment was directed towards Trixie, and with wide eyes, I scoffed, shaking my head. "Seriously, brother? Are you not going to tell her?"

Trixie looked between Pollux and me, and he shook his head once more, not saying anything. I couldn't help but laugh. My brother, the man who had been all about mates his entire life, was finally paired with his, and he wasn't going to take the initiative.

"Wow. Are you fucking kidding me? This is what you've waited for forever, and you're not going to say anything?" I was in shock and complete, utter disbelief at how my brother was acting. It honestly didn't make any sense.

Unless it was because she wasn't a shifter.

Considering this thought, I narrowed my gaze at him and was absolutely pissed that he would reject her because she wasn't a shifter. "If you're not accepting because—"

"Go fuck yourself, Cassie," he snapped, cutting me off, "keep your fucking mouth closed."

He stormed off, and I watched him disappear from sight. I wanted to chase after him and beat him for how he was acting, for how he was treating Trixie, a girl who was nothing but kind to me—who was nothing but kind to everyone.

"That fucking asshole." The muttered response from my lips caused confusion to pass over both Sansa and Trixie, who cleared her throat with her arms crossed her chest waiting for a response.

"What just happened?"

Here I was with my own issues, and now I had to deal with my brothers. It was absolutely bullshit how he acted, and he knew it. With a groan, I closed my eyes, pinching the bridge of my nose, trying to figure out the best way to address this current situation. "Why is it always me?"

"Why is what always you?" Sansa asked. "Can you tell me what's going on?"

I hated being looked at to provide answers to something that wasn't really my place, but neither of these girls was going to let this go. Both of them are going to want to know what I knew and why my brother was being an asshole.

"Okay, I'll explain," I sighed, glancing around at all the listening bodies that stood nearby. "But not here."

Trixie and Sansa both looked at each other before Trixie smiled. "Coffee shop?"

"There's a coffee shop?" I was stunned once again this place had something as simple as a coffee shop just like they had back home.

"Yeah, I already told you before that this place isn't much different from the human realm." Trixie laughed as she looped her arm through mine. "I can't wait to hear what is going on because, honestly, I could use some good gossip."

Trixie had no idea what she was asking for because this wasn't the kind of gossip she wanted. It was far more complicated, and as much as I wanted to tell her, I was conflicted about how she would take the news.

Part of me thought she would take it well, but then... the other part worried she would be heartbroken. I wasn't sure how pixies picked their mates, but I hoped she wouldn't take this the wrong way when I told her the truth.

When I said I wanted to go to a coffee shop, I honestly dodn't know what I was expecting. Perhaps it was something similar to the coffee shops I had remembered going to back home. Coffee shops that had coffee machines, countertops filled with delicious foods, and a variety of different music with high-top tables for you to gather at.

However, a coffee shop in this place was more like walking into an old bookstore that happened to serve coffee and tea cakes. The building had rustic decor and antique pieces lined with cobwebs high up on shelves. The walls were burgundy with white accent trim, and a lady with fiery red hair and golden eyes served steamy cups of addicting coffee at the counter with a smile.

I was intrigued by how people moved in and out of this place. The leather seating seemed to line the walls, and were filled with other students mingling. But as the girls and I collected our drinks and sat down, I couldn't help but wonder if perhaps I should put off telling them what I was going to tell them at all.

Sipping on my coffee, I tried to look anywhere but at Sansa and Trixie. After a moment, though, Sansa cleared her throat, and my eyes gazed up to meet both of theirs.

"Are you going to explain, or are you going to sit there and keep avoiding the situation?"

Sighing, I nodded. "Sorry, I just didn't think I'd be having to do this shit."

Trixie gave me a soft gaze of understanding as she nodded her head. "It's okay if you don't want to talk about it, Cassie."

"It isn't that, Trixie," I said with a smile. "It's just that my brother should be here explaining this, and with everything going on with Lucas right now, I just didn't expect I'd be the one telling you."

Opening and closing her mouth, Trixie frowned. "What are you talking about?"

Glancing quickly at Sansa, her eyes widened as she gasped in shock. "Oh my god. OH MY GOD, are you FUCKING KIDDING ME?!"

"Nope," I replied, popping the 'p'. "It would seem that fate has deemed it so."

Again, Trixie didn't seem to understand what Sansa and I were talking about, and rolling her eyes, she sighed in a very dramatic fashion that caught both Sansa's and my attention. "I have no clue what you're talking about."

"Trixie, how does the mate thing work with your kind? Do you guys have mate bonds, or do you like pick who you want to be with?"

It was probably better to understand more about her people before just spilling the tea, so to speak. I mean, there was nothing like confusing the girl by blurting out that my asshole brother was her mate without her first understanding what the hell that actually meant.

Puzzled by my question, she laughed, shaking her head. "What the heck does that have to do with anything?"

"Just humor me," I pleaded, rolling my eyes. "Please?"

She pondered over what I said and nodded. "Well, we don't have mates like you guys do. We do bond ourselves with who we choose, but there is usually a long courtship, and we choose to tie ourselves to our mate, as you call it."

I had kind of suspected what she said, just simply through stories my mother had told me as a child. Of course, I thought they were just fairytales, but I soon learned that all stories came from the truth at one point in time.

"Okay, so you don't feel any kind of way or anything before you mate with these people?" I questioned, hoping to lead her in a direction she might understand.

Laughter escaped her as she shook her head. "No, that's silly—oh, I mean..." She seemed embarrassed by what she said, realizing it was how we detected our mates.

I couldn't help but smile and laugh at her comment, though. I could see why some people might find it odd or out of sorts to detect the person you're supposed to love like that, but we all had our own way, and it was refreshing to learn a bit about ours.

"Well, when Pollux and I turned eighteen, I quickly found out Lucas was my mate. I honestly never wanted one—that was more my brother's desire. However, when I found my mate, and he didn't find his, he became so angry at me."

Trixie gasped softly with sorrow-filled eyes. "How could he be angry? That isn't your fault or his. Doesn't he know fate makes things happen for a reason?"

Shrugging my shoulders, I thought of Lucas, and how I had treated him. "I guess in the end, we both didn't. The problem was that when we got to this place, he gave up hope of finding her. He used to proclaim she would be the perfect shifter mate."

The three of us giggled over the notion of him saying that, and as I thought more about it, I couldn't get Lucas out of my mind. It actually upset me. I hadn't seen him all day when I had started growing used to seeing him every day.

"You and Lucas will fix things, Cassie," Sansa said softly as she placed her hand upon mine. "Everything will work out. You just have to give it time."

With a soft scoff, I shook my head, trying to push past the idea of Lucas and I ever being normal. "That's wishful thinking, but back to my brother—"

"Oh yes, please continue. I do love stories," Trixie replied cheerfully as she sipped on her drink. "This is getting so good."

"It sure it is," I muttered with a grin. "As I was saying, Pollux did find his mate when he got here. I wasn't sure the first night I saw the look he gave her, but after today..."

Trixie hesitated, staring in confusion before looking at Sansa. "How was I standing there and completely missed seeing him looking at his mate?"

As Sansa's eyes met mine, she laughed, shaking her head. "Girl, if you don't tell her already, I'm going to because this is just too good."

She was right. I couldn't just keep dragging this out. It was better to rip the bandaid off and get over with it because, honestly the longer I held, off the worse I felt about the situation.

"Trixie, you're my brother's mate." I watched as shock registered on her face. "What the fuck?!"

Denying the Bond

Cassie

Trixie's outburst caught both mine and Sansa's attention. She jumped to her feet, huffing and puffing, and I could have sworn her eyes turned brighter than usual. It was as if a flip switched in her, and she was slowly spiraling from it. The guilt that filled me over her looking upset, tore at my heart. I had never meant to hurt her, and biting my bottom lip, the confidence I usually felt slowly dissipated.

"Trixie, I'm so sorry. Please don't be upset."

"Upset?!" She scoffed with laughter. "I'm not upset because I'm his mate."

"What? Then what's wrong?" Confused beyond belief, I tried to understand what was going on. Why was she acting like this if she wasn't upset by the news?

Shaking her head, she paced around the little seating area we were in with her hands on her hips. "I never wanted a mate, Cassie. As surprising as that may seem, in my world, when you take your mate, it means you start popping out babies, and just because my older sister wants to do that doesn't mean I want to."

Trixie's confession was slightly unexpected. She was usually so sweet and bubbly, and right now, she was acting completely different. "Trix—"

"No, Cassie," she sighed, snapping her gaze at me. "Let me finish."

I gestured with my hand for her to continue. After all, who was I to honestly stop her? It was obvious the girl was on a mission, and as she ranted about how people always treated her like she was stupid and how her mother wanted her to settle down, I couldn't help but think of how similar we actually were.

"If your brother thinks for one minute he can disregard me, regardless of me not wanting to mate anything, well, he has another thing coming."

"Whoa–what?" I gasped, coming back to reality at her words.

What the hell was she talking about?

"You heard me, Cassie," she replied with a triumphant smirk on her face. "I'm going to take a chapter out of your book."

Sansa kicked my shin, causing me to gasp as I sent a daggered glare in her direction. "What the hell was that for?!"

"Look what you did!" she groaned, gesturing to Trixie, who pulled out her phone and seemed to look at herself in her reflection. "She has lost it!"

Mouth parted and eyes wide, I shrugged as if to ask her what she wanted me to do. It wasn't like I asked for all of this shit. "Trixie, what are you planning?"

When I spoke, my eyes spotted a figure walking past the store I had wanted to see all day. Lucas walked casually down the sidewalk in the same dark jeans and t-shirt I had seen him in the other day, which confused me more than anything.

It meant that he hadn't been home or anything.

"Guys, I have to go." Standing to my feet, Sansa called after me as I bolted from the cafe and out the door, looking in both directions for which way he had gone. The thought of finding him was the only thing pushing me forward as I turned left and headed up the street in the direction I saw his figure disappear.

My eyes searched the area for any sign of him, and when I thought I'd never find him, a firm arm reached out from within the shadows of an alley and pulled me in, the seductive, sultry scent I had grown used to wrapping around my body.

Pushed against the wall, I stared up into Lucas' dark steely eyes. My heart was racing at the feeling of his body pressed against mine as his breath fanned across my cheek.

"Why are you following me?" he snarled through a narrowed gaze.

"What—what do you mean, why am I following you? I have been looking for you all day."

The comment seemed to shock him as his gaze fell, and he let up on how tight he was holding my wrist. For a moment, I hoped this moment might turn sweet, no matter how much my affection for him confused me, but that didn't happen.

Instead, he scoffed and stepped back from me, running his hand through his dark hair as he always did when he was going to be a sarcastic asshole.

"I don't know why you are, Cassie. It's not like we have anything to talk about." His words were hurtful, and as the hollow pit in my stomach opened, trying to swallow my heart, I refused to believe him.

Did I care for him more than I thought? Maybe—I didn't know.

Curling my lip, I glared, trying to understand what the hell changed his mood so quickly. He seemed different today as if something had happened, and he no longer cared about me being his mate. "Maybe because I wanted to talk to you about—"

"Stop," he snapped, baring his fangs.. "We have nothing to talk about."

"Nothing to talk about?" I gasped in disbelief, "we have a lot to talk about."

Lucas had nothing but amusement in his eyes as he stared at me with a smile on his face. I wasn't sure what the hell his problem was, considering he literally had fucked me stupid last night, and now he was acting as if I was the last person on the planet he wanted to see.

"Cassie, you and I both know this won't work, so stop pretending and move on to some other poor, unsuspecting soul who has time for your shit."

"Excuse me?!" I exclaimed. "What the fuck is your problem?"

Shaking his head, Lucas turned and started making his way out of the alley like he hadn't heard what I just said, but I had no plan of letting him go. Grabbing his wrist, I stopped him in his tracks, and as he turned, I reared back my hand, slapping him across the face. "Go fuck yourself, Lucas."

Without warning, Lucas snatched me by my hair and pressed me back against the brick building he had pinned me against before. His fangs bared and with lips only inches above mine, a low growl echoed from his throat.

"Don't ever do that again—"

"Or what?" I quickly said, cutting him off. "What the fuck are you going to do?"

With haste, his lips crashed against mine, and as they did, our movements turned into hungry, frenzied motions of wandering hands and heated passion. I wanted him right now, and no matter how much he denied me any other time, he couldn't in this moment.

Grazing my hip with his fingers, he slid his hand beneath my leggings and cupped my aching core that throbbed with the desire to have more of him. I was wet, so fucking wet, and when Lucas realized that, a low growl of satisfaction left him.

"Is this what you wanted, Cassie?" He all but purred in my ear as a smile graced his lips, highlighting the glint of amusement that lay at the forefront of his gaze. "You wanted to be my good girl again?"

"Good girl?" I giggled as I nipped at his bottom lip. "Who said anything about being good?"

Kissing me once more, he brought me closer to the edge as his thumb rubbed circles around my clit. He made me ride out my orgasm with his hand. The euphoric bliss of his actions had me begging for more, but when I reached for his belt, he pulled back.

The empty space now between us had me whining for the loss of comfort he had created. I wasn't sure what made him stop, but as he licked his fingers clean, he shook his head with a grin. "I think I've had enough fun for the day, Cassie. Perhaps find someone to finish you off. I heard there are quite a few men who have been trying."

"Are you serious right now?" I breathed out in shock as my mouth dropped open.

He didn't hesitate to respond as he shrugged his shoulders and fixed himself. "Why would I not be? The woman who was supposed to be my mate turned out not to be mate material, after all."

His words were the metaphorical slap to my face I had been waiting for. Last night we had been so happy, entangled in each other's arms, and then with one simple phrase, he turned into the devil's son who sought to taunt me with my emotions.

"You don't mean that, Lucas. I know you don't."

Laughing loudly, his smile grew wider as he shook his head. "You have no clue."

"Then why don't you enlighten me?" The words left my lips without thinking, and for a moment, I really thought he was considering what I said. But then, as if he had remembered something, the amusement turned to disgust.

"I'm not telling you anything, Cassie. Just do me a favor and stay away from me. I don't have time for your shit anymore."

It was the comment I had waited so long for him to say. A rejection without a rejection, and one that, as much as I thought I wouldn't care, I did.

Tears filled my eyes the moment he disappeared from the alley. The overwhelming emotions of how he made me feel and how he broke my heart filled my mind. I had wanted him not to want this, and then when I actually connected with him, I lost him.

Perhaps the situation wouldn't be as rough had I actually known what it was that I did wrong. Was I a bitch to him before? Yeah, but I wanted to change for him.

Trying to be the person he wanted to be with, considering I was his mate.

Yet, that wasn't good enough. Nope, instead, he wanted to pretend I never existed, just like every other man who I had ever tried to bare my heart to.

They were all good at coming in and taking what they wanted, but the moment you tell them it's okay, and you're interested, they run away.

Debating on going home or back to the coffee shop, I hesitated and then exited the alley, turning left.

I wanted to be alone, able to process all of this myself. Yet, as soon as I got closer to the building I stayed in, a familiar voice came from behind me. "Cassie?"

Turning, my gaze landed into that of Silas, and without saying a word, he quickly wrapped his arms around me, embracing me into a hug. I didn't want to seem weak being here, but everything that had happened since the day I turned eighteen seemed to flood me, all at once breaking the dam that held back my emotions.

For the first time in a long time, I cried hard, and there to comfort me wasn't the person I wanted. But instead, the one person I would never have expected.

Words with Silas

Cassie

I hadn't expected to run into Silas on the way home, but now that I was faced with him, I was actually pleased. I had allowed myself to face a moment of weakness by letting my heart play tricks on my mind. To think the mate thing was actually possible with Lucas was a stupid decision to begin with.

Pulling from Silas, I quickly wiped away my tears and pushed a smile on my face.

"God, I feel completely stupid," I whispered as I gazed up into his hazel eyes, "uh–so how are you?"

Silas gazed down at me, giving a small chuckle as he reached up, rubbing the back of his neck as if hesitant to speak. "I'm okay. I actually was coming to see you, but I can see that whatever I had to say can wait... what's going on? Why are you crying?"

He was coming to see me? The thought was sweet, but I wasn't sure why he would have been going out of his way to see me. "Uh, nothing. I'm not sad, more angry than anything."

"Angry about what?"

Shrugging my shoulders, I turned and made my way toward a small bench that sat off the edge of the sidewalk. "Men—in more precise measures, Lucas. It's all stupid and not important, honestly."

Silas followed my movements as he came to sit next to me. He didn't bother to push for more information and instead nudged my shoulder with his own, causing me to smile.

"Well, the topic of men was the reason why I was coming to see you. I wasn't sure if your brother had spoken with you yet, but I wanted to explain myself."

Confusion filled me as I furrowed my brow, staring at him, trying to figure out what exactly he was talking about. Taking a moment, I thought back to when my brother confronted me in the hallway at the school, and suddenly what he had said dawned on me.

"So when he said the guys were talking about me, that was you?" The sheepish grin that crossed Silas's face at my question let me know it was exactly what he was talking about.

Obviously, my brother had overheard a conversation between him and somebody else, which caused the entire scene in the hallway. Not only that, but the word had gotten out, leading to Lucas hearing what he had heard.

Words seemed to travel very quickly around this place, and that was something I did not like.

"It wasn't what you thought. I don't know what your brother told you, but I promise... Nothing was bad," Silas said quickly, causing me to halt and what I was going to say next.

Taking a deep breath, I closed my eyes and allowed myself to think very thoroughly through all of this. Silas didn't come across as the kind of guy who would just say shit for no reason. And in fact, if he was the Playboy kind of guy. Why would he even bother to come here and try to explain himself and then also comfort me when I was at my weakest moment?

"What exactly was said?" I asked him as I opened my eyes and stared back into the bluish-green haziness of his own.

Rubbing the back of his neck, his eyes darted around before they finally met mine once again. "A few of the guys saw us talking the other night, and because of it, they assumed that we were hooking up, which of course, we didn't. And then, they saw Lucas act the way he did toward me. Guys are going to make assumptions."

Whatever his words as he spoke, and nodding my head, I followed along the best I could, trying to understand his point of view. However, if these guys have made assumptions, why had he not corrected them? Because obviously, they were letting people believe that more happened than actually did.

"Ok. And did you correct them to prevent them from spreading these ridiculous rumors over something that didn't even happen?" Silas gave me a meek smile, and that smile let me know he hadn't entirely told them the truth, which pissed me off even more.

Not only did I have to deal with the shit Lucas and my brother were putting me through, but on top of that, I had to deal with everything else in my life constantly spiraling out of control. And now this issues with Silas because people seem to think I'm a girl who likes to sleep around.

This place was supposed to be about growing into the person we were meant to be, and instead, it reminded me so much of high school, so much of the drama I was glad to get rid of when I graduated.

Standing to my feet, I shook my head and quickly turned, heading back down the path toward the building we stayed in. The last thing I wanted to do was say something mean to Silas and cause even more drama.

My mom always told me if I didn't have anything nice to say, it was best not to say anything at all. So that was what I was going to do.

However, Silas had other plans because as soon as I started heading down the sidewalk, he was on his feet rushing after me, his hand gripping my upper arm as he stopped me in my tracks and turned me to face him.

"Please don't walk away from me. I want to talk to you about this. In fact, there's a lot that I want to talk to you about," he said softly.

There was nothing but sincerity in his gaze, and as much as I wanted to tell him to go fuck himself and never put his hands on me again, part of me couldn't help but want to give him that chance to explain and fix things.

"How do you expect to fix what has already happened, Silas? What else is there that we need to discuss? You made it very clear the guys here, and probably a lot of the girls, are assuming I'm somebody I'm not."

I had never claimed to be this badass girl people thought I was. I was 18 years old, trying to figure out my life and where I wanted to go.

Did I have a rebellious nature? Absolutely.

But that didn't mean I was ready to stand toe to toe with the world as if I had my shit together. What I wanted was to be able to come here and heal from everything that had happened, including losing Melissa, the woman I had loved all through high school.

I had pushed the thoughts of losing her to the back of my mind, not trying to dwell on it what had happened because it was a situation I couldn't fix. However, this place turned out not to be the solace I was looking for, and instead, had become just as much a nightmare as where I had lived before.

I took a moment to think about what I had asked him, and he opened and closed his mouth as if he wanted to say something but wasn't sure. "Will you please just have dinner with me? I can explain everything then."

I'd be a fool to agree to have dinner with him, but I was curious to know exactly what it was he was going to do to fix things. Taking him up on this offer was not going to make anything better between Lucas and me. But honestly, after the way Lucas had treated me today, regardless of what he assumed to be true... I had no reason to say no.

Nodding my head slowly, I shrugged my shoulders, gesturing with my hand that yes, I would. A bright white smile crept across Silas's face at my acknowledgment to go to dinner with him. He was pleased, and honestly, I wasn't surprised he was.

He was a very strange man in a way. There was something dark and mysterious about him that pulled me in, but I couldn't help but feel he didn't just look at me like a person but as a prized possession to own, which was a little unsettling.

He hadn't actually done anything to make me feel that way. It was simply the gaze he gave me was as if I was a piece of gold littered with jewels he wanted to have.

Which perhaps was normal because he was a dragon and they were known to be very materialistic.

"Great. I'll come by and pick you up at 7. I promise you won't regret this." He quickly turned, not giving me a moment to decline or say anything else, and disappeared from my sight. And once again, I was left alone to ponder my thoughts.

I, of course, instantly regretted I had agreed to go to dinner with him because it would only add fuel to an already blazing fire. I sagged my shoulders and continued walking down the path in the direction I was headed.

The only thing I wanted to do was curl up in my bed and take a nap. The day had been long and draining. I was still slightly hungover, and with everything that had taken place, I didn't know what to do with myself.

It was the first time in a very long time I had wished my mother was present. That I could go to her for advice, have her bring me a hot cup of tea, and sit on the bed and talk to me.

My mother and I hadn't been close in years, and once upon a time, we had been. When I was little, I was everything to her, just as Pollux was, and she was everything to me. But then, of course, as I grew, we grew apart, and it became more complicated than we would have liked.

Our relationship was strained, and it became more strained the day I turned eighteen.

She may have fought for me to try to get me and Pollux to stay, not wanting to have us leave, but honestly, I believed a part of her was relieved I was going because, for once, she could try to live normally without worrying who I was going to hurt if I got upset.

The moment I stepped into my room and closed the door, tears began to flow down my face. Everywhere I went, everything I did, I caused problems. I had to figure out how to fix myself, and perhaps it was time I changed slightly who I was.

Instead of being the girl who stood out among the masses, perhaps it was time I tried to blend in. At least then, if I blended in, I wouldn't stick out with everybody wanting to have a piece of me or something to say about me.

Because the girl I was, was not a girl she would want to be proud of.

Date with a Dragon

Cassie

When I agreed to go to dinner with Silas, the last thing I had expected was for him to go completely all out. The moment I stepped out of the white-pillared building I stayed in under Oden's watchful eye, I was met with Silas's smiling face.

He wasn't dressed casually like I would have assumed, but instead was dressed in black slacks, a dark purple button-up shirt rolled up to his sleeves, and even dress shoes. His entire outfit screamed money, and from the glimmer of lust hidden beneath his gaze, I felt completely underdressed in my blue sundress.

Stepping slowly down the stone staircase, my hand gently sliding against the railing, I stared at him with hesitation and uncertainty.

"Uh—I thought you said that we were going to dinner. Why are you so dressed up?"

Laughter escaped him as he spun in a small circle holding his hands out as if to give me a better look. "Well, I wanted to impress you, Cassie. Did it work?"

Impress me? Why the hell would he want to do that?

The guy barely knew me at all.

As laughter escaped me unexpectedly, I nodded, shrugging my shoulders. "You can say that. You look like you're ready to go somewhere fancy. Is that what we're doing?"

Asking him where we were going only led to an even bigger smile. I honestly didn't see how his lips could spread that wide across his face, but he did look absolutely ravishing when he smiled like that. "I can't spoil the surprise, Cassie. You're going to have to trust me."

Trust. That wasn't something easily given, but deciding to try and take my own advice, I ignored my head telling me to cancel the whole thing because it was wrong, and instead went with my gut urging me forward.

The night was cool, and the clear skies above made for a perfect evening. The realm didn't have cars or any form of motor transportation like the human realm. Everyone seemed to walk here which allowed for tons of conversation.

To which Silas never ran out of. "So, tell me a bit about yourself."

Glancing to my left, I let a small breath escape me as I tried to figure out what to tell him. It wasn't like I was comfortable when it came to speaking about myself, but if I was going to try and be more 'trying' if you want to call it that, then I would have to be.

"Well, there is a lot to know—can you be more specific?"

"Sure." He chuckled as we passed building after building, heading down the cobbled street. The only dim lighting around were the fire-lit street lamps that stood along the road. "Why don't you tell me what your old school was like? I take it you just graduated."

"Um, yeah. I mean, I'm pretty sure it's no different than your schools... I mean, I don't know which place you came from—"

Silas continued laughing, finding amusement in my quickly stuttering response as I tried to redeem myself from sounding any stupider than I already felt. I wasn't sure how all this worked, and even though I was told a little about Asgard, I wasn't told much.

"Cassie." He smirked, nudging me with his shoulder again. "It's okay. I'm not like the others around here. I know you don't understand how it all works."

Hearing him say that made me feel a lot better about my current situation. As much as Silas reminded me of the fuck boys back home, so far, he didn't seem that bad.

Maybe looks really could be deceiving, or I was just being stupid and he was a wolf in sheep's clothing. Either way, I was fucked because the look he kept giving me made me feel like he was seeking more than just friendship.

"Thanks." It was the only thing I could think to say under the awkward circumstances, but before I could open my mouth, I realized we had left the street of the city, and ended up walking down more backroads that led towards a grassy green clearing. "Where are we?"

Letting my eyes gaze around my surroundings, I took in the shadows of the trees and the darkness that hid beneath the floral bushes. No matter where the darkness looked through, the double moons above let light glisten around the area shimmering off the lake that lay just beyond the tree's clearings.

"It's beautiful, isn't it?" His question caused my gaze to shift in his direction as I quickly closed my gaping mouth.

"Yes, it is. But why are we out here? I thought you said we were going to have dinner?"

Taking my hand in his, he led me forward and past the treeline closer to the water. It was then I saw what he had set up, and the breath was slowly taken from me. Upon the ground laid a lush purple blanket with gold pillows and a low sitting table.

The table was piled with different fruits, meats, and cheeses elegantly placed with such precision that if Silas had really done all this himself, it must have taken a lot of time. "This is amazing, you did all of this?"

Turning to face him, he stood behind me with his hands in his pockets as he shrugged his shoulders and smiled. His hair fell softly in front of one eye, causing him to quickly brush it back on top of his head. "I wanted to make you something special. Since the moment you got here, it seems like you haven't found it easy to adjust, so... I wanted to do something nice for you."

No matter the words he said, this definitely wasn't just a friendly dinner.

Walking towards me, he gestured for me to take a seat, and without hesitation, I did. This was one of the nicest things anyone had ever done for me, and the more I spent time with Silas, the more I realized how I had completely misjudged him.

"You're really not like how I expected you to be."

"What, you mean a pretty boy that only cares about himself and wants to get in your pants?" He chuckled, raising a brow at me.

A soft blush settled over my cheeks from the embarrassment of my question. I felt foolish to have thought what I did, and then, of course, voiced it. Silas, however, didn't seem bothered at all. In fact, he stared at me with those hazel eyes that held so many questions and yet asked none.

"I'm sorry." Waving his hand, he smiled, picking up his goblet of dark red fluid and drinking it down. I wasn't sure exactly what it was, but from the glass decanter in front of us, I assumed it was wine.

"As I said before, Cassie... I know you're not familiar with things yet. And to answer your comment from earlier, I actually come from your realm. However, my upbringing was much different."

Shock flowed through me upon hearing him. "How? I mean—you came from my world?"

"Yeah." He laughed, shaking his head. "Is that hard to believe?"

"Well, no, but no offense, you don't seem like you did."

It was true, he didn't seem like he came from my realm but nodding his head, I had a feeling he was going to explain. "That's because when I was there, the atmosphere was probably much different from how it is now."

Lips parted, I tried to understand his meaning. "Different?"

"Yeah, let's just say that I'm much older than my boyish good looks."

I never that it was possible for wolves to live for a long time, but part of me had never considered other creatures lived for a long time as well. The way Silas said he was much older had me flush, thinking of how old he really was.

"I see. I take it you come with a lot of experience in life, then." The statement caused me to pause as I instantly thought of how wrong it came out. "That's not what I meant—"

"I'm sure." He grinned with a lust-filled gaze that made a heat rush through me I hadn't expected. It was weird how easily I was able to fall into conversation with him and feel comfortable. Initially, when I met him, I felt drawn, but this was so much different than expected.

Almost as if he and I had known each other in a past life.

Clearing my throat, I turned my gaze away from him and down at the grapes in front of me, quickly picking one off the vine and popping it into my mouth. The sweet flavor of the red seedless grape caused me to moan, and as I did, Silas quickly adjusted where he sat and cleared his throat. "Are you okay?"

"Yeah, I'm fine," he replied, catching my gaze again, "so, is there anything you want to ask me?"

"You mean besides how old you are?" I grinned, watching him chuckle at my comment. There was a lot I wanted to know, but I just wasn't sure how to ask.

"Do you really wanna know—"

Shaking my head quickly, I laughed as I picked up the drink in front of me, "no, no... not yet anyways. I'll just keep pretending you're like twenty."

"I definitely haven't been that old in a very long time," he muttered playfully. His eyes gazed up to the clear star-filled sky above us. "Shall I simply just tell you some things about me?"

His solution sounded way better than any questions I could ask, and nodding my head quickly, he made himself more comfortable laying back on the golden pillows staring up at the sky. "Okay, then let me see where to start."

"Maybe just the basics?" I offered, causing him to glance over at me from where he was lying. The urge to lay against him was strong as he pointed a finger at me and smiled.

"Good idea. Well, as I said, I came from your realm, or Earth as you call it. However, I come from a much older earth. I came to Asgard with a friend who has since returned to the realm, a place I wasn't keen to go back to. I actually love being here in Asgard, and if you want to know—I have been at the school for a long time."

"I have never seen you in any of the classes, though. You must have gone through them all a hundred times by now." The idea of someone wanting to take classes that much shocked me. There was no way I would do something like that.

Silas chuckled, though, shaking his head, and I quickly realized I was wrong.

"I'm no longer a student, Cassie."

"Well, then what are you then? Because I mean, you use the training field and hangout there all the time." My question was valid, and watching Silas open and close his mouth, he hesitated in his next words.

"I'm a guardian, Cassie. It's what dragons are known to do. My ancestors helped to defend the realms and, in return, were granted immortality."

I was shocked to hear his admission and would never have expected someone like him to be what he was. He looked so young and well—put together, like a preppy rich kid.

"So, you are a dragon shifter... which means you actually turn into a dragon?"

The question sounded dumb, but I had honestly never seen a dragon, so how was I supposed to know that they were real? Jumping to his feet, he brushed himself off and stepped off the blanket onto the grassy clearing.

"If you want to see a dragon, then I'll show you a dragon, but if I shift Cassie... you're going for a ride."

Flying for Love

Cassie

Eyes wide, I stared at Silas in shock. "Ride? What do you mean ride—you mean on you?"

Silas slowly unbuttoned his shirt and as he did, the laughter that left his lips made me flush even more than I had before. I couldn't tear my eyes from the curves of his muscles and the rippled way his abs glimmered against the moonlight. Everything about Silas was hypnotizing. Never had I met a man who acted the way he did.

"What are you doing?" I whispered softly, watching him watch me as he undressed.

Something about the moment of him undressing captivated me, making my heart race as the blue-green hue of his eyes took me in as if I was a treasure he desired more than anything.

The moment he removed his pants and stood before me in just his boxers, his eyes flashed a golden red and steam came from his skin. I was nervous and slightly unsure, but with a roar, he shifted, and the beast he became was something I would never forget.

Black and red scales encompassed the massive form of the dragon in front of me. He stood taller than a one-story house with golden scales upon its stomach and flecks of gold scattered down its tail.

Slowly, I stood to my feet, making my way across the blanket we had been sitting on towards the beast that loomed in front of me. Never in my life had I ever thought I'd see a dragon, and now that one was standing before me, I was speechless.

It wasn't just a dragon. It was Silas.

A man sinfully attractive, and yet so different than I had expected.

"Holy shit, Silas... you're a dragon!" I exclaimed, stating the obvious as if I hadn't already known what he was. Making a grunting noise that sounded almost like a scoff, he turned his head towards me and bent low before nudging me with his nose.

He had said he wanted me to ride him, but honestly, I wasn't sure if I wanted to. He was a fucking dragon, and I definitely didn't fly. "Silas—I can't..."

I wasn't given another choice when he nudged me again and gripping the scales of his face, I was hoisted upon his back with a soft scream leaving my throat in the process.

"Silas!"

My words were useless as he climbed higher and higher into the sky. The clouds quickly surrounded us as I clung to him for dear life. The last thing I wanted was to fall off and plummet to my death, even though I was fairly sure he wouldn't let me die. At least, I hoped he wouldn't let me die.

By the time he reached a height he seemed happy with, his flapping became more even, and instead of rising, we soared through the night sky. Asgard loomed below us with dimly lit twinkling lights from the homes where people still lay awake. It was beautiful, and with the wind rushing through my hair and against my skin, I felt free. More free than I ever had, which was a feeling I never wanted to let go of.

As a smile washed over my face, I held out my arms and closed my eyes, trusting Silas would keep me safe. I wasn't sure why I wanted to trust in him, but it felt right, and as we soared through the sky, I couldn't help the satisfied at-home feeling rolling through me.

Perhaps through all the evil that has consumed my life up until this point, this was a place I could call home. A place where I could change things.

******

I wasn't sure how much time had passed by the time we hand landed on the ground, but the moment I slid from Silas and my feet hit the ground, I knew something was wrong. There was something about the space we had once been laughing in was off, and glancing around the area, I peered into the darkness for its source.

Stepping from the shadows, the red-haired figure of a woman caught my gaze, and staring long enough, I realized it was the head mistress of the school, Inanna.

"Change back now," she demanded.

A low growl emanated from the dragon behind me as the snapping of bones resonated through the air. I wasn't sure why she was upset, but from the glare on her face, she didn't seem pleased we had a midnight rendezvous in the sky.

"What is the meaning of this?" Silas snarled as he stepped forth, buttoning his pants, still shirtless and without shoes. He wasn't pleased by her tone, and as he stepped in front of me, her eyes flashed slightly gold.

"What are you doing flying around with her," she snapped in a low tone, "you know that isn't allowed."

Allowed? Were we supposed to have gotten permission?

"If you don't recall, Inanna, you have no authority over me."

It was clear as day Silas and Inanna didn't like each other, and as her eyes turned to me, she gave me a sickly sweet grin as she raised a brow crossing her arms over her chest. "No, but I do over her."

"Say what–" I muttered softly as Silas held out an arm holding me back to which I clung. Tension was high, and the woman I had seen before around school didn't seem like the same woman in front of me now.

"She is still a student at our school and, therefore, under my control and protection."

Tired of the drama currently unfolding, I shook my head in disbelief as laughter left my lips. I wasn't trying to be disrespectful, but as both of them turned to me, I planned on making one thing very clear—I took orders from no one.

"Look, lady, I'm an adult and under no one's control."

Inanna didn't like the fact I spoke to her the way I did as her smile fell, and she narrowed her gaze. Again, I wasn't trying to be disrespectful, but for her to speak about me as she had, as if I was still a child, was uncalled for.

"You obviously don't understand how things work here—"

"Stop," I quickly snapped, cutting her off. "I have gotten the gist of it, and honestly, you're interrupting our date. So do you mind?"

The fact I was speaking to her like this seemed to shock Silas, but with a small smile on his face, he turned his gaze from me back to Inanna and shrugged his shoulders. He wasn't obviously going to argue with what I said, and with a scowl on her face, it didn't seem Inanna was either.

"No more flying, Silas. Get her home now."

Turning on her heels, she flipped her hair over her shoulder and continued back the way she had come. I wasn't sure why she felt the need to come out here like she had, and from how Silas looked at her when she left, it seemed he may have been confused as well.

"What was that all about?" I asked him, watching his gaze hesitate a little longer on where she had disappeared before turning to me.

"Honestly, I don't know," he muttered, turning back to where we had been enjoying ourselves. Reaching down, he picked up his shirt and continued getting dressed, a sense of tension now spiraling between us as he remained silent.

I hated how the wonderful evening we were having was ruined because Inanna had shown up throwing a fit about Silas taking me up in the sky. None of it felt right, and yet as he pulled his shirt on and slowly began to do the buttons, I felt a pull to him I had avoided in the past.

Stepping towards him, I slowly reached up, letting my hands brush against the muscles of his back, causing him to freeze in his spot before turning slowly to face me. I wasn't sure what I was doing, but something inside me told me he was more than he let on.

"What is it that you're not telling me?" I whispered, staring at him for some sort of answer. I was tired of people keeping secrets from me my whole life, and as much as I was growing fond of my conversations with Silas, I didn't want him to be another person on the list of people who hid shit from me.

"I don't know what that was about, Cassie. However, I think you may need to dig more into who you are to find out. It seems there are things even I don't know here."

His hand brushed strands of my hair from my face before he reached down and kissed the corner of my lips ever so gently. Part of me wanted more, but from the way he pulled back, staring down at me, I knew that wouldn't be the case.

"Silas–" I whispered again, only for him to shake his head no.

"It's time to get you home, Cassie. Tonight didn't turn out the way I expected, but under no circumstances will I be like other men. You're a treasure to be loved and not a prize to be won. That was never my intention."

It was gentlemanly for him to say what he did, and he took my hand, pulling me towards the brush and back out onto the cobblestone road. I couldn't help but wonder what would or could have happened had Inanna not come and interrupted us.

"I had fun tonight," I admitted glancing at him as we reached the garden by where I was staying. "We should do it again sometime."

Silas chuckled as he nodded his head, pushing his hands into his front pockets. "I'd like that, but perhaps next time, something slightly different for fun."

"Yeah, maybe." I laughed as I swayed from foot to foot, trying to hide the awkwardness I felt. "I will leave it up to you to surprise me, though."

"Me." He chuckled as his eyes went wide. "Do you like my surprises then?"

"I do."

The smile that crossed my face was all he needed before he fidgeted with his hands and then turned, making his way back down the path we had come up, disappearing without another word. He was such a strange man, it turned out, and one with so many stories to tell that completely spun my mind.

Turning, I made my way back inside the building and down the hall towards my room, thinking about everything that had happened. I wished my night wasn't over, but of course, things never went the way I wanted.

"Did you have fun, Cassie?" a cold voice said from beside me as I passed Lucas' door. I was surprised to see him, not having really had a conversation with him since earlier in the day when he decided I was nothing to him.

I wasn't sure what his issue was, but the cold glare he gave me wasn't like anything I had ever seen before. He was my mate, and regardless of my friendship with Silas, I knew something was wrong.

Stepping forward, I opened my mouth to speak, but as I did, a glare crossed his face I hadn't expected. "What? Can't find anything to say?

"What is your problem? You wanted me, had me, and then didn't want me. What is it you expect from me when you keep acting like this?"

I was confused in so many different ways, and the emotional rollercoaster Lucas had me on wasn't enjoyable. Granted, I knew I wasn't the easiest person to get a lot with but something had to give. We at least had to draw clear lines or something.

Laughter escaped him as he shook his head. His hand pressed against the door frame as if something inside him snapped. "My problem? Perhaps you need to look at yourself, princess."

"What the fuck is that supposed to mean?" I snapped at him, cocking an eyebrow.

"It means exactly what I said," he all but spat as he stepped closer to me, "you're all the same."

I had no fucking clue what he was talking about but with a look of disgust, I decided not to play whatever sick fucking game he was looking to enjoy tonight. "Go fuck yourself, Lucas. I don't have time for your shit."

The moment I turned away from him, I was snatched back by my arm and pulled close to his chest. His dark eyes loomed down at me as if he was searching for something he couldn't find. "You leave when I tell you to leave, Cassie. I'm far from over with you."

A sudden rush of fear washed over me as he kept his grip firm on my arm. My heart raced like never before as I struggled to free myself from his grip. "Lucas, let me go."

Concerned and on guard, I stared into his gaze when Lucas broke into maniacal laughter I had never experienced in my entire life. Something was wrong, and I wasn't sure what it was but from the moment Lucas and I shared the night we did until now... something happened.

Something dark lay inside Lucas, and I had to save him.

Dancing with Darkness

Unknown

For years I had been waiting for the moment I would regain my freedom, and with every passing second I survived in a world that didn't want me, I dreamt of the day I would get my revenge.

The day I would be able to regain who I truly was and make my way back into a world I would punish for treating me the way it did. Power, it was the ultimate sacrifice, and with the death of so many, balance would be restored.

The distant dripping of water from the pipes within the darkness was the only thing that reminded me of where I was. I was unfairly punished for trying to correct the evils of the world. Evils the gods themselves didn't deem important enough to be tampered with.

Sitting upon the small cot in my cell, I stared off into the darkness, waiting for anything to remind me I wasn't alone in the plans of my rebellion. Day and night, for years, I had been formulating my plan. Making sure nothing could happen to detour what needed to be done.

A plan that would get me back to my one true love. A woman with raven black hair as deep as the night, with eyes so blue they reminded me of the sea. Her love was the only thing that made me feel mortal in a world of souls who didn't die.

I had no doubt she was waiting for me. No doubt when I got back to her, she would be in the same small cabin we shared in the woods, anticipating when I would walk back through its front doors.

It was funny what love could do to us in the weakest of moments. How one single kiss could change your entire life, and how quickly that love could be snatched away from you when you least expect it.

"M'lord," a soft voice called from within the darkness, "things are more complicated than we would have liked."

My eyes darted to the red-haired woman I was all too familiar with. "Inanna…"

The moment she came into view, she dropped to her knees before me as if to worship who I was, even if she was technically my equal in a way. As her golden green eyes gazed up at me from the floor, I couldn't help but see how truly wicked she was.

"The girl… she isn't doing as we would have hoped."

Of course, she wasn't. She was just like her mother, and that was something I expected.

"So what are you going to do then?" The question posed made a blank expression cross her face as her eyes shifted from side to side, and her heart rate increased.

"M'lord," she stuttered in confusion, "shall I kill her?"

"Kill her?" The anger that crossed me over the comment was graciously expected. How could this woman think I would want the girl killed? She was important to my freedom, and without her, I would be held here indefinitely.

"Yes, I can arrange—"

"You will do no such thing!" I growled in frustration, "have you not been listening to anything I have told you over the past few years? She is important to what I need."

Taken aback by my outburst, Inanna's brows furrowed slightly as she shook her head. It was clear she was confused, and as she opened her mouth, I braced myself from the stupidity that was sure to follow. "She does deserve to die in the end—"

"How do you come to that conclusion?" I asked, trying to understand what exactly she had against the girl. Yes, she had shown interest in her over the years but never truly explained why her sudden interest in killing her had been so high.

Opening and closing her mouth, she pursed her lips together and grinned instead. It was a clear sign she wasn't going to say anything to me, and when she finally did open her mouth, I wasn't surprised. "Your son has taken the news of you well."

Diverting the question as usual. "That's good. Does he seem open to what we are asking him to do?"

Shrugging her shoulders, she slowly stood to her feet, flicking her hair over her shoulder with a grin that spread softly across her lips. "I have been... helping him to understand."

"Your mind tricks aren't what I asked you to do, Inanna."

"I know," she hummed as her gaze glittered in the dim lighting, "but it's working, so what does it matter?"

She was cocky in her approach to do what we had planned and knowing she played with fire when it came to the pawns in our game, I was concerned. However, unlike so many others I had played with before, she was effective when it came to getting what she wanted.

"Very well," I sighed, shaking my head, "just no more complications."

Pausing in her step, her eyes met mine with another glimpse of hesitation, and I knew that something else had happened she had come forth to tell me. "What is it?"

"The dragon," she said slowly, "he's become a complication and a possible issue."

"Dragon? You mean Silas?"

Nodding her head, I sighed with frustration. Silas had once been a friend of mine and over time became an enemy as our views on certain things changed. He didn't see the cause I was trying to fight for, and it wasn't a surprise he would put his nose into things that didn't concern him.

"I see. Handle it. Put some space between him and whatever complication he is creating. I'm sure your creative nature can think of something, Inanna."

Lucas

The moment Inanna had stopped me in the garden after I spent the evening with Cassie, I knew she wanted something. However, I hadn't expected her word to be true about meeting my father. The dark eyes that looked back at me were the same as my own, and everything about him was untrusting.

Lucas.

The sound of his voice when he said my name that night was something that would forever haunt my dreams. There was no way I had come from that, but the more I thought about it, the more I knew it was true.

He was my father, and I was filled with more darkness than I realized.

The moment I returned to my room, I reeled over the conversation I had with Cassie. I hated I was being cruel toward her, but the last thing I wanted was for her to get hurt. For the darkness inside me to lash out and destroy her in some kind of way.

She may have been a lot of things, but deep down, I could see her heart was purer than most of us here. Even if she did hide it behind a wall of sarcasm and cruel intentions. No one can blame someone for lashing out in unkind ways because of what they have been through, and I knew that better than anyone.

The moment I slept, I dreamt of the dark world I belonged to. Whispers of hatred and unhappy endings swirled through my mind as I saw the destruction the past brought and the future held.

A world of flames and chaos which would consume everyone I loved if I didn't keep my distance from her. Cassie would be the one to do it, and it would be because of me.

However, as I tried to keep my distance, something dark inside me sought to complete our bond. Sought to force her into submission, and as much as I tried to fight it, I couldn't. My lycan tried to push himself to the front and craning my neck now as I stared at her, all I wanted to do was taste her blood.

Feel her heart beating against my own as I fucked her into submission.

"Lucas, let go of me," she cried out softly as panic filled her eyes. Panic I was enjoying more than she knew. "You're hurting me."

"Hurting you?" I growled as she stared up at me with the same blue eyes I had fallen in love with so many times before. "How many people have you hurt?"

Shock swept through her face at my comment. She had definitely not been expecting me to ask her that, and honestly, I was pleased with her reaction. Yet, disgusted with myself as well. What the hell was wrong with me?

"What happened to you?" she whispered as her eyes brimmed with tears. "How can you say something like that to me? You wanted me as your mate, and then you treat me like shit... what the fuck is wrong with you?"

"Wrong with me? There is nothing wrong with me. I feel better than I ever had."

Shaking her head, she refused to accept my answer, and as she tried to pull herself free again, I tightened my grip on her. My hand slid up to her throat, causing her to whimper in both pleasure and fear. "Lucas, please."

"Oh, don't pretend you don't like being treated like this, Cassie. I can smell your arousal, and it's so fucking delicious."

A soft moan escaped her lips as a single tear fell down her cheek. I knew she could use her powers to hurt me if she wanted to, and that battle waged behind her eyes as she tried to contain the anger that wanted to lash out. "Please, let me go."

Before I could answer her, I was roughly hit from behind. My hold on Cassie loosened as my gaze turned murderous and was spun around to find Pollux had pulled Cassie behind him and was staring down at me with a newfound hatred I found deliciously enticing. "Pollux," I chuckled with delight, "how good of you to join us."

Narrowing his gaze, he bared his fangs at me, "I don't give a fuck if you're her mate or not. If you ever put your hands on her like that again, I'll fucking kill you."

Laughter escaped my throat at his comment as I felt the shift wanting to take over me. Every part of me wanted to kill this boy for putting his hands on me, but I knew that wasn't possible. Odin and the other gods wouldn't allow that to happen.

"Pollux, please... let's go."

Her soft voice caught my gaze and her hand on his arm. Regardless, if it was her brother, it pissed me off more than anything. "You're not going anywhere, mate."

The moment I went to step forward though, I was frozen in my place, and stepping from around the corner came a flash of blue hair and glowing grin eyes. The same girl I had seen with Cassie so many times stood with her hand gently in front of her and a grin on her face.

"Oh, isn't this interesting," she purred, turning her gaze to Cassie and Pollux for a moment as I stood, unable to do anything. "Cassie, why didn't you tell me your mate was part darkling."

What did she just call me?

Cassie's brows furrowed in confusion as she let her gaze fall from me to her friend. "What is that?"

Chuckling, the blue-haired girl looked to me again with a mischievous smile. "Let's take this conversation into his room, shall we? It looks like we have a lot to talk about, and the hallway isn't the best place to do it."

Waking Lucas

Cassie

Shocked by everything going on, I didn't know what to say when Trixie froze Lucas in place and referred to him as a darkling. Moreover, I didn't know what to think about Pollux coming to my rescue. It was evident something was wrong with Lucas by the way he was acting, but never did I consider myself to be weak in a moment where I shouldn't have been.

With his hand on my back, Pollux ushered me into Lucas' room as Trixie used her powers to glide him backward and then lower him onto his bed. She seemed almost entranced with her movements as her powers radiated through the space, catching me by surprise. Of course, she had powers, but this... this was something else entirely.

"How did you do that?" The question left my lips before I could actually contemplate what I said and as she touched her hand to Lucas' forehead, his eyes closed before hers turned to me.

"It's part of my powers, and he is asleep. Not sure how long as I have never tried to use that on someone but we can hope for the best." She pushed a strand of hair behind her ear as she glanced at my brother and quickly looked back at me.

They were mates, and the flirting gesture made me smirk before realizing I had to figure out what was happening. "What's a darkling?"

Trixie and my brother both looked at each other before looking at me. My brother knew, and that was honestly unexpected. Usually, he didn't know anything like that, and I was the one filling him in. Opening and closing his mouth, he glanced at Trixie, urging her with his head to say something, to which she rolled her eyes and groaned. "You're no help, are you?"

"Oh, just fucking tell her," he snapped, rolling his own eyes. Both of them acted as if they were closer now than they had been before which was weird considering it wasn't that long ago he was being a dick.

"It means that he is the child of a God who plays within the shadows. There are a few, but it's rare to find the children as they are often killed."

As if her words held magic, Freya walked into the room with a smile on her face. Her long hair was braided in sections and adorned with small flowers. She glanced at Lucas with a raised brow and turned towards me. "I'm glad you all finally figured it out. Too bad he wasn't aware."

My mind was blown by the fact everyone knew and I hadn't, nor had Lucas... at least we were assuming he hadn't. "How do we fix him?"

Freya furrowed her brows and sighed, "I can't tell you that I'm afraid but I can say you have friends who can help."

"Why are you here then if you're not doing anything?" Pollux snapped, saying exactly what I was thinking.

Freya shrugged her shoulders with a smile and as she turned towards the door and then looked over her shoulder, I knew for sure she had come for a reason. "Odin wants to see you, Cassie... you weren't in your room so I figured you might be here with your... whatever you want to call him."

She didn't bother to wait for a reply before she was out the door, leaving me there wondering what the hell was going on. Turning to Pollux and Trixie, I stood dumbfounded. "What the hell am I supposed to do... I can't leave right now."

"So then don't," Pollux sneered, rolling his eyes as he crossed his arms over his chest.

Trixie, however, was quick to shake her head with wide eyes, "You can't refuse Odin, Cassie. Just go. I think I know what we can do to try and help Lucas. I can't promise it will work long term, though."

"You can't leave Trixie in here alone with Lucas," Pollux scoffed with laughter.

Smirking, I turned to him, "That's why you're staying here with her. I'm sure you can protect her from Lucas if something happens."

Pollux's mouth dropped open as he glanced at Trixie, who was beaming with a mischievous grin as I turned and made my way toward the door. I wanted to look back and admire Lucas one more time before I left but I couldn't. I had to stay focused.

Step by step, I made my way down the hallway toward the hall where Odin resided. I didn't know my way around this place very well but I did the best I could to get by. So when I finally approached and my eyes set upon the golden throne Odin sat on, I couldn't help but admire him and also shake in fear.

Was he going to kill me for what I did?

Or was he going to help me... the question was one often unanswered.

Pollux

The moment Cassie left, I was in shock. Trixie, my gorgeous mate who wasn't a shifter, seemed nothing but pleased with the situation I was currently in. The idea of being alone with her was driving my beast crazy with the desire to claim her, but I refused.

How was she going to help me lead when she couldn't take care of herself?

It was a joke, honestly. A mistake by fate.

"You don't seem pleased to be here with me," Trixie stated, causing me to focus my attention on her and taking in every detail of her face down to her enchanting eyes. Never in my life had I wanted to kiss someone as much as I did then, and as I fought the urge to do so, I scoffed in response.

"I had things to do, so don't think it had to deal with you."

"Right." She laughed. "Whatever you have to tell yourself."

She was quick to go back to what she was doing, her figure pacing around the room as I watched her. She had reached out to someone, but I wasn't sure who the hell it was. There was something about her I loved and couldn't get over, and the realization I didn't know what it was frustrated me.

"What are you doing?" I asked, watching as she waved her hands up and down Lucas' body as if she was doing witchcraft or something.

"Do you always ask this many questions?"

Taken back by her response, I stood there for a moment. "Excuse me?

Trixie sighed with annoyance as she turned towards me, placing her hands on her hips. No matter how sweet and bubbly this girl was, I could see behind the front she had a fiery attitude which was not something you wanted to mess with.

She proved that when she quickly put Lucas in his place before he could do something to Cassie or me. Even though she wasn't a shifter, I had to admire her for her strong-willed nature. "You heard me, Pollux."

Pollux? No one here called me by my first name but Cassie, and yet the moment this woman said my name, I felt my balls tighten with anticipation.

"Look, just tell me what the plan is. I don't want to argue." Changing my tone with her, she smiled brightly before a knock came at the door. Trixie didn't look surprised by it, and in fact, got excited as she quickly answered the door.

"Sansa!" She squealed excitedly as the light-skinned girl entered the room. Her eyes fell on me and then darted toward Trixie with a raised brow as if she was unsure of what she walked into.

"I was going to ask why you were in here with Lucas, but seeing Pollux is in here as well, I want to remind you I'm not up for group orgies—"

"Oh my god, no!" I quickly exclaimed, cutting the woman off causing her and Trixie to laugh at my outburst.

"Calm down, Lux... I'm only teasing," Sansa replied as she walked toward the bed, pulling a brown satchel from her shoulder and setting it down. "So, we need to strip his mind of darkness... sounds like fun."

I wasn't sure what she was talking about, but Trixie walked around to the other side of the bed, looking down at Lucas with a quizzical glare that made me slightly uncomfortable. "You know, for an asshole, he is attractive."

"Yeah," Sansa sighed looking at Lucas as well, "Cassie definitely got a keeper."

Scoffing, I rolled my eyes, pulling both of their attention toward me. "Can we get to what we need to do, please? I have other places I'd rather be."

"Are you jealous, Pollux?" Trixie asked me as she slowly made her way from the bed toward me. "Do you not like me making comments about other men?"

I was frozen in place, unsure of what to say. The primal dominant in me wanted to put her in her place and show her who she belonged to and who was in charge. But the other part of me refused to break down from the expectations I had upon myself since youth.

I was an Alpha with a pack to protect.

I couldn't have weaknesses within my reign, or my pack would fall and I would fail.

Taking a deep breath through my mouth, trying to not let her amazing aroma of jasmine and honey flood my senses, I shook my head and kept a calm neutral expression. "Why would I be jealous over you, Trixie? There is no reason."

Sansa quickly snapped up from where she had been bent over, and a fire in her eyes showed how angry she was at that moment. "Who the fuck do you think you are speaking to her like that?"

Trixie quickly glanced over her shoulder, shaking her head at Sansa for her outburst. Something I hadn't been expecting her to do. "It's okay, Sansa. I'm not bothered by what he has to say. In fact, the pain of the mate bond only affects him. So if this is what he wants, I'm fine with that."

Hearing her reply to the situation gripped my heart and twisted my stomach. How could she think that? She should be enraged!

"Nice to know you don't care. Makes things easier," I snapped at her, but instead of her being hurt by my outburst, she simply laughed and walked over to the bed as if everything that happened just then between us meant nothing.

"Sansa, are you ready to wake dear Lucas?" she asked her friend, my presence quickly put into the background as the two women got ready to do whatever witchy shit Sansa had planned.

"Sure am... now, if only I didn't have to worry about another dick in the room... not that I can promise this won't backfire and take another man for payment."

Her eyes darted toward me with amusement as I tried to understand what she meant. There was no use in the end, though, because before I could open my lips, she placed her hands on the side of Lucas' head, and she spoke the words to set him free.

"Come forth from darkness, and fill the light—"

The Latin that left her throat after her first bit of words went by in a flash, and with a blinding white light that lit the room, Lucas gasped for air and shot upright in the bed. His breathing came in ragged as he glanced around looking more confused than I had ever seen him in my entire life.

Golden shimmers in Darkness

Cassie

The last thing I wanted to do was see Odin, my supposed grandfather, when I had more important things to worry about, like what was wrong with Lucas. However, here I stood before him, watching as he took me in from head to toe, running his hand over his beard as if he had something on his mind. "You called for me?"

Nodding, a smile crossed his wrinkled face. "I did... I know our last meeting didn't go as I had planned and I wanted to clear things up."

Stunned this was why he called me, I opened and closed my mouth, trying to find the words needed to make sense of why I was here. Of course, I wanted to talk to him, or at least I thought I did, but right now wasn't the time to do it.

"I'm not sure what you want to talk about..." It was true, I didn't know what he wanted to talk about considering there wasn't really much to say, but by the look on his face, he wasn't pleased with my remark.

His brows narrowed at my words as he sat a little straighter. I had no doubt he wasn't expecting me to respond the way I did, but it was irrelevant. Pollux and Trixie were waiting for me and being here wasn't going to help the mass of mysteries we were trying to figure out.

"Castor," the sound of Odin saying my first name was a distraction. No one called me Castor but my mother, and that was usually when I was in trouble.

"Odin..." I replied, holding my chin high. "I'd say that we can do this all day long, but I honestly have something else to tend to." I refused to backdoor or show any weakness. If he had something to say, he could get on with it.

Chuckling, he shook his head with a smile that made my brows furrow in confusion. "You have such a strong will to survive, Castor. So much confidence and yet it is perfectly balanced by the soft, sweet side of you that you hide away."

"Showing weakness gets you killed," I replied quickly. That was a lesson my father taught me long ago, and something I made sure I didn't do.

"There's more to life than simply hiding behind what you fear. We really do need to have this conversation, but I can see by the way you are moving from foot to foot you would rather be elsewhere than actually having a conversation with me. Am I correct?"

"You would be correct," I quickly said with an eyebrow raised in his direction. Gesturing with his hand, he showed me towards the door, not saying another word. I wasn't sure if this was a good thing or if I possibly made a huge mistake in disregarding whatever conversation he wanted to have with me.

Turning towards the door, a heavy breath escaped me as I thought over what I was possibly doing. Was this going to be a negative mark against me, refusing to have words with Odin? Or would it be a positive thing to where he maybe wouldn't look at me again, and therefore, I could go undercover or do whatever it was I needed to do without his watchful gaze upon every move I made?

Regardless of all of it, my mind went back to my brother and friend, who currently watched over my unbonded mate, who lay in a bed full of darkness, and I had absolutely no idea what had happened to him.

Was I angry at him for the way that he had acted? Yes.

Then again, deep down, I knew I was not the easiest person to live with.

Making my way down hallway after hallway, taking turn after turn, I found myself closer and closer to Lucas's door, and as I opened it upon my arrival, I was shocked to see the sight before me. Lucas, upright in bed, was snarling at Pollux, his eyes completely black as if the Onyx depth of despair had filled him and not a single bit of light was left.

I didn't have the slightest clue what was going on, and the last thing I wanted was for the gods to figure out what it was. It was bad enough that Freya was obviously well aware of the situation if she said anything to Odin.

There was a chance Lucas could be imprisoned here.

Which, no matter how much you pissed me off, wasn't something I wanted for him.

Gazing around the room, my eyes fell on Sansa, and with a wide, shocked expression, she shrugged her shoulders. "I have no idea what happened."

"What happened while I was away? I was literally gone for fifteen minutes," I exclaimed in anger. How was it we calmed the chaos for a moment, and I came back to a shit storm brewing in his room?

Lucas's eyes darted directly toward me as I spoke. "You," he growled in anger.

I wasn't sure what his problem was, besides the obvious, of course, but slowly he slid off the bed, and as he did, I made sure not to freeze in front of him again. I wasn't going to be a victim this time.

Letting the power that flowed through my body come alive, he stopped in his tracks and growled at me again, the problem was my stupid ass brother didn't know I had everything under control, and as he tried to rush Lucas, he got blasted back by something I hadn't expected to see.

A power that almost mimicked mine, but one of nothing by obsidian darkness.

Trixie screamed out my brother's name as she and Sansa tended to his unconscious body. He wasn't dead, and that was simply by luck. But knowing Lucas hurt my brother pissed me off, and without a second thought, I charged him, only to have him toss me onto the bed and pin me beneath his body.

With his claws at my neck and only inches between our faces, I felt myself break. I wanted to hurt him, hell part of me wanted to kill him for hurting Pollux, but I couldn't.

"Lucas, let me go. Look at what you have become!" I shouted at him, trying to get his attention, trying to do anything I could to make him see he was losing control of who he was.

"Me?" he laughed maniacally. "You're the cause of all of this, Cassie. You're the burden on not only the human realm but this realm as well. If it weren't for you and the power inside you, so many people would still be alive,"

"What—" I gasped, my eyes instantly filling with tears at his words. "Lucas, stop... it wasn't my fault."

"Nothing is ever your fault, is it? Poor Cassie, she can't take the fall for anything, can she? What a pathetic use of godly power."

Lifting his other claw high into the air, I wondered if the end was coming. I wondered if I was going to die, but a roar, unlike anything I had ever heard, rattled the room, and as it did, Lucas was ripped from my body and tossed toward the far side of the room.

It took a minute for me to process what had just happened, but as I looked toward the figure currently stalking Lucas's body, attempting to get up from the floor, I took in a sight more magnificent than anything I had ever seen.

Silas stood there, a golden shimmer encompassing his body. Fiery irises burned in the center of his eyes. "Under the command of Odin, you are to be taken."

"What? No, Silas..." I didn't want Lucas imprisoned, nor did I want him hurt. He wasn't himself, and I could see that. Hell, I could feel it from the small bit of our bond. Something was wrong with him, and I had to find a way to save him.

But before Silas could even get hold of him, Lucas quickly lept out the nearest window. My heart jumped in fear as I scrambled to where he had just been and looked out, expecting to see him dead. Only he wasn't.

In fact, Lucas was nowhere to be found, and his lingering words rattled through my mind like a plague of pain that pounded down upon my heart.

"Cassie, are you okay?" Looking over my shoulder, Silas was back to his normal self, and with a sorrowful expression on his face, I couldn't resist hugging him. My arms reached for him without hesitation as I buried my face into his chest.

"Thank you, but how did you know?" Glancing up, he looked at me with a smile and shrugged his shoulders.

"Odin," he said softly, making my blood run cold. "He knew something was wrong, so he sent for me to find out what it was."

"If it was Odin, why didn't he or the other gods come to help us? Why would they let it happen and not step in to help us fix this?" None of it made sense, and as a sigh escaped him, his eyes turned to Sansa, who quickly stood to her feet, rolling her eyes.

"You want me to give a history lesson?" she asked, crossing her arms over her chest, "that's bullshit."

Silas groaned with irritation as he gave her a death stare that amused even me. After a moment of reluctance, she rolled her eyes and sighed. "Okay, fine. The gods don't interfere because the mortals–even the half-bloods—must know how to handle our own problems, in simpler terms. They only step in when it directly affects them."

"That's the stupidest thing I have ever heard," I muttered to myself, but obviously loud enough for the others to hear. "What's the point in all of this, then?"

"What do you mean," Silas asked as he stared at me, "this is how this realm works."

"Yeah, and it's beyond stupid. Are you telling me they just let everyone do whatever they want? I mean... something is wrong, and they won't help. That's fucking stupid. I don't even get the point of being here. I'm not learning anything, and honestly, all it reminds me of is being in high school again."

My outburst definitely surprised the others in the room; even Trixie frowned at my comment. My brother groaned and with that, caught everybody's attention. And I was thankful for that—considering I did not want the attention on me. All I wanted was to be able to go off on my own, back into the human realm, without anybody around to tell me what to do to try and live a normal life.

I had hoped coming to Asgard to live with the gods, to learn from people like me, would be beneficial, but in the end, it hasn't been. I was stuck here trying to figure out who I was and grow from the mistakes I had made, and in the long run, ended up with problems that involved my brother and my so-called mate.

Why was it fate couldn't just let me be normal for once?

Rejected

Cassie

For two days, I didn't see hide nor hair of Lucas. In fact, all of us had looked for him, and yet... nothing. I was worried, which the others thought was crazy, considering Lucas attacked me, but in reality, I tried to attack him first, and so did my brother.

Guilt swallowed at me, wondering if he would ever be normal again. Even if he didn't want me anymore, it didn't mean I didn't care to know if he was okay or not. Frustration filled me as I tried to focus on my current task at hand. The endless lectures on how to use effective magic was something so far from my thoughts, and yet my teacher's rambling still echoed in the distance.

The moment the bell rang, a sigh of relief washed over me as I collected my book and moved from my seat. My stomach growled for food, considering I had barely eaten the last two days, and instead moped around like a pathetic loser hoping for the attention of one person who, at one point, couldn't stand to be around me.

Stepping into the hall, I instantly dreaded this place. The whispered conversations and stares of the people around me made my skin crawl. Everyone heard about what had happened with Lucas, and I wasn't sure exactly how they had heard, but it may have had something to do with the fact Zia had seen Lucas jump from the window.

She was an absolute bitch, and the more she glanced at me and made mocking comments, the more I wanted to cut her eyes from her head and shove them down her throat. She had already tried twice now to taunt me, telling me I didn't deserve Lucas and that she would happily take him off my hands.

As if I would ever reject my mate, even if he were a bit of an asshole since we slept together. A moment I thought of very often.

He was mine, and I was his, even if I didn't want to admit it to myself.

"Cassie, what are you doing here? I thought I told you to go back to your room?" Sansa said as she grabbed my arm, stopping me in the hallway between the bell.

"I can't miss class because of all this," I explained as I adjusted the bag strap on my shoulder. "Plus, I'm starving and really need to get something to eat."

Her eyes went wide at my words as if my wanting food shocked her in some way. She was literally the one who scolded me this morning for not eating. "Oh well, why don't we go to the cafe down the street where we got drinks that one time and we can grab something there?"

The cafe was a good fifteen-minute walk from here, and honestly, I didn't have the energy to do that. All I wanted to do was to go down to the cafeteria where everybody always ate lunch, grab something there and then move on to my next class without bringing any more attention to myself.

If that was possible.

"No, I think I'm just going to grab a sandwich or something down in the cafeteria," I replied as I gave her a small smile and attempted to walk past her, to which she quickly stopped me once more.

"Oh, come on, it'll be fun. We haven't done it since that day, and there's been so much else going on. I think we should do that. We could even find Trixie."

Laughter escaped me as I shook my head. "As amazing as that sounds, maybe we can do that this weekend. I honestly just want to grab something small from the cafeteria and just move to my next class. I can't be late."

Hesitant about it all, she quickly let me go but kept at my side the entire way there, still trying to convince me that going to the cafeteria was only going to be boring and that we should go have fun somewhere off campus.

It wasn't until they got to the cafeteria doors Trixie popped up with a smile on her face, and I suddenly realized something was going on.

"Hey, I was just coming to find you guys. I actually ordered us some food down the street. Why don't we go ahead and take a walk and go pick it up, and then we can get to class, and we won't be late," she said without a breath, causing my suspicion level to rise even higher.

"What the hell is going on with you two? Why are you acting like this?" Both Sansa and Trixie looked at each other, giving each other a questionable gaze that was undeniably a sense of warning, if you will, between the two of them.

I wasn't sure what was going on, but I sure as hell was going to find out. As I pushed past Trixie, opening the door to the cafeteria, I got a front-row view of exactly what had them so out of sorts.

Lucas sat at the table with Zia and a couple of the other populars—if you want to call them that–who showed off around school. His arm was draped over Zia's shoulders as she leaned in close to him with only inches between his lips and hers.

Upset didn't even begin to explain the way I felt the moment I laid my eyes on him and Zia. Only two days ago, he had literally tried to kill me, and yet he was sitting here amongst all of these people, acting as if everything was fine and nothing was wrong with him.

Shock and anger consumed me as I tried to think of what to do or what to say. Anyone else would have run out of there crying in tears that their mate was lounging on another woman, but my and Lucas's situation was far different than the typical mated couple.

Hell, we weren't even actually mated it yet. Of course, we had sex, but thank God I didn't let him bite me. I could only imagine what the mate bond would feel like right now. "Are you fucking kidding me?"

My muttered response did not go unnoticed. Trixie and Sansa had heard me, and as his eyes met mine, I could assume he heard me too. Trying my hardest to think clearly on this matter, I held my head high, averted my gaze from his look of disgust, and marched down the center of the cafeteria, straight towards the buffet of food that lay on the far back wall.

The last thing I was going to do was allow him to fuck up the rest of my day. I had already spent the last two days completely worried about him, on whether or not he was alive, if his mind was too far gone and how I was going to be able to help him. And yet he sat here with those people with his arm around another woman, acting as if everything that had happened between him and I had never existed.

"Cassie, you don't have to be here going through this," Trixie's soft, gentle words were a push of encouragement and understanding. But at the same time, I wasn't going to allow him to get what he wanted. I wouldn't allow him the satisfaction of seeing me break.

Turning my gaze towards Trixie with a croissant in hand, I smiled at her. "I already wasted enough time trying to figure this man out. I'm not going to continue doing it. If he wants to figure his stuff out with her, then let him. I have better things to do with my time."

I didn't really. Honestly, it was killing me inside, knowing he would prefer the company of another woman than allowing me to talk to him so I could try to figure out what the fuck was wrong.

Turning back to the food in front of me, I made a small plate and grabbed a drink and as I turned, hoping to make my way out of the cafeteria without causing any kind of disturbance, I found Lucas standing before me with a sinister grin upon his beautiful plump lips.

"The fuck are you doing in here?"

Staring at him for a moment, I held up my plate of food, raising one brow as I shrugged my shoulders. "What the fuck does it look like I'm doing?"

"I thought I made it clear I didn't want anything to do with you, so I don't know why you're here bothering me," he spoke loud enough for the people around to hear what he said, and as I took in his comment, I couldn't hold back the laughter that escaped me.

So instead, I decided to play his game. "Bother you? I'm pretty sure you're the one who just walked up to me. I didn't say anything to you, nor did I approach you. I walked right past you and got my food, and yet you're the one standing in my way from leaving."

Lucas' eyes narrowed as a sneer marred his lips. He couldn't deny the truth in what I said. I hadn't said a single thing to him, and yet he was the one who left the comfort of his new toy and friends to come over and address me as if I was the one bothering him.

It wasn't the smartest move on his part, considering everybody around heard exactly what I said. It left him standing there looking like the fool he really was. No matter the fool, though, in the gaze he laid upon me, I saw the darkness seeping within him, and every part of me wanted to help.

But I couldn't. It was obvious Lucas had made his choice, and had he wanted my help, he would have allowed me to give it to him two days ago when he tried to kill me.

"You are a delusional bitch. I will never be with you. Get that through your fucking head," he growled as his eyes shifted between gold flecks and Obsidian chaos.

Taking advantage of the opportunity, I stepped closer, making sure he got a good wiff of my scent as I gazed up and down his body taking in every single curve of the ripped muscle beneath his shirt. As well as the same well-defined arms that had once held my naked body against him.

"If you don't want me, then reject me and get it over with."

I didn't really want Lucas to reject me as his mate, but at the same time, I was tired of this back and forth battle with him. It was absolutely pointless, and as he seemed to contemplate what I was offering, a smile spread across his lips.

"Fine. I, Lucas, reject you, Castor, as my mate."

The stinging pain of the tear of our bond echoed through my heart. Thankfully our bond hadn't been completed, and I was for once grateful I didn't allow him to mark me completely. "You will regret doing that one day."

"Accept the rejection, Cassie," he snapped as he stood waiting for me to say something further, but instead of accepting right away, I pushed away my pain and smirked.

"When I'm ready, I will. For right now, though, you don't deserve it."

He cringed in pain himself as I quickly pushed past him making my way down the hall with all eyes upon me, whispers escaping those who had witnessed our reaction. I had to learn to ignore everyone like I used to do with Melissa, and as I took a deep breath, it worked—for a moment.

Zia stood from her seat as I passed her, a look of pure satisfaction upon her face.

"Looks like you finally got what you deserve," Zia called out, with nothing but amusement in her tone.

Halting in my tracks, I stared at the double doors in front of me that was my escape to freedom, wondering what choice I was going to make. I could continue through the doors and be known for the girl who got dumped during lunch, or I could turn and make her eat her own words.

Both were things people would eventually forget... but right now, I didn't care.

"Cassie, don't–" Sansa and Trixie said in unison. "She's baiting you."

Pushing back the pain in my heart, I glanced at my friends with a smile, "I know... and she is going to eat her fucking words too."

Challenging Zia

Cassie

Handing over my plate of food and drink to Sansa, I slowly turned to face Zia. Her long hair flowed in waves over her shoulders. Her piercing eyes stared back at me with a smug expression on her face, the only thing I could think about was what it would look like beaten in.

Perhaps that was a slightly aggressive thought for me to have, but she had pushed my last fucking button like no one would believe.

"What is your problem?" I asked her, trying to remain calm as everyone waited for her explanation. A scoff left her lips as she sat there, rolling her eyes with her arms across her chest. She had to always be high and mighty when she was around her peers, something girls like her would never get tired of doing.

"I don't have a problem. It's you who's jealous Lucas and I are, well, eventually going to be together," she replied mockingly.

The last thing I had was time to spend on a woman like this, but I was sick and tired of her pushing my buttons. I was sick and tired of her spreading false rumors and more sick and tired of just dealing with her shit in general.

I hadn't even been in this place that long, and it was like she was completely threatened by my presence here and sought to try and make my life a living hell.

"You have high hopes for someone who's second best. Is that what you do with your day, Zia? Do you dream of taking the men of other women just to make yourself feel better when they don't give you the attention you want?"

Shocked by what I had said, her mouth dropped open wide as her eyes narrowed and an angry glare crossed her face. "What the fuck did you just say to me?"

Snorting with laughter, I glanced over at Trixie, who was just as shocked as Zia. It didn't come as a surprise to me no one had ever stood up to this girl. She was pathetic, honestly, and I didn't understand how she could be the way she was when, in today's age, we should be working with each other, not against.

Regardless of how she should be, I couldn't help but stand there staring at her in annoyance. "I'm pretty sure I didn't stutter, and I said it loud enough for everybody in here to hear. So I don't understand where the confusion is coming from."

Stomping her foot, she screamed in irritation as she stormed past people toward me. I knew that look in her eye. It was one of a woman on a warpath, and if she wanted a part of me, then she could have one.

"Enough!" Lucas' roar was enough to make me shudder. With our bond still technically in place, for the most part, I let the shiver of his tone run down my spine before he stepped in between Zia and me with his glare pointed at me. "Give me what I want."

"No," I snapped with more determination in me than I ever felt. "You're not you right now, and I won't let you make a choice when you're not thinking clearly."

Laughter escaped him as he looked at Zia and a few others before turning his gaze to me again. "You never even wanted this, Cassie. Why hold on now?"

"Because I won't let you do something you might regret."

My reply made him flinch as his angry scowl dropped for a moment before reappearing again. No matter what I said, he refused to see what I was saying for truth. The more I thought about it, the more I couldn't help but wonder what had happened for him to act the way he was.

The night we spent together flashed through my mind, and though he tried to break our bond, I refused to accept him. Which meant neither of us was going to move on.

Zia's slimy fingers wrapped around Lucas' arm as she leaned in and kissed the corner of his lips. As much as I wanted to remain calm and not let her see how much it was affecting me, I couldn't. A low growl emitted from my throat enticing the beast within Lucas because behind his gaze—a flash of gold—let me know his beast wasn't pleased with the choices he was making.

"Oh, is someone jealous?" Zia hissed, causing me to roll my eyes and laugh.

"Jealous?" I smirked. "That would call for me to have someone worth being jealous over. I wouldn't really call you competition, Zia. You're more like... a gnat that doesn't leave when you swat it."

Crossing my arms over my chest, I watched her eyes narrow at me as a look of shock and disgust crossed her face. She couldn't believe what I had said to her, but honestly, she had no one to blame but herself. In a moment of amusement, I thought the argument was over, but as I looked at Trixie, whose expression matched so many others, I misjudged the situation.

The punch Zia threw caught me off guard, and as her fist connected with the side of my face, I stumbled. A wave of anger rushed through me. My eyes connect with her's, causing an 'oh shit' expression to come forth in her eyes.

"A sucker punch... really, Zia?" I snarled at her with fists clenched at my sides, my nails extending, cutting into my palms as I thought of the many ways I was going to demolish her.

"Cassie, calm down right now," Lucas said warningly as he pushed Zia behind him.

"You would protect her after what she just did, Lucas?"

Opening his mouth, he was silent as if contemplating what he was going to say next, and even though he hesitated, he quickly sneered once more, gritting his teeth as the eyes of everyone in the cafeteria watched on.

"You're not my mate, Cassie. So why would I care what happens to you?" he replied, causing my heart to clench in agony. Yet, no matter how hurt his comment made me, I didn't allow others to see its effects.

Zia began to laugh at Lucas' comment, and any idea I had to walk away from being the bigger man escaped my thoughts. With a fit of anger rolling through me like a typhoon, I reached out past Lucas and snatched Zia by her throat.

My claws dug into her skin, causing droplets of blood to drip down her flawless skin. "Find something funny, Zia."

She gripped my hand, trying to break it free as she gasped for air. Lucas was too stunned initially to do anything, at first. Yet, he did come to terms with the fact that if unstopped, I'd probably kill Zia. My brother already had his arms wrapped around my waist, trying to break me free of the hold I had on the girl.

I was a hunter, and she was my prey. My instincts to kill on an all time high as I dug my nails deeper into her skin. "Let me go!" she gasped, "someone help!"

"Cassie, let her go now!" Pollux screamed at me, trying to get me to focus and loosen my hold. My will and drive to high to acknowledge him.

"She has crossed a line that's unforgivable. I will not tolerate disrespect."

The sound of my own voice sounded foreign in the moment, and as I realized what I was doing, I quickly let go of Zia and was pulled back. Her friends ran to her rescue as she pretended to be dying from what she had gone through.

"That bitch tried to kill me!" She whined as fake tears quickly started to fall down her cheeks. "Someone better do something! I want her gone!"

"Too bad that will never happen!" I yelled back, thrashing in Pollux's arms as Trixie and Sansa tried to help him calm me. My eyes still locked onto her wanting to rip her apart. No matter what the consequences would be, Zia was going to pay for what she was doing. "Enough!"

A voice yelled, catching the entire cafeteria's attention. "What in the hell is going on?"

The voice came from the main door to the cafeteria, and as I looked toward it, I spotted an older face I hadn't ever seen before—a man who looked to be in his late forties, accompanied by Inanna at his side.

He was a graying man with dark stubble and blue eyes. His whole characteristic screamed shifter, and I had no doubt he had to have been some type of cat shifter by the way he was dressed and carried himself. It was as if he was the king dick on campus, and everyone needed to bend to his will.

"Well?" he said again, glancing around with his hands on his hips. "Who the fuck is going to start explaining?"

As I opened my mouth to speak, Lucas stepped forward, and addressed the man. "Nothing, the girls were just showing each other new moves."

"Lucas—" Zia called out before he snapped his angry gaze toward her shutting her up.

The older man hesitated as his eyes shifted from Lucas to Zia and then to me. "What do you have to say for yourself?" he asked me.

As much as I wanted to rat everyone out, that wasn't who I was, and honestly, the last thing I wanted to do was get myself in trouble. I may not have cared for this place, but it didn't mean I wanted to have any other kind of issues before I was able to go back home.

"We were just practicing... nothing happened."

"Are you sure you want to go with that answer?" the man asked with a raised brow as if he knew I was lying but wanted to see if I'd admit to something.

"That's enough, Lyonal. She said it was nothing, and that's where it will be left."

I didn't expect Inanna to speak up. The nasty look she gave me as she brushed past me and placed her arm on the upper left shoulder of Lucas' chest made me furrow my brow. It was an intimate gesture, and whatever she whispered to Lucas made him narrow his gaze at me.

Turning without another word, she exited the hall, and Lucas quickly tended to Zia before the both of them followed behind Inanna.

I had no clue what the hell was going on, but the gesture between Inanna and Lucas was something I hadn't expected. There was something going on, and I couldn't help but wonder if the way Lucas had been acting was because of Inanna.

The chatter of the cafeteria quickly returned back to normal as I stood in my place with Pollux, Trixie, and Sansa at my side. The three of them talked about what happened as I continue staring at the closed door, trying to figure out what it was I was missing.

"Cassie." The sound of Silas' voice was welcoming, and glancing over my shoulder, I watched him stride towards me with a concerned expression in his eyes. "What happened?"

"It was nothing," I replied, shaking my head. "Just a misunderstanding."

"Misunderstanding?" he said in an unbelieving tone.

A heavy sigh escaped me as I forced a smile on my face, and nodded my head. I tried to figure out how I could explain to him what I had noticed. It wasn't like it was an easy thing to tell anyone. "I think Inanna has something to do with Lucas."

My response caught not only the attention of Silas but Pollux, Trixie, and Sansa as well. "What are you talking about?" Sansa asked with curiosity.

"I don't know," I muttered again, "but I'm sure as hell going to figure it out."

A Pack to save Lucas

Pollux

I had never seen my sister as upset as she was, and to be honest I thought she was going to kill Zia before I jumped in to pull her off the poor girl. Perhaps Zia was a wicked pain in the ass and deserved every bit of what she got but I wouldn't let Cassie be the one to pull that trigger. I wouldn't let her live with the guilt.

The problem was I hadn't anticipated the way things ended, and as Cassie said she thought Inanna, the head of students, had something to do with what was wrong with Lucas. I didn't want to believe it.

"Cassie, you can't be serious." I scoffed, shaking my head. Her eyes darted around the room before she gave me a sharp glare and nodded with her head for us to follow her. I wasn't sure where we were going, but when we stepped outside into the cool afternoon air with no one around us, she let go of a sigh and turned to face us.

"Okay, now that we are away from prying ears, I think Inanna has something to do with what's wrong with Lucas."

Glancing at Silas, he seemed just as skeptical as I was. He crossed his arms over his chest and opened and closed his mouth as if trying to formulate words to make sense of all of this. "Cassie, we can't jump to conclusions like that."

"Yeah, Cassie," Trixie drawled as if not believing her, "Silas has a point..."

Cassie groaned, rolling her eyes as she shook her head. "Look, I know it sounds crazy, but I'm telling you... something is definitely going on with that woman."

"Cassie, that's just how she is," Silas replied quickly trying to make my sister see reason. He did have a point. Even when I met her in her office when I first started that was how she came off... as someone a bit odd but who cared.

Frustration grew within my sister's eyes as she looked at each of us before glancing at Sansa as if searching for at least one of us that would believe her. However, even Sansa seemed skeptical, and I wouldn't doubt her for feeling that way. Cassie was my sister, and at times I was even skeptical of how she acted.

"I can't believe you guys don't believe me—"

"It's not that I don't," Silas quickly interjected as he stepped toward Cassie, "we just have no proof, and you can't go around throwing accusations out like it's the most obvious thing without having proof to back your claim."

Proof. That was something that was going to be virtually impossible to get, and even if we did have it, who would we turn it in to? Inanna was the head of the school.

"We can get it," she said with an excited smile, "we can get proof."

Tilting my head, I gave out a frustrated groan. "We can't just assume people to be evil and go on a witch hunt for proof because you have a feeling about something, Cassie."

As much as I wanted to believe in my sister, I just couldn't. I couldn't come to grips with the fact that Inanna, someone who was well-known and respected in this school, would have something to do with changing students for her own personal gain. She was technically a celestial and specialized in education.

That didn't exactly speak highly of her being a criminal mastermind.

"Why is it you always have to be negative about everything?" she asked me with a disgusted look. "Can't you just jump on board the ship again?"

"Cassie, you know what I mean."

The more and more she stared at me with a determination in her eyes I had seen so many times growing up, I knew damn well she wasn't going to let this go. If we didn't help her, then she would be fine. She would continue with the pursuit of her idea.

"It's okay, Pollux. You don't have to come." She sighed, shoulders sagging as she turned and walked through the courtyard toward our building. She was on a mission for sure, and I was curious to find out what she had planned.

<u>Cassie</u>

I couldn't believe they didn't believe me. No matter what they said, I knew what I saw. The connection between Inanna and Lucas wasn't like a normal teacher-student relationship. She was controlling him, making him dark... and I would fix that.

Making my way across the courtyard, the calls of my friends rushing after me could be heard clearly through the softly blowing wind. Part of me wanted to stop and see what they wanted, but the other part of me was just too eager to continue.

"Cassie, stop for a moment," Pollux said harshly as he grabbed my arm, stopping me in my tracks. "Look, I don't know what's gotten into you, but you need to chill. You're worrying people, including myself."

"No, Pollux. You may not want to believe it, but I'm not lying. Something is wrong, and he isn't acting the way he is because he wants to. It's like his judgment is clouded."

Running his hands through his hair, he scoffed again. "You're delusional, Cassie. Lucas rejected you, and you need to let him go. You can't force someone to be with you and think it's because someone else is clouding their mind."

His words hurt, and after he spoke, Trixie quickly smacked his arm and glared at him. "What the hell is wrong with you?"

"Ouch, what the hell is wrong with you? Why did you hit me?" He whined as his eyes darted toward her.

"Because she's your sister no matter what has happened in the past, and she is trying to save someone she cares about. Just because you don't believe in it doesn't mean you can't support her until she figures out what she needs."

Once again, Trixie was sticking up for me when I didn't know how. It wasn't like me to be weak and unwilling to stand up for myself, but since I came here, I had felt myself grow and change slowly into someone I wasn't sure I wanted to be.

Taking a deep breath, I composed myself, unwilling to allow myself to falter, unwilling to allow tears or any emotions to fall, even though the little girl in me that had once always dreamed of a mate like my mother had was breaking inside.

Yes, I had said once upon a time I didn't want a mate. That I never had wanted it, but honestly... it had only been because I was scared. Because I was worried my powers would be to much to control, and I would end up killing them.

Now I see the idea was ridiculous, and even though it's to late to fix my mistakes, it wasn't to late to save Lucas and allow him to make his own choices.

"Pollux, maybe you're right, but I have to make sure. I can't explain it to you, but deep down inside, I can feel him. He isn't the Lucas we knew back home.

Something has changed in him, and you saw the darkness in his eyes that day in his room. You can't tell me that the entire thing felt off."

Pollux stood there, staring at me for a moment as if searching for the truth in what I was saying. After a moment, it seemed to be he finally accepted what I said because I wasn't going to back down.

"I have never seen you so determined before, Cassie," Pollux whispered as he glanced over his shoulders to look at them, "they are both worried about you."

I understood his concern, but I wasn't going to just let it go. There was something seriously wrong going on, and the more I thought about how Inanna acted, the more I wondered what kind of person she really was. "I have to do this."

My soft response seemed to settle within my brother as he sighed heavily and nodded his head. "Okay... well, how are you going to prove any of this?"

I didn't have the slightest clue how I would prove anything if I had to be honest with myself. I barely knew my way around this place. Which was a problem if I wanted to snoop around or learn anything about this place that could help me.

Glancing at Silas with puppy dog eyes, he chuckled, hands up in defeat. "Okay, okay. I'll help you on your quest to solve this mystery."

My brother quickly turned to Silas, glaring at him as if to ask him why he was agreeing, and all Silas could do was shrug his shoulders, smiling. "Hey man, I can't say no to her."

"Well, you better start learning how to," Pollux replied, pinching the bridge of his nose. "Okay, Cassie... I guess I'll help... even though it's against my better judgment."

Shocked that my brother, who currently hated me, was going to help was something I hadn't expected, and the shock that crossed my face didn't go unnoticed by Trixie and Sansa, who quickly took to either side of me and pulled me close to them.

"Don't worry. We will figure it out." Trixie smiled, leaning against me, "we will get your mate back."

My mate? Lucas had rejected me and therefore wasn't technically my mate anymore. However, no matter the situation of him wanting to be with me or not, I still couldn't allow him to be used the way he was. He had to be free to make his own choices, and with his mind obviously clouded, there was no way he was.

Not that I would ruin Trixie's moment by telling her that. "Thanks, Trixie."

"Welp, I suppose we should sit down and try to figure out what to do first." Silas finally popped up as he glanced around at the four of us. The tension hung heavy in the air as Pollux stared me down before finally giving in.

I was grateful for Trixie, who nudged him gently. It was clear that something was going on, and I was happy for them if they were planning to figure themselves out. He was my brother, and Trixie had become a good friend of mine. They may have come from different species, but in the end, they were mates.

The fate of our future was unpredictable, and we can't hold back from what we really want or ignore what's in front of us if we have it. Even if it isn't what we were hoping for, which made me realize how stupid I had been for pushing Lucas away to begin with.

"Maybe we should start in the library?" I suggested, not that I knew where any library was beside the one at the school.

Silas hesitated momentarily, glancing at the school and then back to me. The wheels turned in his mind as he opened his mouth, "actually... I know just the place."

Sansa raised her brow as she stared at Silas with nothing but amusement on her face. "You know somewhere with a library?"

"Yeah," he replied, rolling his eyes. "Come on... I may be a sexy Dragon with style, but I'm far older than all of you. So, of course, with spare time on my hands, I know where one is. I happen to love reading very much."

Laughter broke out amongst our ranks, and as Silas stepped forward with his arms open wide, I quickly accepted his offer and let him pull me into a warm embrace. The day had been more than emotional, and chaos was slowly brewing in the distance.

That much I could feel deep in my bones.

If I was going to save Lucas and get to the bottom of what was going on, then I was going to need all the help I could get. Nothing was ever easily accomplished alone.

Anna

Cassie

When Silas told me he knew of a place for us to go, I was expecting something fancy or perhaps something that was more... elegant, marble, and who knows what else. What I wasn't expecting though was for him to take us to an old brick building with broken windows that looked wildly out of place to be within Asgard.

Pollux, Trixie, and Sansa decided to stay behind and snoop around the school to see if they could find anything that might be useful. With them looking around, no one would suspect them for doing anything, me, however, they would.

Yet, even though they were busy looking for information, I wished they were here with me. I wanted Pollux to see this building, to see how beautiful and strange the land around it was. One thing about my brother that no one knew but me was his love for history–a love for the past because the past makes us stronger.

The building reminded me of old ruins of castles in a way with its intricate archways and carved designs within the stone. I couldn't help myself when I passed them to reach out and let my fingers brush against the ancient markings. My mind wandered to who these people must have been because it was far older than anything here now.

"Where are we?" I asked softly, my eyes turning to Silas, who smiled down at me with amusement. As if he knew a million secrets and wanted to tell me but didn't know how.

"This is a structure from another realm, one that we no longer speak of because of the battle that commenced there thousands of years ago," he replied as he gazed up at the structure running his own hands against the broken rock. "During the battle, they sought to escape and when the portal was opened, it moved the earth they stood on and anything else around."

"Who is they?" I asked curiously, trying to understand how anyone could be so powerful that they could move all this earth and even structures.

Silas chuckled though as he glanced back at me. "You don't know any of the stories, do you?"

I wasn't sure why he was amused by me not knowing the stories of this place, and shaking my head, he pushed open the large wooden and brass door before us. The creek of the wood echoed against the silent air around Silas and me. I found myself stepping into a hall of darkness filled with cobbled steps and cobwebs.

Silas moved forward down the cobbled steps further into the darkness, and I hesitated for a moment, I took a deep breath and forced myself forward. One thing people didn't know about me was the internal fear I had of darkness. Not that anyone would suspect it—I hid my fears very well.

"Silas." I called out into the darkness having lost him in my delay as I reached the bottom step. My eyes strained to see through the black void that filled my vision in front of me. "Silas?"

"Over here!" The dim lighting of a torch coming into view as he came around a corner, and once again I was able to see his smiling face. "Come on, what are you doing?"

What am I doing? Jesus, like I meant to get lost.

"Nothing, right behind you," I replied, pushing a smile onto my face as I watched him turn, my steps right behind his. There was no way I was going to allow myself to get lost in this place again.

After a few minutes of walking, we came to another archway that opened up into more darkness. Silas stopped in his tracks and turned to the right, letting the lit flame of the torch to touch something on the wall, and as it did a wind blew through the room lighting every torch in sight.

A gasp left my breath as I took in the sight before me. Bookcases reached high into the ceiling, multiple levels of books as far as the eye could see. Never in my life had I seen something so beautiful, and I felt the soft gentle brush of Silas' hand.

"Do you like it?" he asked, causing me to turn to him in awe.

"Like it? Silas, I love it," I said, my voice echoing, "how is this kept like it is? I'm surprised people don't come here every day."

Shrugging his shoulders, he looked around as if contemplating what I had said. "It's been forgotten, honestly. Not to mention the school explained to the gods it wasn't a safe place for students to be. So it went vacant for a thousand years."

Taking one step after the other, I wandered around the room, admiring everything there was to admire. From hand-carved tables with toppled chairs, tons of books that littered the floor, as well dust that laid blanketed upon every surface in the area.

Never had I seen something so old and beautiful at the same time. I let my fingers brush over some of the multicolored spines as my feet crunched upon scattered papers, I was curious as to what had happened here to leave it in such chaos.

"So within all of this, you think we will find what I need to figure everything out?"

My words bounced off the walls, and as I turned to look at Silas from over my shoulder, he stood watching me. "In a way, I suppose."

"In a way?" I repeated, furrowing my brow, "what do you mean?"

Stepping forward, his arms falling at his sides he stared at me, and the intensity of that stare made my breath catch in my throat. I didn't understand what it was about him that made my heart flutter like it did, but twhen he stepped inches in front of me, a wave of nervousness washed over me I hadn't expected.

"In order for you to find out about current things... I think it's best for you to learn about the past. About the gods, and more importantly about who you are, Cassie. Odin and the others have been hiding the truth, but it's wrong."

His words confused me, and the sincerity in his eyes let me know he was telling the truth. Yet, knowing Odin–my grandfather–and the others were hiding things from me didn't sit well in my stomach. "Why are they hiding things from me?"

He brushed his hand down my shoulder gently before moving a strand of hair from my face. "Because they don't think you're ready to know. I was ordered never to tell you, but I can't keep things from you... not with..."

On a heavy exhale, he didn't finish his sentence, but with the way he was looking at me, I could almost tell what he was going to say. He was going to tell me how he cared about me, but I didn't need him to tell me for me to know. I should have been disgusted with him advancing on me because I was supposed to be with Lucas but I wasn't.

Part of me wanted him to kiss me... part of me wanted him to take me and make me his.

"Tell me who Anna is, Silas," I whispered, clearing my throat and trying to divert the sexual tension currently flowing between us. He let a small smirk cross his lips as he stepped back, and picked up a chair setting it up right then gesturing for me to take a seat.

"If you want to know, I will tell you," he replied as I took a seat in the offered chair, watching him move about the room to a bookcase as if he had been here so many times before.

"You know this place well?"

Chuckling sounded from within the bookshelves as he popped his head back out and looked at me. "You can say that."

"What do you mean?" I asked, opening my mouth only for him to quickly come striding toward me with a brown book covered in emerald stones.

"I can explain everything in time... for now, first things first—Anna."

He took a seat next to me and flipped the book open to a drawing of a woman with reddish brown hair and blue eyes. She was strikingly beautiful, but what stayed with me the most is how much she looked just like me—or well, a mixture of my mother and me.

"This is Anna?" I asked, tearing my gaze from the book only to see him staring intently at the woman as if seeing her face brought back memories he hadn't seen in forever. "You knew her, didn't you?"

Blinking quickly, he averted his gaze from the woman and frowned. "Something like that. Anyways... I guess it's best to start from the beginning."

I didn't bother to say anything, and as I watched him flip the pages, I settled in for whatever story he had to tell me. If it would help me get closer to figuring out what was wrong with Lucas, then so be it.

"So a thousand years ago, there were two people who ruled your kind in a way the world had never seen. The Alpha's name was Bjorn, and his Luna was the lovely Anna. She never wanted to be his, and her union to him was actually formed in a blood promise her mother had made before she was born in return for Bjorn saving her life. He was a man many feared, but over time, Anna grew to love him and she was the only one who could control Bjorn when he lost his mind."

Drawing after drawing Silas showed me the images of Bjorn and many other people explaining how the twos' life played out. How they bared many children, but in the great war, something happened that changed Anna's life forever.

"Anna loved Bjorn, but when their eldest daughter died, Bjorn lost himself. His daughter was everything to him but his best friend killed her. A man he trusted, and Anna would have died too had Bjorn not got there in time to save her."

The look he gave when he said Anna would have died was heartbreaking, and I realized he definitely knew her on a more personal level. However, if that was the case, then that meant he was far older than I expected.

"Silas, you knew her personally, didn't you?"

Lifting his gaze to me, he opened his mouth, "I did."

"That would make you over a thousand years old!" I gasped trying to wrap my mind around how old he really was. However, laughter left him as he shook his head no.

"I'm definitely not that damn old, but I am a few hundred years old."

"That doesn't make sense, Silas. She lived here a thousand years ago," I replied, trying to understand what he was saying. The math didn't add up, and as much as I wanted to know about her, I had to understand the truth behind him.

"Look... why don't you let me finish what I'm telling you first before you assume things," he suggested causing me to nod, deciding not to continue asking him any more questions.

"Good, as I was saying... Bjorn lost his mind, and when he did, Anna fled with the rest of her children, hiding them around the world out of fear that they may be hurt in his rage. Now, Bjorn didn't take kindly to what Anna did... he saw her as a traitor, and wanted back what was rightfully his. So he sought to battle with her to find them, and then forced her into submission."

Thinking back, I remembered Priscilla, a woman I saw as a grandmother, telling me similar stories about two people named Bjorn and Anna. "They were the reincarnated version of Geri and Freki?"

Silas's eyes widened at my words as a smile spread across his face. "Yes... so you do know them?"

"No," I laughed, shaking my head. "I just remembered a story my grandmother had told me a long time ago. About the wolves of Odin..."

Opening his mouth, he didn't speak and simply scoffed with a smile. "Yeah... Odin."

I was curious why he remarked the way he did but chose to stay silent hoping that when he was ready, he would tell me what it was he was hiding.

"Look, it's been a long day, and there is so much about that battle you should learn. Why don't you take this book with you, Cassie. Read what you can about Anna, and then I can fill in the rest where you have questions."

"Silas, what's wrong?" Confusion washed over me, wondering why he was suddenly acting the way he was. He had been so eager to tell me the stories before and now he simply wanted to end the conversation.

"Nothing, Cassie... I just remembered I forgot to take care of something."

Silas looked at me for a long moment as he stood to his feet and handed over the book to which I took and placed it into the black leather satchel at my side. There wasn't a point in carrying on the conversation if he didn't want to have it, and so when he turned to make his way for the exit, I stayed quiet.

Silas was more mysterious than I could have ever imagined, and every part of me wanted to know the secrets he was hiding.

After all, why was it so important I learned about Anna?

A Pixie for an Alpha

Pollux

I was never a man who cared for envying other people, and in all honesty, I had been a complete asshole over the past few weeks. Not only while being here, but also before we came here. My sister was my twin, and even though we were completely different and irritated the shit out of each other, I couldn't tell her no.

The way she looked at me with pleading eyes asking me to help her because she believed more than anything that Lucas was being controlled, I couldn't say no. I couldn't let her down and not help her when she needed it most.

Even though I thought she was full of shit... even though I thought this was all pointless.

"You're doing the right thing, Lux." Trixie's voice pulled me from my thoughts as she came to sit next to me at the table in the dining hall. I had been so against her initially, but the last few days, I had spent more time with her because of everything going on with Cassie.

She wasn't like I had expected her to be and when I stared at her glowing green eyes and electric blue hair, I saw a woman far more exotic and beautiful than I ever saw before. A woman who was capable of so much, and yet had been so vastly misunderstood.

"Am I, though? I can't help but feel she is wasting her time."

Trixie sighed as she stared at me. I didn't understand why she was so willing to stand by Cassie in this charade of trying to help a man who didn't even want to be her mate. It was embarrassing, and all she was doing was hurting herself even further.

"People act weird when they are in love, and even if he doesn't want her, Cassie has a good heart. If you haven't been able to tell already, Cassie sees things in people others overlook."

There was something in Trixie's eyes as she spoke that made me wonder if she was slightly directing that at me. If she wasn't trying to say I overlooked things, and maybe also that I was acting weird.

All of it confused me to be honest, and as I tried to wrap my head around everything going on, Lucas walked back into the dining hall with Zia on his arm and every part of me wanted to lose control. Every part of me wanted to rip him apart for what he was doing to my sister, and he must have felt my anger because when he looked at me, he smirked.

"Don't..." Trixie softly placed a hand on my arm, "let it go. We are supposed to be helping her, not making things worse."

"I can't fucking stand him. Even before we came here, Lucas was nothing but a thorn in my side. So many times I had the chance to get rid of him, and yet... I couldn't."

Standing to my feet, I gripped the edge of the table and stared at Lucas, who sat with a group of kids on the far side of the dining hall. His arm, still draped around Zia. She kissed his neck as if they were thoroughly in love.

The entire sight sickened me, and it made me want to rip him apart even more. But before I could do anything, Trixie stood beside me, her hand tightening around my arm. "Come on... let's get out of here."

Every part of me was screaming the moment Trixie touched me. Begging to leave with her and forget all of the troubles I had. Yet, I was scared.

Scared of what my future would be like and how people would view me because of her.

"Okay," I sighed as I let her lead me from the hall. "Where are we going?"

She smiled, giving a small laugh as we made our way towards the front door of the school, and out into the evening air. "You're going to go back to your room. You have had a long day, and the last few days haven't been easy–"

"My room? Trixie," I replied softly as she gripped my arm tighter and pulled me forward.

"No buts about it, sir. You are Mr. Grumpypants right now, and that isn't safe for anyone." Her teasing remark was cute, and hearing her speak the way she was made me smile.

Silence filled us with small bits of banter here and there, and I finally found myself feeling comfortable with a woman for the first time in a long time. She was so different from the other women I had known, and honestly, it was refreshing.

"Can I say something?" I asked her, listening to her chuckle as she nodded her head.

"You don't have to ask if you can ask me something, Lux. Just ask the question."

Glancing at her, the amused smile that crossed her lips made a warm rush of feeling pass over me. Even in a simple pair of leggings and an oversized shirt I was pretty sure was designer—even though it looked like it came out of the garbage—she was hot.

"Right," I smiled, "well, if you want, you can come up... I'm just going to catch up on some work. Maybe you can help me with some of the magic stuff."

One may have thought my mind was in the gutter, but it wasn't. I enjoyed Trixie's company even though she was energetic at times and often annoyed others around her. To me, I found it comforting to be around her.

Maybe the mate bond pulled me closer to her, or maybe it was just because she was a nice girl and our conversations were usually entertaining.

Taking a moment to consider what I offered her, she smiled, nodding her head with her hands clasped behind her back. "Sure, I mean, from what I heard, you suck at magic."

Laughter escaped me at her words, and though at one point in time I would have been pissed by what she said, I wasn't. She had a point, and in all honesty, my magic was nowhere as strong as my sisters.

"Well, maybe with your tutoring, I won't suck."

As we walked up the steps to the building Cassie and I stayed in, I carried on the same casual conversation I had with her before. From magic spells to summoning objects, she filled me in on everything going on and also what I was doing wrong.

"No, you're not supposed to do that. You need to take deep breaths before releasing..."

"Is that right?" I asked her as we stepped into my room. Her mischievous eyes rolled as she shoved me a little and began to let her eyes scan my room, taking in every inch of what I had around that gave way to who I was.

"You have so much stuff," she murmured, letting her fingers dance along the photos on the wall and the items on my dresser. Since being here, I had been able to get someone under Odin to acquire a few more things from my home, including family photos and sentimental items.

All things Cassie had no idea I had gotten, seeing as she was being a bitch to me.

"Yeah, I had someone collect some things for me from my house," I replied, averting my eyes due to the guilt slowly forming thinking about Cassie.

"Your sister doesn't have any photos or anything," Trixie murmured as she turned to me. "You had these brought recently?"

Confusion caused me to furrow my brows as I tried to understand how it was she knew I had recently gotten these things. I hadn't let anyone know I did simply because it wasn't their business, but for her to know this meant she had been in my room before. "How would you know?"

"Because I was the one who decorated it to begin with," she said as a smirk fell across her lips that made my gut twist with anticipation.

My entire life, I had waited for my mate, and since I had first laid eyes on Trixie, I had avoided taking her as mine. I avoided letting our relationship bloom because I wanted something unattainable. Something fate didn't mean for me to have. That guilt alone ate at me, but now with her standing before me...

I didn't want to hold back. I didn't want to waste any more time with her.

Rushing forward, I let my hands grab the side of her face as I crashed my lips against hers. Her soft, plump lips moved against mine as our tongues battled for control—the taste of her driving my wolf crazy as I sought to have more.

Walking her backward until the backs of her thighs hit the bed, she fell, panting as she looked up at me, her hands helping her crawl backward a bit until I came down over her. My body hovered over hers as I took in every inch of her face.

"I want you," I whispered, watching a smile cross her lips I had been worried about seeing. Part of me thought in the end, she might be disgusted about being my mate, but looking at her now, I knew that she wasn't.

"I wondered how long it would take for you to accept me," she whispered as her hands reached up to the sides of my face, slowly pulling it down towards her own. "Let's not wait anymore."

Letting my lips gently press against hers, our tongues danced in a gentle motion, my hands running up and down her body as I relished in the moment with her. The moment I had waited my entire life for. The moment I would be with my mate and claim her as mine forever.

Piece by piece, our clothing was stripped from our bodies and fell to the floor. Our limbs weaved together in a battle for dominance as I made her moan over and over again. Her back arched as her perky round breasts bounced with every thrust I made inside her.

She had accepted me, and as I allowed the knot in my cock to form, locking us in place, I pulled her up closer to my body, impaling her harder and harder until she was crying in pain, begging for her release. With a scream of ecstasy and a roar of pleasure from my throat, I sunk my teeth deep into her neck and marked her as my own.

A pixie for an Alpha and a mate for a lifetime.

A losing battle

Cassie

A few days of going to the secret library Silas had brought me to hadn't brought me any closer to figuring out how to help Lucas. However, I learned a lot about Anna. Including just how close Silas was to her when he came to Asgard to begin with.

"So you were her guard?" I asked, staring at Silas, who walked around the library tossing an old brown ball up in the air before catching it.

"Yep, it was my first job here. It wasn't exactly what I had expected... when I came here she had already been here for a long time. I was young and rebellious. I hated the world because of how I was treated, and she saw something in me others didn't."

"But... that doesn't make sense. She would have been ancient by then—"

"Around seven hundred years old to be exact," he hummed as his eyes twinkled with amusement.

I was astounded. From the stories, she was supposed to be human or so I thought, but then lived that long. It didn't make any sense. "How, though?"

"How was she that old?"

Nodding my head, his smile widened, "Anna was one of Odin's creations, Cassie. She was a descendant of one of his wolves."

I had heard many things over the years about Odin, and some of the stuff he did but this... I had never heard before. Odin's wolves were famous, and the entire reason our species was created. In order to protect the wolves hunted by humans, Odin bestowed his wolves to gift them with the ability to turn into to humans to hide amongst the same men that tried to kill them.

"We are all descendants though," I whispered looking back down to the painting of her I have found in a scroll on one of the many bookshelves. "That still doesn't explain how she lived so long."

"Odin bestowed a gift on her when she lost Bjorn and two more of her children. When she came here, three of her children had died, and she wanted death as well. Her anger consumed her, making her hate the life she was given. However, Odin wouldn't let her give up on life. He knew she had more to offer so he made her immortal until she could see that even through the darkest of days life has beauty even in the darkest of shadows."

Sila's words were always poetic when he wanted to explain something important. Letting a smirk crest the corner of my lips, I rolled my eyes and went back to trying to read the faded writing on the parchment. However, the words were foreign and far more advanced than anything I knew, and I was left wondering what they were instead of actually knowing.

"So, he made her immortal until she appreciated life?"

Nodding his head, he picked up another book and made his way toward me, laying it down. "This is Anna's journal from her last year here. When you have time, you should read it."

Picking up the purple fabric-bound book, I ran my fingers over the spine, admiring the intricate designs. It was beautiful, and my mind was curious to know what she had to say but right now, I had more important things to worry about.

"Maybe once things are better, I will. For now, we have more important things to figure out, like how to save Lucas."

The reminder made his lips part as he nodded again. "Of course."

He seemed to hate the fact I kept reminding him, but it was important to figure out if I was ever going to fix what was going on. Every single day Lucas was the way he was, I felt the distance grow between us within the little bit of bond we had.

Perhaps it was a good thing, but I felt an emptiness inside me I didn't like. "So we have been here for days at this. What is actually going to help me?"

Silas sighed, shaking his head, "Inanna was here when Anna was. The two women were friends at one point, but Inanna was strange..."

"So that makes her a villain?" I laughed.

"No," he smiled, "but her acting the way she was set Anna on edge. I worked closely with Anna, and through all of it, she felt Inanna and her were growing distant. That Inanna was up to something dark, and when she began hanging out with the wrong people, Anna became wary of her."

Glancing down at Anna's portrait, I took in her dark hair, celestial blue eyes and pink plump lips. I was shocked. The first time I saw her photo I realized how much she and I looked alike. The only difference was she seemed to smile all the time where I did not. Anna didn't seem like the kind of person whose smile ever fell, but of course, this was reality, or it was her reality once upon a time.

"So did she ever confront her?" I asked without looking up at Silas. My fingers once again brushed over the purple book he had given me.

"Yep," he replied quickly. "It turned into a huge fight, and the next day... Inanna and a few others were gone."

Letting my eyes dart up to Silas, I furrowed my brows. "What do you mean they were gone? Someone doesn't just vanish."

He shrugged his shoulders and took a seat in the chair across from me. "Back then, the vale between realms wasn't as confined as it is now. It was easier to slip out, but that was because Odin didn't worry about things like he does now I suppose. At least, since everything with Loki."

"Loki?" Hearing the name rang internal bells as I remembered the stories I had heard growing up of the battle my parents went through with him. How they wanted my brother and me but our parents fought to protect us.

"Yeah, Loki was dangerous, but thankfully, Odin imprisoned him."

I opened and closed my mouth, considering what Silas had said. As far as I remembered, it was my mother who had thrown Loki back into Asgard, but then again, who was I to correct the history they knew? "Oh, right."

Unsure of what to say or do, I simply rolled back up the portrait and retied the ribbon around it that had once held it closed. I was learning a lot being here but it wasn't helping me like I wanted. While I was here doing this... Lucas was out of his mind with partying and fucking with Zia.

He was never that kind of person before, and I was never the person I am now before.

"Are you okay, Cassie?" Silas asked as I moved towards the bookshelves to replace the scroll with Anna's portrait on it.

"Not really, just a lot on my mind."

"You know you can talk to me, Cassie. I can help you through whatever is bothering you," he said as the sound of his footsteps echoing behind me let me know just how close he was to me.

I placed the scroll on the shelf and turned to face him. "As I said before, Silas... how does any of this help me?"

"Because... Inanna acted like this before, Cassie. How she is acting now with Lucas, she did it before."

For a fleeting moment, I thought I had hit a brick wall with what to do. I had found myself lost wondering if I would ever find something to get me closer and then Silas finally lets this bit of information out. "What?"

Taking in Silas with much irritation, I watched as a quizzical glance of amusement danced in his fiery eyes while the corners of his lips turned up into a wide smile as if he thought what he told me was the most insightful thing ever. What he didn't know was I was more than irritated with him because that was information he could have told me long ago.

"Right. I mean, it shocked me at first. Back then, I didn't want to believe—"

Shaking my head, I couldn't believe he thought I was interested in the details. "Stop. You didn't think to tell me about Inanna before?"

Stopping with his mouth wide open, Silas gave me a confused look before closing his mouth with a sigh. "I guess I should have."

"Then why didn't you?" I asked, trying to understand why he wouldn't. That was something I could have used to steer me closer in the right direction but instead, he had said nothing and let me float around in unanswered questions.

"I guess I didn't think about it, honestly... there is much you still don't understand."

Resting my hand on my forehead, I closed my eyes and breathed through the outburst that desperately wanted to leave me. I wanted to shout at him, scream and curse his name for dragging me around for days and giving me a history lesson instead of telling me but I knew I wouldn't get anywhere acting like that.

"Who did Inanna act like this with before... the people she was with, who were they?"

Glancing at Silas again, I watched him tap his fingers on the table. "I may have been Anna's guard, but I didn't know everything that was going on. I just saw and heard certain things."

I found it hard to believe that Silas didn't know more, considering the fact he had told me so much already. Granted, he could have read a lot of it in books, but I had a feeling everything he told me was first-hand information.

"Okay, then answer me this... how many years has Anna been dead?"

The moment that the question left my lips, Silas froze. He stared at me with such a blank expression I began to wonder if what I said was not in English. After all, he was staring at me like I had grown three heads. "A hundred years ago... three years after Inanna left the realm."

The conversation was clipped, and with the last of his words, he turned quickly and made his way toward the main door. I wasn't sure why it was his attitude changed but shoving the purple book into my bag, I quickly made my way after him.

"Silas!" I called out in confusion, "Silas, stop."

My feet carried me forward, and by the time the moonlight filtered over me once more, I barely had caught Silas', arm stopping him in his tracks. He was angry, and as he gritted his teeth with a clenched jaw, he stared down at me. I didn't understand why.

"Let me go, Cassie," he said sternly as he pulled his arm from my grasp. I had no clue what had happened. All I did was asked when Anna died. One minute he was laughing and telling stories, and the next, he was pissed off at the world.

"Dude... what's wrong? Why are you acting like this?"

He turned away, taking a moment before glancing back at me. "You just... you remind me so much of her and thinking of the day she died... the day she left is not something that brings back happy memories, Cassie."

There was so much emotion in those last few words that suddenly made me realize why he was so dead set on telling me about Anna, how he knew so much about her to the point where most of the memories brought a smile to his face.

Silas had cared for Anna... maybe even loved her at one point, and when she died, it left an empty place in his heart. One that the thought of death caused nothing but agony.

"Silas, I'm so sorry."

Holding up his hand, he took a deep breath and shook his head, "I'm trying to help you, Cassie. If you're not careful, you're going to end up like Anna."

"What? What do you mean I'll end up like Anna?"

Staring at me, his entire body sagged as if the weight he was carrying was too heavy. "She allowed herself to fall for darkness and in the end, gave her life for it. Something you will do if you don't find a way to separate your emotions and let go of what you can not change."

Silas & Lucas

Cassie

Staring at Silas's blush green eyes tinged with streaks of red and gold, I couldn't help but wonder what was running through his mind. He had obviously seen something back then that bothered him and while I wanted to listen to what he was saying, I didn't know how to follow his words. I had a goal to achieve, and though Anna's life ended that way didn't mean mine would.

"I'm not Anna, Silas," I said softly as I watched him. His concerned emotional state quickly vanished as he formed a blank expression. It was clear he wasn't pleased with how quickly I was brushing off what he said.

"I know you're not. Trust me."

Turning from me, he continued walking and left me feeling slightly clueless as to what I did to upset him. All we had been doing was having a normal conversation, and suddenly he flipped his mood and stormed off. Something completely out of character from how he normally acted.

Left in the darkness of the night, I stood feeling foolish and void of answers. Not only did I have Lucas upset with me, but now Silas was upset at me as well.

With a heavy sigh of frustration, I pushed forward down the gravel and dirt road back toward the main lights of the town. There was no point in staying at the ruins when Silas wasn't with me. Sure I could have investigated further on my own, but the place was creepy in a dark and mysterious kind of way and even if I considered myself a badass... even I had limits.

As the moon lit the path for me, I relished the feel of the cool breeze against my skin and the way the leaves rustled in the distance. It was beautiful outside, and with the silence of nature around me, it gave me time to think about everything I had gone through over the past few weeks.

I'd made a mess of things, and a lot of what happened was my fault. First, the arguing with my mom, and the fact that she was probably terrified of me after what I did on my birthday, and then losing Melissa. The thought of my friend made my eyes water, and as I quickly blinked them away and let my mind drift to Lucas.

The way he looked at me the night of my birthday, the way he kissed me, and then filled me with so much passion was something I would never forget. So when the rustling of movement from within the treelines and the sound of distant voices caught my attention, the last thing I expected to hear was Lucas talking to someone.

"I'm taking care of it..."

The sound of his frustrated voice was not what I expected, and stopping in my tracks, I turned towards the treeline and carefully moved closer to see who it was that he was talking to. I was curious to know if it was Zia or maybe even Inanna, but as I stepped over fallen branches and moved by brush as quietly as possible, I peered through the darkness, letting my eyes peer into the clearing ahead.

Lucas stood there alone, talking out loud, but with no one I could see around. Furrowing my brows, I glanced around again trying to understand, and the more I listened, the more concerned I became.

"I can't...she doesn't deserve that..."

The way he stood with his fist clenched at his sides and his dark hair swept in front of his eyes, it was captivating but also concerning. Lucas looked like a madman talking to himself, and the more I watched, the more I knew I had to do something.

Glancing around behind me, I bit my bottom lip and let out a heavy breath before stepping forward. I wasn't afraid of him or anything like that, but I couldn't help but feel awkward talking to him after everything that happened at the school.

"Lucas?" I said as I stepped forward from where I had been hiding. His dark eyes quickly darted to me as his claws lengthened and he bared his fangs at me.

"What are you doing here, Cassie? Are you spying on me?"

The growl that emitted from him made me halt in my tracks. "No," I said slowly, shaking my head. "I was walking by, and I heard you... are you okay?"

Scoffing, he shook his head, retracting his claws. "I'm fine. Why are you out here?"

He was far from fine, and anyone with eyes could see that. "Just heading back to my room. It's getting late."

"That doesn't answer my question, Cassie," he growled as he stepped closer to me. The moonlight slipped through the tops of the trees, illuminating the spikes of his obsidian hair and the ripples of muscle beneath his skin tight black shirt.

"It doesn't matter why I'm out here," I replied firmly as I pulled the strap of my bag tighter to me as I broke eye contact with him. "If you're okay, I'll just go."

"What the fuck is your problem?" he snapped, grabbing my arm as I turned to leave.

Shrugging him off, I narrowed my gaze, "I don't have one, but you obviously do. You're not okay no matter how much you try to tell people you are."

With a sneer of disgust, he stepped back in anger. "You have no fucking clue what you're talking about. I'm not the one with a problem... you are."

"Look, if this is how you're going to act I'm just going to go. I don't have time to deal with you being a dick." Reaching out, he grabbed my jaw, halting me in my next words.

Never had he grabbed me like this, but when he did pull me close to his chest, my heart began to beat rapidly. Lucas was much bigger than I was, and though he had me in physical size and strength, my magic was far stronger.

"You're not going anywhere until you tell me where it is you were at, Cassie. People don't walk out this way without a reason."

Unsure of what to say to him, I stared at him blankly, opening and closing my mouth as if I wanted to tell him, but at the same time couldn't because I didn't think he deserved to know.

"Get the fuck off me, Lucas."

Snatching my arm away from him again, I narrowed my gaze, trying to understand why he thought he had a right to order me around as if he still had some kind of say. He revoked his claim to me, whether willingly or not, and therefore had no say over me anymore.

"Damn it, Cassie! Just fucking tell me!" he roared in frustration.

"I was with Silas!" I yelled back, Lucas' eyes going wide as if what I said took his breath away. Never had I expected my relationship with Lucas would be like this. It was exhausting going through the same shit over and over, but as soon as I said Silas' name, Lucas slowly began to lose his shit.

"You were with the dragon?" he snarled, "are you fucking him now?"

Gasping, my mouth dropped open in shock. "Excuse me?"

"Oh don't act like that, Cassie. You're a fucking whore, just like I knew you would be."

Lucas had some audacity to call me such things, considering he was the one who fucked me then suddenly decided he didn't want to be with me. "Go fuck yourself, Lucas. It doesn't matter what I do with anyone... I don't belong to anyone."

"That's where you're wrong, Cassie. You're mine and nothing but a disappointment."

His words left a hole in my heart, and as my angry scowl fell, I felt my emotions rise. I had never been someone to show my emotions like I had lately, but hearing him say I was a disappointment was too much. "Fuck you."

Laughter erupted from his throat as he nodded then shook his head, "I knew it... nothing but a whore, just like I was told by others. I should have rejected you."

Part of me wanted to scream at him that I accepted the rejection so he felt exactly how I did when he rejected me, I couldn't. I couldn't be cruel like that to him, no matter how much I wanted to be. "You know nothing of who I really am."

My comment was bold, and I squared my shoulders, staring at him. He seemed taken aback by my response as if expecting more of a fight from me. Yet, I could expect the frown marring his face. It was rare to ever see him truly smile in my direction, unless, of course, it was his signature smirk.

The same smirk that made my heart skip a beat every time I saw it.

"You think you're clever, don't you," he sneered as his dark eyes narrowed in my direction, his rigid jawline firmly squared as he stepped back. "You're wrong though, Cassie. I know exactly what kind of person you are... just like your mother."

My mother and I had plenty of issues sure, but at the end of the day, no one talked shit about my mother. "Watch your words, Vega..."

The moment I called him by his last name instead of by his first, he began to laugh. I didn't expect this reaction, and as he shook his head and loosened up his shoulders, an evil glint crossed his eyes that worried me. "Oh, someone angered the pretty puppy."

"Puppy?!" I scoffed, "my, how the mighty have fallen. Once upon a time you were a man who was highly regarded in some aspects. Women wanted you... men hated you because they envied you. And now—"

Gesturing with my hand to the length of his body from head to toe, he rolled his eyes and chuckled. "There is nothing wrong with me."

"Yet, the fact you think that is a problem on its own."

It was clear this conversation was going nowhere, and from what I could tell he was just out here talking to himself. Which was something I needed to tell the others.

"You're a pain in my ass, Cassie. You need to face facts that this will never happen with us. Accept the rejection," he replied sternly, causing my frown to deepen.

"Maybe one day... but not today." Turning, I made my way from where we had been talking in the treeline back towards the main road. He didn't stop me this time for which I was grateful, and when I glanced over my shoulder once I hit the road, I couldn't see him anymore.

Every day spent here in Asgard, I felt my usually cocky nature slipping. My demeanor slowly disappeared as the weight of my life crushed down upon me like a future impossible to change.

No matter how much I hated it, there was no way to change anything. At least not any time soon, and as my feet finally hit the city street with the sound of happy chattering from those who still lingered about, I knew that if anything were going to change, I would have to do it myself.

For now, I'd seek the advice of my brother because even though he and I often fought... he was still very wise at times. The knowledge of our fathers Hale and Damian having rubbed off on him quite a bit.

Seeking Help

Pollux

The last few days I had spent with Trixie had been amazing. I had marked her as my mate. Right now, I lay on the bed watching her walk around my room with her hair hanging down in ringlets over her shoulders in nothing but a see-through black robe. All I wanted to do was take her again.

She was beautiful and smart, and to think I thought ill of her made me disgusted with myself. How could I have ever thought that way about my mate when fate destined her to be with me?

Regardless of what species she was.

Pushing aside the guilt that had formed over my initial behavior towards Trixie, I relished the sweet moments I had with her now. It had only been a few days since we mated, and the entire time we spent wrapped in each other's arms, learning more and more about each other with every waking moment.

She was strong, and I had no doubt now when the time came for me to return home, she would make a fierce and amazing Luna to my pack.

"Pollux, I'm starving. Maybe we should go get some food." She looked over her shoulder at me from where she had been looking in the mirror, absorbing the mark I left upon her shoulder.

One thing about this woman that constantly amused me was her love for food. She loved to indulge herself, and looking at her, you would never think that considering she had to have been barely one-hundred and twenty pounds soaking wet.

"Food?" I hummed to myself as a smile spread across my face. "All I need is you to eat, and I'm a satisfied man."

The comment was true but also meant to make her laugh—which it did.

"Is that right?" she purred as she turned to make her way toward me seductively, making my cock jump at attention. "I'm pretty sure I would be down for some more fun."

Before I could land my lips on her, a banging at my bedroom door made us both jump. It was late in the evening, and the last thing either of us was expecting was company. Our only agenda was the pleasure we took in each other.

So for someone to be here, it was either important or someone fucking with us.

Hopefully, it wasn't the latter otherwise, I wouldn't be able to control my anger at someone interrupting my moment with my mate.

"What the fuck..." I groaned, rolling my eyes as I slid from the bed and quickly threw on a pair of gray sweatpants. "This better be fucking good."

Trixie laughed at the interruption as I watched her plop onto the bed. Her hand on her chin as she lay on her stomach with her feet kicking in the air. "Stop being grouchy. It may be important."

"I'm not being grouchy—" The moment that I opened the door, Cassie bounded in, looking out of breath and panicked. Her eyes scanned the room between me and Trixie as her mouth opened and closed.

"Oh, shit, I'm sorry."

"Cassie," Trixie replied, quickly getting off the bed, "what's wrong? What happened?"

Cassie's hands fidgeted as her eyes brimmed with tears. "I don't know what I'm doing..."

Confused about why my sister was acting this way, I closed the door and strode towards where my concerned mate stood with her. Only once had I seen my sister this panicked before, and that was the night Melissa had died. The night I saw her come out of the woods with Lucas.

It was something I would never be able to forget. At the end of the day, she was my sister, and despite our issues, I'd kill someone if they hurt her.

"Cassie, I need you to take a deep breath and tell me what happened," I said calmly, trying to make sure I didn't lose my patience. The first week of mating was always the most testosterone-driven, and male wolves–especially Alphas—were very territorial during this time.

Even towards those who were family, and right now, with my mate touching her, my beast was going crazy.

"I saw Lucas in the woods near the edge of town, and he was acting all weird. Like he was talking to himself, and then when he saw I was there—well, he just wasn't himself. Something is going to happen, Pollux. I can feel it."

She rambled on frantically as she looked between Trixie and me. The moment my mate's eyes met mine with concern, I knew I was going to have to do something. She wasn't going to let me brush this off and part of me hated that she and Cassie were close. It did make for interesting conversation but also harsh realizations that my mate would do anything for my sister, even if I didn't like it.

With a heavy sigh, I pinched the bridge of my nose, trying to focus on the situation at hand and not on the hormonal shit running through my head. "Cassie, why were you near the woods at the edge of town?"

Cassie quickly shut her mouth as she looked at me hesitantly. I knew she wasn't going to give me a direct answer.

"Taking a walk."

The comment was quick, and my sister—who couldn't lie to save her life—was trying to avoid my question at all cost. "Cassie-"

"It doesn't matter why I was there. Did you hear what I said? Lucas is not himself."

Snapping, I glared at my sister with irritation. "Lucas hasn't been himself in a fucking while, Cassie."

"I know this," she replied, shaking her head. "But I'm telling you now, it's getting worse. We have to do something."

I couldn't understand why my sister couldn't get it through her head that Lucas had made his choice. There was nothing to be done about the situation. He may have seemed normal to her at first, but the moment he got here, he changed. He allowed his powers, his beast, to take over him, and in doing so, became the arrogant asshole he was always meant to be.

I had no sympathy for Lucas, and unfortunately, my sister was blinded by the idea of her mate being uncontrollable to see that. I highly doubted anything was wrong with him. The only thing wrong was my sister couldn't let go of a mate who didn't want her.

"I don't know what you expect me to do, Cassie."

"What to do?" She shook her head in disbelief. "How about helping me save one of our pack members, my mate, Pollux? While I've been out there trying to find some reasoning behind what is going on with him and what is going on with some of the others, you're in here with Trixie fucking around, and I need both of your help."

A growl escaped my throat as I clenched my fist at my side. She was being disrespectful, not just to me, but to my mate, and that was something I wouldn't tolerate no matter who she was. "You will watch how you speak to us."

Standing there with hesitation, her lips parted. She gave me a disgusted look before turning away from me. "You act like you're in control, Pollux, but the reason why you're here is because you couldn't be the leader or pack needed."

Without thinking, I grabbed her arm, spinning her around to face me. A snarl escaped me as my canines lengthened. How dare my sister speak to me like this? After everything I've tried to do for her over the years, this is how she would treat me in front of my mate.

"Just because your fucking mate didn't want you doesn't mean you can be disrespectful to mine. Perhaps you should start accepting what is given to you, and then you wouldn't lose everything around you."

"Pollux!" Trixie yelled, causing me to glance at her. An angry scowl marred her beautiful face, and seeing it, I realized quickly perhaps I had gone too far.

I didn't understand my sister's reluctance to tell us what she had been doing. Instead of her coming here and telling us exactly what happened, she made a mess of things like she always did, and now my mate wasn't happy with me.

"I'm sorry," I gritted out as I rolled my eyes. "Let's start from the top."

There was a smile on Trixie's face as I adjusted my behavior towards my sister. She was definitely a peace, love, and dream kind of girl, and while that would be great for the future of my pack, I was going to have to educate her on how things worked in our world.

"Ignore him, Cassie," Trixie said as she caught my sister's attention. "You said you saw him in the woods, and he approached you. He didn't hurt you, did he?"

Shaking her head she replied with a no. "He wouldn't hurt me."

I couldn't help the scoff that left my lips at her words. "Don't say that... you never know what he could be capable of."

"He wouldn't, Pollux. He's my mate!" she shouted in frustration, "he is just... confused."

Going to open my mouth, Trixie gave me a wide-eyed look as if to tell me to shut the fuck up. The entire situation was frustrating, and as I stood there trying to understand what to say or do, Cassie frowned and moved toward the door.

"Cassie, where are you going? Please don't go."

Hesitating, she stopped at the door and glanced over her shoulder at us. "No, I think it's best that I go. I'm sorry I interrupted your evening. I think I'm just going to get some sleep. Maybe I'm just tired and overthinking things."

Not giving Trixie or me a chance to say anything, she was out the door in a hurry and quickly closed it behind her. There was definitely something going on, and multiple questions ran through my mind.

One, why was my sister near the edge of town?

Two, what happened with Lucas that put her in such a state as she was?

Turning to Trixie, her eyes stared after where my sister had been as if she was just as lost as Cassie had been when she arrived at my room. There was still a lot I didn't know about my mate and the type of creature she was, but something I did know was Trixie could sense things even I as an Alpha couldn't.

"What is it?" I whispered as I came up behind her, wrapping my arms around her waist. A soft sigh escaped her as she leaned back against me.

"Pollux, your sister has a point. Something is going on, and we have to do something about it—"

"No," I snapped before pulling away from her. "There is nothing to be done."

Trixie didn't hesitate to whip around and glare at me with her arms crossed over her chest. The last thing I wanted was for my mate to be upset at me, but I wasn't going to cause an issue when there wasn't one.

"We can't just let her go about this on her own. She could end up getting hurt."

Laughter escaped my lips as I ran a hand through my hair. "I don't think Cassie will get hurt. It's more likely she will end up hurting someone else. My sister is reckless and always has been, and now she won't accept the fact that Lucas—the man who was supposed to be her mate—doesn't want her. But I mean, I can't blame the guy after how she treated him."

"Pollux, you're being unreasonable. Not everyone's relationship starts the same. Look at us... you didn't even want me when you found out I was your mate, and you can't deny that."

The hurt in her eyes was something I didn't want to see. She was right, and I hated that she was. It still didn't stop me from thinking this whole thing with my sister was ridiculous. "Fine... I'll go talk to her in the morning."

Trixie smiled brightly once more, and as she moved, she wrapped her arms around my neck to place a kiss on my lips. I wondered what our future would be like. This woman already had me wrapped around her finger, and our relationship had only just begun.

Silas' Desire

Cassie

The moment I left my brother's room, I couldn't help but feel a little hopeless in this entire situation. I've never been the kind of girl to be weak. I was always the girl who stood out, who didn't take shit from anyone. And the one time I really did need my brother's advice, he dismissed it as if I was the one who had a problem.

I didn't understand it. I had been there for him countless times over the years. Even though we had our differences, it didn't matter. I still came to his aid if he needed it. And the one time I needed him, all he wanted to do was be balls deep in a girl who was supposed to be my friend.

Tears streamed down my face and quickly I wiped them away. This was nothing but a sign of weakness. At least that was how I was raised. And right now, more than anything, I kind of wish I had my father's here to help guide me through all of this.

I know for fact my father, Talon, would be a little disappointed in how I was acting. He had raised me to be strong, to not take crap from anyone. And even though he had raised me that way, I still had that weakness of emotional instability.

Or at least that was what my therapist had called it when I was younger.

I stepped into my room and closed the door behind me, sinkin to my knees. Perhaps Lucas didn't want me, but I couldn't help but feel a little jealous over the fact everything I was doing wasn't good enough for him to realize I was trying to help him.

Yes, it was my fault I had acted the way I did and pushed him away.

I didn't meant to. I was scared initially when I found out he was my mate and now I regret the way I acted. I was stubborn and impulsive, andI had a hard time adjusting to the reality of things sometimes. But that was my own selfish intent causing me to be that way.

Thinking back to Melissa, my best friend who died at my hands, I couldn't help but wish she was here now, that she was able to be by my side and guide me through what I needed to do. She wasn't just my friend back then, she was like a sister to me in a way even though I had wanted her to be my mate. I would have been fine with her simply being my friend.

The soft, whooshing sound of the wind swirling outside alerted me, and as I quickly stood to my feet, the curtains of my balcony billowed from the breeze coming through my room. A shadowed figure stepped from the moonlight and into the dim lighting of my bedroom.

Silas stood there. He was the last person I had expected to see after everything that had happened at the library. But with here, part of me felt kind of hopeful. "What are you doing here?"

The moment his bluish-green eyes locked with mine, I felt myself slightly weakened. Through this whole time I had known him, there was always something about him that made my heart skip just a little bit more, and it was something I never understood.

Watching his tall, muscular form stride towards me very slowly, I couldn't help but take a step back, only to find the door blocking any chance of escape. Stopping inches from me, he let out a soft sigh and shook his head as he cast his eyes to the floor.

"I'm sorry that I left you the way that I did, Cassie," he muttered before his eyes locked with mine. "Your question simply brought up memories I had hoped never to think of again."

"Oh." It was the only thing I could manage to get out as he stood there, trying to explain himself to me. "I'm sorry I wasn't trying to upset you."

"You have no reason to apologize to me," he replied as he lifted his hand to gently brush down the side of my face.

I wasn't sure what to do with him being so close and the delicious smell of him swirled around me. It fogged my mind, making it hard to think. "Why do you make me feel this way?"

I hadn't meant to ask that question out loud. It was supposed to be internally done, but unfortunately, my brain and my mouth right now were not communicating properly and with me asking that question, he let out a soft chuckle that made me blush.

"How do I make you feel?"

The question alerted me to reality and caused me to quickly step around him and out of his touch. My mind raced with a million and one thoughts of Lucas, of Silas, of my brother and Trixie, of everything that had happened since I came to this God forsaken place.

"I don't even know how I feel about things, let alone know how you make me feel or anybody else. And I have a mate. I don't understand this. Why is it that I'm so attracted to you?"

He stood staring at me for a moment, as if he was contemplating his next words with another heavy sigh escaping him as he nodded, gesturing for me to take a seat on my bed. "I think I might be able to explain things to you in some kind of way. But first, I do want to say how sorry I am that I didn't tell you sooner. I prolonged our visits at the library because I wanted to spend more time with you, which was selfish of me."

"Are you saying you withheld information from me that could have possibly sped this up a lot faster because you wanted to hang out with me?" I grumbled, anger slowly bubbling inside of me realizing this could have all been sorted out long ago.

Opening and closing his mouth, he nodded his head. "Kind of. It's a little more complicated than that, but if you give me a chance, I'd like to explain everything to you."

I wanted to protest to tell him to get the fuck out of my room because he had wasted so much of my time, but I wanted to know what he had to say. I wanted to hear his explanation because part of me longed for him, thought of him day and night, just as I did for Lucas, and none of that made sense to me.

"Fine, explain. But make it quick because right now, I'm more upset than I was when I walked into this room." I reluctantly replied. However, as I waited his brows furrowed in recognition of what I had said.

"Why were you crying? What happened?"

He was completely ignoring I had allowed him to explain himself and instead was going back to why I was upset when he walked in here. If he hadn't noticed when he walked in here, then why was he asking now?

"It doesn't matter. Just please tell me what you were going to explain," I replied with frustration before slowly standing to my feet, not able to sit down anymore as I started to pace the room. "I need to hear what you're going to say."

"Fine," he huffed out, clearly not happy with the fact I was not going to tell him why I was upset. "Since the moment that I saw you, I couldn't stop thinking about you, Cassie. Everything about you pulls me in. Everything about you makes me want to know you more, and at first, I didn't understand it either. But honestly, the only thing I can think of is that we were destined to be together."

I was taken back by the forwardness. It wasn't what I was expecting. I knew he enjoyed being around me, but with the lust-driven look he was giving me right now, I found myself completely speechless.

"Silas, I have a mate," I whispered as he stepped closer to me.

"Yes, one who doesn't appreciate the woman that you are. I do, though I can be that man for you."

Every part of me wanted to run, wanted to tell him no but I couldn't. I was attracted to him, just as he was attracted to me, and there was an undeniable pool that wanted to be even closer to him.

With every step that he took, I watched, unwilling to move from the place where I stood. And as his arm wrapped around my waist, I found myself lost in his touch. While the carnal desire within his eyes sought to eat every inch of me.

Not resisting what he was doing, I let his lips crash upon mine, and as they did, the taste of his tongue within my mouth hypnotized me. It pulled me in closer, and before I knew it, my arms were wrapped around his neck, and I was pressed so hard against him that the only barrier was the clothing on our bodies between us.

With a deep growl coming from the belly of his throat, I was quickly lifted and tossed upon the bed, his body hovering over mine as the talons he had for nails ripped through my clothing with pure ease. This carnal desire between us was absolutely raw, and I loved every moment of it, moans escaping me.

With Lucas, there was a primal feeling between it, but there was also passion and aggression. With Silas, though, it was different. It was as if we couldn't get enough of each other, as if an eternal flame had brought us together over years and centuries of love and passion.

And as much as I didn't understand it, it didn't matter, because the moment his mouth descended upon my core, I lost control, my eyes rolling into the back of my head. My back arched in absolute bliss as his tongue flicked against my sensitive bud.

I hadn't noticed before he had a forked tongue, but the way it flicked across my clit caused ripples of pleasure to caress my skin as my heart began to race and my legs begged to close from the sensations he was creating. The entire thing was undeniably erotic. "Oh fuck–" I gasped. "Oh my god, yes!"

The more I praised him for pleasing me, the more aggressive his tongue moved. The carnal hunger running through him brought me closer and closer to the edge until I couldn't take it anymore. The grumbled roar of the dragon came to life as he tipped me over the edge. The blinding dots of my orgasm filled my eyes as I screamed louder than I ever had.

Yet, he wasn't done with me.

The moment I glanced down, his eyes connected with mine, I knew I was in for far more. Standing to his feet, he smiled at me, licking his lips as he pulled off his shirt, revealing iridescent scales that glimmered when the light hit him the right way. It was beautiful, but mesmerizing. I wanted more than anything to run my fingers against those scales and would have until he stripped off his pants and my mouth fell wide open.

I had been curious about what a dragon's cock may look like, and staring at his enormous dick adorned with thick veins and spikes along its ridges, I felt fear course through me. "Calm down, Cassie... I promise they won't hurt... in fact... you will love it."

He didn't give me a chance to process anything else as he grabbed my legs, flipping me over onto my stomach. My heart was pounding as his hands gripped my waist, pulling my ass high into the air so I was displayed on all fours like the heated bitch I was.

I was scared yes, but caught in the lust-filled pleasure he put me in, I wanted him. I wanted him to make me scream again, and as the head of his cock gently pressed against my tight cunt, I wasn't sure how he was going to fit.

The pressure of his erection hurt slightly as he pushed in, but that was until the spikes slid into my core as well. Then I realized what he meant. With a sudden thrust of ecstasy, I gripped the sheets as he shoved the length of his rigid, spiked cock inside me. The vibrations they gave off made me gasp as I closed my eyes, relishing in the way they felt pressing against the walls of my tight cunt.

"Fucking hell!" I shouted before a smack came down upon my bare ass that turned me on even more.

Silas didn't hesitate to thrust in me rapidly, and as I held tight to the blankets on my bed, I let him take me for a wild ride. The sensation of the spikes mixed with the fullness of his cock was more than I could handle, and as he fucked me relentlessly, I screamed in pleasure over and over again.

"Fuck, Cassie..." The words made me push back against him, working my hips to bring us both to the edge. "Yes, just like that... you're taking my cock like no one ever has."

I was surprised he talked dirty to me, but it turned me on and the more he did it, the faster I moved. I wanted him to cum just has hard as me, and as I bounced my ass up and down, allowing my tight cunt to take him fully, I felt the swell and vibrations of his cock increase until I didn't think I could take him anymore.

A few rough thrusts and he reached his peak, emptying himself inside of me. The feeling of his thick, hot cum coating the inside of my womb made me panic and I couldn't help but orgasm one last time.

I had never given much thought to having children of my own, but when he pulled out, I spun around with wide eyes, looking at him in fear. "You came inside me... why would you do that?"

"Calm down," he laughed, shaking his head. "You're not going to get pregnant."

I didn't understand what he meant, but as soon as he finished wiping himself off with a towel, he climbed naked into my bed and pulled me against his chest. My fingers instantly went to his skin, imagining the scales hidden from the dim lighting. It was crazy how his skin felt so normal now, and part of me wondered if it was because while we were having sex, he seemed to be restraining the beast within him.

Glancing up, I frowned with confusion. "How can you be sure?"

Raising one brow, he smiled at me. "Because with dragons, you can't just fuck and get people pregnant, Cassie. There is a ritual, and you also have to be mated completely. If it wasn't like that, there would be dragons everywhere. Our species is known to have a very high appetite for sexual pleasure."

I was shocked to hear what he had to say, but confused. "Oh, I guess that's a good thing."

"Mhmm, it's a very good thing. Otherwise, Anna would have been pregnant multiple times by me."

Shock filled me with his words. I hadn't expected them, and as I shot up and glanced over my shoulder at him, I realized quickly he hadn't meant to say what he did. "Cassie, please, I can explain... I didn't mean that."

"You only had sex with me because I look like her, didn't you?!" I screamed as I climbed from the bed, grabbing my robe off the chair in my room and quickly putting it on.

Silas was quick on his feet, and shaking his head. He opened and closed his mouth to try and justify what had happened. "Not at all, Cassie. You're completely misunderstanding me. I would never do that—"

"Silas, you need to leave. You need to leave right now."

Stepping towards me, I quickly stepped back. "Cassie, please. Don't be like this... we just had—"

"We had sex, Silas! You tricked me into feeling a certain way, and I should be focused on Lucas. Now please get out of my room."

Trying as hard as I could not to cry, Silas stood there before he put on his pants, grabbed his shirt, and left my room, slamming the door behind him.

I hadn't meant for things to go this way, and yet I kept allowing myself to be stupid. How was I ever going to learn if I didn't stop and think about what I was doing before I did it? Shaking my head, I made my way toward the balcony attached to my room.

The cool evening air bellowing through caused a heavy breath to escape me as I helped back the sobs that wanted to follow. All I wanted were for things to be right again, and staring up at the sky, I prayed that one day they would.

That was until a hard hit from behind caused pain to radiate through my head as everything slowly began to go black.

Kidnapped

Pollux

Trixie made it clear last night that she wanted me to speak with my sister and correct the wrongs said during our argument when she came to my room. I had no interest in really talking to Cassie about all of this, but the more I thought about it, she did look quite bothered last night.

I wished she would give up on this relentless journey of trying to save Lucas. There was nothing wrong with him. He was simply being the asshole I always knew he was, and toying with my sister was probably just his way of getting back at me for all of the bullshit I put him through in the past.

Freshly showered and with my mate's scent wafting around me from our lingered experiences together the night before, I made my way down towards my sister's room, my feet moving slowly until I approached the door.

With a heavy sigh, I lifted my hand to knock. Before I did, I glanced over my shoulder to see Trixie standing down the hallway with a bright smile on her face, the yellow dress she wore illuminating against her skin as she gave me two thumbs up and nodded her head eagerly for me to go ahead and knock.

If it weren't for Trixie, I wouldn't be standing here right now. But I knew she cared about my sister very much as her friend, and because of that, I was doing this for her and nobody else.

Knocking upon the door, I waited. There wasn't a sound from inside. After a few moments of knocking again, I became irritated. "Cassie, it's me. Let's talk about all of this going on. I'm ready to listen."

There was no sound from the other side of the door again at my comment. I blew out a huff of frustration, banging upon it with my fist. "Cassie, open the door and stop being like this. I—I'm sorry I acted the way that I did. Can we please just talk about this?"

Still, there was no response whatsoever to my attempts to get her to answer the door. Before I knew it, Trixie was at my side. I glanced at her—a worried expression of confusion had crossed her face as her beautiful eyes stared at the closed door.

"Something's wrong," she whispered as she reached for the handle, finding it unlocked, and quickly pushed open the door, entering inside.

Glancing around the room upon first entry, the smell of sex lingered in the air. It was Cassie scent and another male's I wasn't too familiar with. I glanced around at twisted bed sheets, blankets on the floor, and the open balcony door. I was curious where my sister was.

"Perhaps she's already left for today," Trixie said to herself as she glanced around the room, the same as I, and then looked at me, her eyes locking with mine with a simple shrug of her shoulders.

"She might have."

Trixie walked towards the bed. "Well, if she did, at least we know she had fun last night. This bed was absolutely ravaged. Kind of reminds me of what you and I did in your room."

Chuckling to myself, I crossed my arms over my chest. The last thing I wanted to think about was my sister getting fucked senseless, but it did make sense that whoever she had been here with, she had had a good time. The only problem was, I couldn't shake this feeling in the bottom of my stomach that told me something else was at play here.

Before I could open my mouth to say anything, the door was pushed open and I quickly turned to see Silas standing there with a bunch of flowers in his hand. His mouth partially opened as his eyes met mine, realizing he had been caught in a situation he hadn't expected to.

"Are those flowers for me? Are you here to see my sister?"

Silas rolled his eyes at my comment, entering the room with nothing but confidence as he held his head high. "Your sister, of course. Where is she?"

"Obviously she isn't here, so why are you?" The reply I gave was completely sarcastic, and as his glass eyes glanced towards the bed and then back to me, I gave him a smug smile.

It was clear he saw exactly what I did, and unfortunately for him, no matter how much he liked her, she must have had fun with Lucas last night and rekindled whatever argument that they had.

"Do you know where she went?"

Rolling my eyes, I shrugged my shoulders as a gesture to the bed. "Obviously with her mate who fucked her senseless last night."

Silas look to the bed again, and as he did, he couldn't contain the laughter that ended up erupting from his lips completely, catching me off guard. "You think Lucas did that to her last night and that's why the beds all messed up?"

I suddenly felt as if I was the elephant in the room who had absolutely no idea what was going on. As Silas sat the flowers down upon the dresser, I glanced at Trixie and realized I was incorrect.

Trixie's face flushed red as her eyes widened in shock at what Silas had said. She had obviously realized exactly what he was talking about and I felt completely stupid. I rolled my eyes with annoyance before stepping forward and grabbing Silas's arm.

"If there's something that you know that we don't, it's best that you go ahead and say it."

Silas glanced down at where my grip was upon his arm and quickly shrugged it out of my hand. "It would be in your best interest not to touch me again."

"Boys, boys, that's enough," Trixie quickly exclaimed as she cleared the room, looping her arm through mine to try and calm me down. "Sweetie, it would seem that your sister and Silas may have a small fling going on."

It took a moment for those words to sink into my head, and as they did, I quickly turned my glare back upon Silas with a narrowed, angry expression. "Took advantage of my sister and one of her most vulnerable moods, knowing full well that she has a mate?"

It was clear that Silas was not the person I thought he was, and as he quickly ignored what I said and made his way around the room as if searching for something, I couldn't help but want to completely destroy who he was in order to gain satisfaction from the entire situation.

Cassie and I may not have been close, but I wouldn't tolerate anybody taking advantage of my sister, especially since she wasn't in the right mental capacity to make decisions like that, considering the emotional stress she had been under.

"Hey, I'm talking to you," I snapped, moving away from Trixie and straight towards Silas. However, before I could even attempt to lay a finger on Silas again, he quickly turned, gripping me by the throat and hoisting me into the air.

He was far stronger than I had given him credit, and as he looked up at me with a sneer upon his face, I could see he was not in the mood to fucking deal with me. "I need you to back the fuck off so I can figure out where your sister is."

The moment didn't last long as he quickly was thrown from me, my body hitting the floor as Silas hit the wall. I was slightly amazed by the power my mate Trixie had and as she came to stand before me, the aura that radiated off of her body was nothing but pure power.

"Silas... Pollux," Trixie said like a stern mother scolding her children. "What did I tell you about getting along? I thought we've had this conversation before. Both of you need to keep your hands to yourself because I'm in a good mood today and I don't need that ruined."

There was no point in arguing with my mate when she said her piece. I had quickly learned a few days ago after I marked her. When Trixie wanted something, she was going to do it whether you wanted her to or not. And if she told you to knock it off, it was best that you did it. Otherwise, you were likely to receive punishment you did not want.

Something that would make her a wonderfully amazing mother one day. But for right now, I felt a little scolded, like a boy who got in trouble by his mother because I wasn't listening.

Standing to our feet, Silas and I brushed ourselves off before quickly turning our attention back to Trixie, who had crossed her arms over her chest with a smile upon her face as she rocked back and forth from heel to toe. "Thank you. Now it's obvious that Cassie isn't here and we need to figure out what exactly happened."

Silas and I were both silent as we watched Trixie walk around the room. She had an uneasiness before she stepped in here, and as she continued to walk around, looking at every little thing that lingered around the room upon dressers or even within the small bookshelf against the far wall, she came to stop eventually in front of the balcony door to which she was hesitant to go out on.

"She went out here..." Trixie muttered softly before pushing herself forward through the billowing curtains out into the sunny balcony that lay just beyond them.

I barely had a chance to move when a sharp yelp escaped her and I quickly went running with Silas following behind me. The moment my eyes landed upon my beautiful mate, her hands over her mouth with a gasp and a look of horror across her face, I knew something had happened.

Letting my eyes follow the line of sight to see what Trixie was looking at, I found the red small splashes of blood upon the cobbled balcony floor laying in wait for someone to find it. "Is that blood?"

Silas rushed forward, bending to his knees as he touched the blood with his fingertips and quickly brought it up to his nose. "It's Cassie's..."

I never imagined my sister's name would follow the word blood, but as it did my heart sank into the pits of my stomach as I realized this situation was far worse than I had thought.

It was clear something had happened to my sister. She had obviously come out to the balcony after Silas left and was attacked. A million and one thoughts swirled through me, and as I tried to put all of the pieces together. There was only one common denominator that didn't make sense.

And that was Silas.

Rushing forward, I gripped him by the front of his shirt and quickly pushed his back towards the wall. "What the fuck did you do to my sister? Where is she?"

The sound of Trixie saying my name, trying to get me to stop filled my ears, but unfortunately my brain had been hardwired to defend my family and the beast lurking under my skin wanted vengeance.

Once again, with the quick thrust, Silas shoved me off, adjusting his shoulders as he straightened his back and narrowed his gaze down at me. "I told you not to fucking touch me, pup. Trixie, get a hold of your mate before he ends up dead."

She didn't hesitate at the command and was quickly at my side, shaking her head. No. She had obviously known Silas longer than I had, and there must have been a good reason for her to say that. From what she had explained to me, dragons were notorious for being absolutely ruthless, and Silas right now was on the verge of losing control, his eyes flickering between the bluish green to a reddish gold.

I had no idea how we were going to find what had happened to my sister. But before I could even open my mouth, as if she had read my mind, Trixie smiled and pulled her phone from her pocket. "Everyone calm down. Let me call Sansa. She'll know what to do."

"You're calling the witch?" Silas snapped as he sent a glare Trixie's way.

Most people would have been intimidated, and she had been for a moment when he demanded she keep me in check. But as she stood to her feet, pushing the phone against her air, she pointed at him with an angry gaze, one that I had never seen as her eyes flashed a fluorescent green.

"Silas, you may be powerful, but do not forget who I am. Piss me off and be disrespectful one more time, and I'll put your ass in a permanent timeout."

Sansa's Gifts

Silas

The moment I had left Cassie last night, my heart absolutely broke. She was everything I ever wanted, and though she reminded me so much of Anna, I didn't want her to think the only reason why I was with her was because she reminded me of Anna.

Anna and I had a relationship far beyond what a normal guard would have with his charge, but with it, that was all it was. A sexual relationship with no emotional attachment because I was not her mate, nor would I ever have been.

Granted, after Anna died, I absolutely broke into pieces, the emotions of losing her too much for me to bear. I begged fate to give me a chance to have a mate of my own, one who looked like Anna and had her kind heart, but with the fire of an internal dragon inside of them.

I knew it was a long shot for me to actually have a mate who filled all of those things, but the moment I laid eyes on Cassie, I knew without a doubt she was exactly what I had been waiting for.

She was sarcastic and witty. She was beautiful, and even though she had a rough exterior that was nothing but walls she had built over the years, she had the kindest heart I had ever seen in any one.

She was the type of woman you wanted to spend the rest of your life with, and the fact her mate treated her the way he did disgusted me. He didn't deserve her, and perhaps fate bringing her to me was the reason why he had rejected her.

At least that was what I hoped for.

The moment I had stepped into our room, when I saw her brother Pollux and his mate Trixie—a girl that I had known for many years—standing in the room with no Cassie in sight, I felt in the pit of my stomach something had happened to her.

Of course Pollux would act like he did, and Trixie would have to get into the middle of our situation to ensure neither of us killed each other. But when I saw the blood, it all made sense.

My love for her was not enough to keep her safe, and I should have fought harder to stay with her last night, I could understand why her brother would be angry and assume the worst of me.

"Call your witch, Trixie," I said softly, staring at her mate with an absolutely distant and voided expression, unable to even think in that moment because the realization of Cassie being gone wasn't something I wanted to believe in.

I was in love with a woman I couldn't have and as I turned away from Pollux and Trixie, I cast my eyes out over the city, looking down below at Asgard, wondering who it was that could possibly want to hurt a woman as kind as her.

"Okay, she's on her way. She'll be here in just a minute."

Pollux stood to his feet, brushing himself off as he curled his lip and anger at me. "You know, my sister came to Trixie and I last night talking about how she ran into Lucas in the woods rambling on to himself or some shit like that. She was on the edge of town. You wouldn't happen to know anything about that, would you?"

Thinking back to last night and the way I had left Cassie back at the library, guilt filled me realizing her encounter with Lucas may have been problematic. However, it did make something clear, and that was if she did have an interaction with Lucas maybe he could have been involved with something like this.

"Partially. I was at the old ruined library on the edge of town. It's a part of the history of Asgard. She and I had a disagreement and I left, which left her, of course, to walk back to town by herself. It's not that long of a walk, maybe 20-30 minutes at max, but I didn't think anything would happen, nor did I know Lucas was out there."

Anger soared through Pollux, and that much I could feel radiating off of him like a tidal wave of uncontrollable power. He clenched his fists at his side as he narrowed his gaze at me. "You left my fucking sister alone out there? Anything could have happened to her, and yet you supposedly care about her."

"She wasn't in any immediate danger and it wasn't like I had vanished completely. I took flight and kept an eye on her from above. I just needed time to clear my mind. But I didn't even see her go into the woods. That's what I don't understand. The entire time I saw her walking along the road."

"Yeah, whatever. There's no way she just magically stayed on the road but magically went into the woods. Obviously, you weren't fucking keeping an eye on her," he scoffed.

We could continue the argument, but Sansa made her appearance at the open balcony door, her eyes darting from Trixie and Pollux to me and then back. "Did I interrupt something important?" she questioned and stepped forward.

"No," Trixie said, turning to her friend with a gentle expression. "These two just have too much testosterone and continue to bicker back and forward. I'm glad you're here. They were becoming irritating."

Pollux's mouth dropped open at his mate's words and I couldn't hide the chuckle that escaped me upon seeing his expression. I found it funny the two of them were mated together. She definitely kept him in check and wasn't what he was expecting. But in the long run I was happy because Trixie was a good woman and if anyone could get him into shape it was definitely her.

I watched as Trixie quickly explain the situation. Sansa's eyes fell to the blood on the cobbled balcony floor. "That's it right there."

She glanced at me for a moment, and as I nodded my head, she bent down next to it, running her hand through the air above where the blood sat. "This isn't just the blood of Cassie, there's someone else's mixed with it."

This was news to all of us. I wasn't quite sure who it was, but I was hoping Sansa would be able to figure it out. That way we might know who took Cassie and get her back safely. She pulled various items from the brown satchel she kept at her side; little bottles of herbs, a couple crystals and some black powder I had never seen before.

"So what are you gonna do? Like some magic spell or something, and it'll tell us where she is."

Sansa, Trixie and I glared at Pollux with utter irritation.

Standing to her feet, Sansa glared at him. There was a thin line across her face where a smile once had been. She wasn't going to put up with this shit and as I stood back with my arms crossed over my chest, I waited to see what it was she was going to say or do, because this girl was very laid back and it was very rare that anybody saw her upset.

"Magic spell," she scoffed. "Is that the only thing that you think we do? Fly on brooms, brew potions, run around dancing naked around fires? Doing nothing but playing with crystals and creating magic potions."

Her head bobbed with so much anger and sarcasm, my own eyes widened as I stood there watching this girl go completely off on Pollux.

"There's more to being a witch than just magic potions, you stereotyping asshole. If you have nothing pleasant to say, then step back and shut the fuck up and let me do what I do." The moment she finished talking, she spun herself to me. "Do you have anything to say as well?"

"Nope," I replied, holding my hands up in defense. "Do whatever you need to."

She took a moment to stare at me as if contemplating on whether or not I was telling the truth. However, as I stepped back away from where the blood splatter was upon the ground, she knelt back down once more, letting her hand hover over the blood as she closed her eyes.

She mumbled something to herself and then her brows furrowed in confusion as she gasped. I had never seen anything like that, and as I watched her, I could feel the powerful aura rating off of her, the celestial blood that flowed through her veins, controlling whatever it was that was going on.

Just when I was about to reach out and touch Sansa to make sure that she was okay, her eyes shot open and she jumped to her feet, stumbling backwards from the blood. But quickly Trixie caught her.

The girl's heart was racing, and I could hear that clear as day, which meant Pollux could too. And as she glanced around at all of us, wide eyed, she placed a hand over her heart and held back a sob in her throat that wanted to escape. "She's in really big trouble, I mean like really big trouble."

"Well, we know that, do you know who did it? Did you see them?" Pollux snapped, causing me to growl at him in disapproval.

"Knock it off, Pollux. What happened to Sansa was that she saw visions. Those are subjective and never clear."

I was slightly shocked I knew exactly what had happened to her. I had seen it happen before, but to Anna, a very long time ago.

Anna had visions and from what she said, they started not long after she came to Asgard. Odin bestowed upon her the gift of our immortality, something she didn't want to have.

"That's right," Sansa replied softly. "I'm not sure where she is, but I can describe it. The visions... it was so confusing. First, I felt like I was with Cassie... or well, seeing everything through her eyes. She has shackles on her wrists, and there is like brick or stone wall. It smelled wet, almost like wet dog but it was weird."

I knew Asgard better than any of them did, and as I wracked my mind to try and figure out where that could have been she continued explaining what had happened to her.

"It's okay," Trixie hushed her. "Just take your time."

"We don't have time, Trixie," Pollux grumbled, earning him an angry glare from the woman he was mated to.

"We make time or I will punish you."

Usually, I would have been amused by the angry banter between them, but right now, I was irritated because I needed to concentrate to focus on the task at hand.

"I saw his visions, too." Sansa's words stopped me and turning to face her again I couldn't hold my tongue.

"Whose, Sansa? Can you describe what you saw?"

Slowly she nodded her head. "Darkness... deep dark eyes and a baby born in snow. A child without a father, and sorrow in his heart for a lost mother. There was a battle... one that caused a lot of death, and he is angry about it. He blames Cassie for the death... but at the same time, he is confused."

I didn't have the slightest clue as to what she was talking about, but as I looked at Pollux, his face went white as snow. "I know who has her—"

"Who Pollux? Who fucking has Cassie?"

His eyes met mine, and as they did he shook his head. "Lucas does... and if its the battle that I'm thinking about—we need to hurry before it's too late."

Prisoner Beneath The Wall

Cassie

Darkness seemed to surround me, and slowly waking from the endless sleep I was in, I realized the sharp pain currently radiating through the back of my head and down my neck wasn't actually from me sleeping wrong. It was because I had been hit from behind.

A low groan escaped my lips as I tried to glance around through the darkness, but my vision was blurred, and the more the pain radiated through my head, the worse I felt. The metallic scent of blood must have been on my clothing. It's scent wafted around me, making my stomach turn.

Slowly, I tried to move but quickly realized I wasn't going to be able to. My hands were shackled to a stone wall behind me, and the cold, dripping wet water flowing down the wall from a crack above had begun to pool beneath my bottom.

I didn't have the slightest clue what had happened. I remembered being on the balcony, having just argued with Silas. The next thing I knew, this pain came from behind, my head splitting as the radiating agony of what had happened traveled through my body before darkness captivated me.

Someone had attacked me; that was clear. The only problem was currently, I was sitting in the darkness alone, without anybody around me, or at least that is what I assumed.

My time here in Asgard hadn't been pleasant so far. I had been cast aside by my family after everything that had happened in the other world, brought here by my grandfather, who rarely even checked in on me. Not to mention the number of issues I had with some of the students and even from some of the teachers.

Deciding not to play helpless victim, considering I was an independent woman who could take care of herself, I simply had to find a way out of this no matter how hurt I was. I used all the strength that I had to push myself up onto my feet.

My wrists were shackled, and it did hurt when I stood, but the moment I got onto my feet, I realized the reason why it was such an inconvenience for me to be able to move beforehand was simply because my chains were twisted.

I had about two to three feet of movement from the wall forward, and that was all the space I had been given. Gazing into the darkness–trying to disregard my currently splitting headache—I searched for anything in my surroundings I could use to try and escape.

The only thing I found was cold, cobblestoned walls and a floor that matched. A few iron bars set off in the distance looked like they could have been cells for prisoners. And on top of that, a wooden table sat in the far corner that had a few metal objects on it, but nothing I could distinctly picture nor get a hold of, considering I was chained to a wall and unable to move more than three feet.

Whoever had placed me here had done so with precision.

My mind tried to reel over who it was that could have done this, and the only thing I could piece together was, maybe, I had misread somebody. I had misjudged them and their capability of what they could do to me.

With so many people I had petty issues with, it wasn't enough for someone to want to kidnap me and bring me down here as a prisoner. Therefore, whatever was going on had to be far more than I could comprehend.

Had I simply gotten too close to something trying to figure out a way to free Lucas from Inanna? Was I captured because I had found something or stumbled upon something in that library with Silas I shouldn't have?

It honestly would make sense as to why I had seen Lucas in the woods near the library, but Lucas wouldn't have done this. Even if he had issues with me, I was sure he would never hurt me.

Just when I thought things couldn't get any worse, I quickly realized with the echoing sound of footsteps I was no longer alone down here in my prison. In fact, there was somebody standing behind the bars in the darkness on the far side of the room, watching me.

With my vision slightly blurred, I tried to focus on the figure. However, the only thing I could really notice was the mesmerizing golden yellow eyes that stared back at me. They reminded me so much of Lucas' beast in a way, and my curiosity piqued, wondering if it was him I was staring at.

Yet as I went to open my mouth to ask if it was him, the sound of a door squeaking open caught my attention. I found myself gazing to my left towards a small light shining down a narrow path of stairs.

The footsteps of heels on concrete echoed through the darkness, and slowly but surely, a figure came into view I had hoped not to see. Her fiery red hair and green eyes stared back at me from the darkness. She stared back with a look of pure evil, and the more I stared at her with her hands on her hips, the angrier I became.

"Inanna." The firm tone of her name made my lip curl into a sneer. "What the hell is the meaning of this? Why do you have me here?"

She laughed, and as she stared at me, I couldn't help but wonder what she found amusing. She was supposed to have been the Dean of students, a person who we could go to who would protect us in a time of need, and instead, she had me chained up against a wall with a smile on her face like a kid on Christmas morning.

"Oh, come on. Did you honestly think that after everything that you've pulled, I would run the risk of missing a chance of capturing you? I have waited so many years to be able to take my revenge back out on the descendants of

Anna, and you just gave me everything I wanted the moment you stepped through that portal."

I didn't have the slightest clue what she was talking about, or that I was a descendant of Anna. As far as I knew, I was just someone who looked like her. Perhaps, I should have given Silas more of a chance to explain things instead of getting frustrated over not getting the answers that I wanted.

"I have no idea what you're talking about. I have done nothing to you."

With laughter, she took a few steps towards me, admiring the handiwork of me being chained against the wall as if I was some type of decorative ornament in her home. "Oh, but you have everything to do with everything. Didn't you know that?"

"You're fucking crazy. I don't even know you, and you don't even know anything about me. So, how did I do something to you?" Pulling on the restraints, I tried with every bit of energy I had left to find a way to escape. But my efforts were simply met with a slap to the face that had my ears ringing and my head splitting further from my previous energy.

"Shut up!" she screamed at me, "how dare you speak like you're innocent. Because of you, my child is dead!"

This woman was beyond insane. I had barely had a few conversations with her, and yet she seemed to believe I had wronged her in some way. The last thing I wanted to do was upset her, but I was growing worried about her mental stability.

Not to mention my safety, the woman already had me chained up.

"Look, lady... you have me mixed up with someone else. I haven't killed anyone—"

The words froze on the tip of my tongue as I paused mid-sentence. I couldn't say I hadn't killed anyone because I had. Melissa was dead because of me, and the more I thought about Melissa, the more I saw something in Inanna that made my breath catch in my throat.

"There it is... the look of realization." Shaking her head, she rolled her eyes before letting a heavy breath escape her. "I had hoped one day she would be here, that she would... or that I would at least see her again."

Inanna didn't seem like the type of person to be sentimental, but staring at her right now, I could tell that her daughter—Melissa, the girl who was my best friend—meant everything to her. "How... how was she your daughter?"

I was at a loss for how Melissa was Inanna's daughter. I had known Melissa my entire life, and as far as I knew, Melissa's mother died when Melissa was a baby. To find out now that wasn't the case was troubling. Especially since that meant Melissa was a celestial half-breed and she never had shown any sign of being like me.

Cringing in pain from the shackles that were digging into my wrists, I watched as Inanna paced around the stone dungeon. "I never meant to leave Earth... but when your horrible mother attacked us, I had to help. I had to save my people, and in the process, I was sent back here."

"Enough!" The booming sound of a male voice caught me by surprise, and even Inanna jumped, freezing in her place as her breathing increased. "The girl doesn't deserve to know everything. You have a job... now do it, and free me."

Small scuffling noises once again echoed from the otherside of the room where the yellow eyes had once appeared, and with his command, Inanna moved towards a wooden torch that laid against the far wall. Her hand shook as she pulled something from her pocket and lit the torch illuminating the room before me.

There, amongst the cobbled walls and stoney floor, were cells with iron bars that seemed to buzz with their own energy. An within the cell directly in front of me stood a man with dark hair and black eyes, eyes that reminded me so much of Lucas.

"Who are you?" I whispered softly, watching a smile cross his face.

"What... you don't recognize me? I would hope you did, considering your mate and I share very similar features." I couldn't stop thinking of how familiar the man looked. How I had seen his face before but wasn't sure where I had seen him before.

"She looks just like Ivy, doesn't she?" Inanna chuckled. The man before me gazing at her for a split second with annoyance on his face. It was clear he didn't care to much for Inanna speaking and as he stood to his feet, I realized where Lucas got his build from.

"You're Lucas' father?"

Nodding his head, he chuckled, "I am... and I do have to thank you for bringing my son with you to this realm. I waited for that moment for a very long time."

Quickly, I realized this was not just any man, but Lucas' father and what he had said before about him and Lucas sharing similar features made sense. He didn't seem like a man who was here willingly, and perhaps that was something I could use to my advantage.

If he was using Inanna to try and free himself, perhaps I could have him be on my side instead. I could make him see she was hurting Lucas, and that would put him against Inanna.

Desperate in my thoughts to try and find a way to escape, I decided to resort to extreme measures to make the man see my side of things. To see if he would be a savior in the depths of shadows that seemed to fill the dungeon around me.

"I didn't–it wasn't like that," I muttered quickly, "please let me go... I need to find your son. Inanna is poisoning his mind, you have to help me—"

"Poisoning?" He laughed, running a hand over his squared jawline. "I wouldn't say that. She simply helped him to see the truth of the past. The truth of why he lost his father, and how his mother eventually died from a broken heart... the truth of the evil that runs in your veins, Castor."

Hearts Desire

Cassie

Evil. It wasn't a word I had ever associated with my family because it wasn't something I had ever seen. Of course, we all had our issues, but my parents were the most caring people I had ever known. They went above and beyond for people all the time and ran our pack fairly. To hear this man, who was caged, proclaim my family was evil was wrong.

"Don't you dare speak about my family. You don't even know them."

Narrowing my gaze, I watched amusement dance on his face.

"Oh, but I do. Your father's were always a pain in the ass growing up. They wanted everything and gave nothing. That is, until your mother came along. She had them all sort of messed up."

"You're here and in prison. How could you possibly know my parents or even have met them? They have never been here before." I was tired of hearing this man spewing nonsense. Pulling upon the chains again, I growled with irritation. "Let me go."

There was no easy way for me to free myself, and with a quick step forward, Inanna raised her hand once more and brought it across my face. This was the second time she had hit me, and if she wasn't careful, I'd break every bone in her fucking hand if she touched me again.

"You will not speak unless spoken to," she snapped, glaring at me with anger.

"If you didn't notice…" I said before spitting blood at her feet, "he had spoken to me."

Quickly raising her hand again, I closed my eyes preparing for another hit but found that it didn't come. Instead, when I opened my eyes I found that from within the shadows, Lucas had appeared and stopped her. She stared at him with wide eyes as if she couldn't believe he would save me.

Lucas' dark eyes glared at her from beneath narrowed brows and with every moment that passed between them, she slowly nodded, and he release her arm before she lowered it to her side. I had thought she would have taken her wrath out on him for stopping her, but instead, she was okay with it.

"Lucas–" my whispered breath caught his attention, and as he stared at me I knew something was different. It was like he was here, but then again, he wasn't. The voided expression he gave me would forever haunt my mind, and as his lip curled into a sneer, I knew the man I once laid with was forever gone.

"Don't speak to me, Cassie. You lost that right."

Lips parted and completely speechless, I stared at him in shock. It was clear he wasn't going to help me, and with the laughter from Inanna and the man behind the bars, I couldn't help but wonder what my fate was going to be.

As the light from the torch flickered in the damn air of my prison, my mind tried to reflect on everything I had done in my life and wished I had done differently. There was no way I could give up, but it didn't stop me from considering my fate.

"What is it that you want from me? Are you going to kill me?"

The words slipped breathlessly from my lips, and as they did, Inanna gazed at me with more curiosity than I had expected. "As enticing as that thought is, we have bigger plans for you than simply killing you… at least right away."

All I could do was watch as Inanna moved around the room, my eyes gazing at Lucas, who stood still staring at me completely unmoving. A statue frozen in time, waiting for his next order like a soldier without a mind of his own.

"Lucas," I whispered while Inanna was speaking to the other man, "please… I'm your mate. Let me go."

No matter the pleas I threw at him, he stood as if my words couldn't break the wall wrapped around his mind, and with a single twist of her body, Inanna turned to gaze between Lucas and me with a smile.

"Before we get started, Cassie I want to tell you a story... seeing as you seem to lack a lot of information about who we are and what has happened."

A story... she had to be fucking kidding me. "What part of all this makes you think I want a story, Inanna? You kidnapped me, hit me over the head, and are plotting my demise."

"I didn't hit you over the head or kidnap you." She chuckled, "that was all Lucas' idea."

Inanna glided towards Lucas, letting her perfectly manicured hand lay upon his shoulder with a grin. She was sick and twisted, no doubt, and the more than she continued with what she was doing, I wanted to rip her fucking head off.

"Take your hand off my mate," I growled at her.

"Your mate? You don't deserve a mate... you don't deserve anything after what you did to my daughter. The only reason you're not dead is because of who your grandfather is, and also because I need you," she replied, flipping some of her hair over her shoulder as if she was fifteen again, and overly confident in her position.

"Enough, Inanna. The childish conversation is beneath you."

Her eyes cast towards the floor as she huffed and nodded her head. Whoever this man was obviously was capable of putting her in her place, and as I looked up to Lucas once more, I found that he wasn't looking at me but at his father with confliction weighing upon his face. "What are you going to do to her?"

Silence filled the room as Inanna looked between Lucas and his father. It was clear Lucas wasn't in on everything they had planned, and like a puppeteer controlling her puppet, Inanna seemed to understand the silence and quickly addressed Lucas.

"Lucas, why don't you prepare the circle for me—"

"No," he snapped with a narrowed gaze. "I want to know what you have planned. You had me bring her here for you, and you said that you would explain how she would be able to free my father. Now start explaining."

The tension in the room between Lucas and the others was a little unsettling. If Lucas thought he was part of whatever Inanna and his father had going on, he was completely wrong. The sinking feeling of doom began to rise in my chest, and with every passing second, I knew I had to escape.

For years I had always expected my future would be my own. That I would end up meeting my mate and eventually we would see the world and then grow old together. Never once did I think I'd end up in Asgard, fulfilling some bullshit knowledge quest to better myself. I mean sure, they had spoken about it while I was growing up, and look how everything had turned out.

I was captive, my brother probably didn't know I was gone, and my so-called grandfather was nowhere to be seen.

How the hell could no one in this damn place know I was in trouble?

Looking between the three people before me, I tried to understand what it was I had done wrong to deserve this. Melissa dying was an accident, and as much as I wish I could take it back, I couldn't.

All I ever wanted was a normal life, one free from my past and unfortunate future.

"Enough," I breathed out, tired of their bickering. "What do you need of me?"

All eyes turned to me, and as a smile crossed Lucas' father's face, I knew this was going to be my end. His father planned to kill me and Lucas... he had no fucking idea.

"Do you even know who I am, child?" he asked with confusion and amusement.

The thought had crossed me a million times on who he could be, and yet I couldn't figure it out. "No, I don't and neither of you have bothered explaining it to me."

"Did your parents ever tell you of the great war in your world?" His question caught me off guard, and as I started to put pieces together, I realized what he was talking about.

"The battle of Loki?" I gasped, my eyes darting to Lucas. "Your father is Loki?"

"Is there a problem with that?" he snapped, narrowing his eyes as he crossed his arms over his chest. It was clear he didn't know the truth of who Loki was, and as Inanna picked up a silver blade with green jade stones in the handle, I realized what they were going to do.

"Lucas... Loki isn't to be trusted," I stammered as his hands fell to his sides clenching into fists. He was angry, and I didn't understand why. "They are brainwashing you."

"Oh, so it's okay to trust you? You're parents are the one that put him here! He did nothing but try to stop your parents from a power trip they went on after he was gone!"

"That's not true!" I cried out in response to his anger, "please... you have to wake up from whatever spell she has you under. You can't let him out... you can't."

Pulling on my restraints, I tried to understand how my grandfather had allowed this to happen. "He won't save you... your grandfather, that is. He isn't in the realm."

"What?" My breath caught in my throat as I looked at her with confusion. I had no idea Odin was out of the realm but the realization he was made it clear there was no hope for me. I was going to be another statistic but in a world that wasn't my home.

Stride after stride, she made her way towards me. "Odin and the other gods got called away to a meeting in the Fae realm. It seems your grandfather and the others are trying to set up something special for you, Cassie... too bad you won't be around to take part. Nor will we be around to answer for what we have done."

Anger and panic boiled through me at her words, and with them, Lucas seemed taken back by the remark. My eyes fell on him seeking some kind of help but I realized wouldn't find any. At least not with Inanna around.

Stepping back, she admired me for a moment, her eyes scanning from head to toe before she snapped her fingers causing Lucas to go blank once more. "What did you do to him?"

"Lucas has been asking too many questions," she laughed softly. "He is needed to complete the ritual to help with freeing his father, and the only way I'll be able to have that done without issues is for him to be... compliant."

The way she smiled and looked at him when she said complaint only further fueled my rage. "You're fucking crazy!"

"Maybe I am," she laughed hysterically, "but there is nothing you can do about that."

Walking towards Lucas, she held out her palm with the jade handle dagger to Lucas. My heart raced as I watched him pick it up while I pulled on the silver shackled restraints trying to break free. "Lucas... you have to wake up... please, Lucas."

"Enough toying with the girl, Inanna. It's her blood that will free me, considering it was her mother's blood that put me here."

"Very well, very well." She sighed. "I do wish I could have played with her longer. Lucas... take care of your mate for me... and bring me her heart to free your father."

Death to those we Love

Cassie

I had never given much thought to how I die, but being faced with it now, I finally realized why it was my parents loved so fiercely. At any point in time, you could walk out the front door and never come home. Fate didn't pick sides, and it never made things fair, but in the end, we learned to live with the futures we were given because, as my mother always said, things happen for a reason.

Watching Lucas walk towards me with the jade dagger in his hand, my heart broke. The moment he realized what he did, he would regret it for the rest of his life because even though Inanna had her claws in him and he tried to reject me, I knew he still felt our bond.

Glancing towards Inanna, who was taking out candles and preparing the altar, to which she would free Loki, I decided to try one more time to get through to Lucas. There was no way he could be unreachable, and with a heavy breath, I focused.

The pull of our slightly broken bond told me he was still there.

"Lucas," I whispered, staring at him with a gentle gaze trying to make him see me. "I'm sorry, Lucas. I'm sorry your mother died, and I'm sorry your father was cast away, but it wasn't me. We aren't responsible for our parent's choices in life, and it isn't fair that we should pay for them either."

"This has to be done, Cassie. I have to save him." Determination sat heavy in the forefront of his mind, and it was that I had to break through.

"I know you do, but I'm your mate, Lucas. Don't I get one more thing from you before I die?" If my words weren't enough to break the hold, I knew one thing that would be.

Halting only a foot in front of me, his dark eyes stared down into mine with knitted brows before a sigh escaped him. "What is it that you want?"

With parted lips, a faint of a smile crossed my face. "One last kiss... one with meaning that lets me know some part of you loved me."

The request was obviously not something he had expected by the way his face softened and his eyes shifted from side to side. "One kiss?"

"Yes," I nodded, "please... I need you."

Lifting his hand, he brushed the matted strained of hair from my face and gazed down at my body. The robe was coming slightly undone, and with a part of my breast slightly exposed, he let his hand run over it. "I wish things could have been different."

"So do I, Lucas... I'm sorry I took so long to realize what I had in front of me."

With that one sentence, his lips pressed against mine, and as he did, he wrapped his arm around my waist, pulling me flush against his chest. The kiss deepened as his tongue moved against mine as if desperate for my touch, desperate for the love he had to give deep down inside.

For a moment, I thought a part of him was back with me, but as the kiss broke and I stood staring up into his deep mesmerizing eyes, I realized that wasn't the kiss. Yes, he was hesitant, but that was because I knew without a doubt he felt the connection in our kiss that I did.

"How is that possible...I rejected you..."

Letting a small smile fill my face as tears streamed slowly down my cheeks, I glanced at Inanna, who was almost done with what she was doing. "I never gave up on you, Lucas... I refused your rejection. If you kill me...you're killing the other half of your soul. Please don't do this, please—"

A deep roar filled the air as the smell of fire consumed my senses. I knew that roar anywhere, and as the stone began to shake, a blast of light filled my vision, knocking me to my feet. Anyone in my past life would have thought an earthquake was threatening to take us all, but as my heart began to race, I knew the truth.

"What the hell is going on?" Innana shrieked as Lucas quickly stood to his feet from where we had both been knocked to the ground.

"Silas," he growled, his eyes gazing toward me. "You almost had me fooled, Cassie. If you cared at all for me, you would never have laid with Silas. You would never have betrayed me."

With no time to respond, the far wall was blown out, and within the debris, I spotted familiar faces I hadn't expected to see. Faces that would be forever imprinted into my mind, "Pollux...Trixie!"

An agonizing scream ripped from my throat as I turned back to Lucas with wide eyes and parted lips. Gazing down, I spotted the jade handle blade sticking out from my stomach and realized what he had done.

"If I can't have you, then no one can, Cassie."

My heart broke hearing his claim, but at the same time, a roar of anger washed over the roam as I clutched at the blade, slowly pulling it from my body. Chaos consumed the area, and with it, the battle began.

I had spent too much time in my life worrying about what I wanted to see that there were people around me that needed things too. People who needed me to be there, but because of my selfishness, I was too blind to see it.

Fire, smoke, and rage filled the area as gentle hands lay upon my skin. Glancing to my left, my eyes met the deep luminescent eyes of Trixie and the tears pouring down her cheeks.

"Sansa!" she screamed, "Sansa, please...Cassie needs you!"

Lifting my hand, I brushed it down the side of Trixie's cheek, catching her attention once more. "It's okay...I'm okay..."

"No, you're not crazy... you better hold on. Don't you fucking dare leave me."

As my head bobbed, a small laugh escaped my lips. I glanced down at the deep red color that stained my robe and shook my head. "I really liked this robe..."

Trixie let her own laugh escape her as Sansa stood on the other side of me, her hand placed over her mouth as her eyes filled with tears. "Oh, Cassie..."

"Don't just sit there...heal or...do something...don't you have something?" Trixie rambled on in hysterics as she took deep breaths, trying to calm herself.

"I can't, Trixie..."

"What—what do you mean you can't, Sansa?" Trixie gasped in confusion, "you can heal people, though."

Sansa looked down at me again for a moment before a sob racked through her. "I'm sorry, Cassie... it's jade. I can't."

It took a moment for things to sink in, and when they finally did, I realized what she was trying to say. The blade was special in some way, and from the way my body wasn't naturally healing itself like it usually would—I was guessing it was spelled or something.

The fact my life was slowly slipping away, and there was nothing I could do to stop it, was heartbreaking. When they say you don't realize what you have until it's gone... well, they were right. I was young and had so much to offer, and with my heart slowly coming to an end, I realized it was all that was needed for the shimmering energy of the cell doors to die, and Loki suddenly stepped free.

A maniacal laugh escaped him as he burst from the cage, grabbing Silas by the neck and tossing him into the wall. Both Sansa and Trixie screamed, and as Trixie went to help Pollux, I watched her be cast aside as well, just as Inanna went after Sansa.

My friends and my brother were all in trouble, and as Lucas and my brother went toe to toe with one another, I realized I had to help. I had to do something to stop this chaos because if I didn't, they were all going to die.

With all of my energy slowly draining out of me every single minute, I found the courage somewhere deep inside me to gradually find my feet. Looking down at the silver shackles that bound my wrist, pinching at my skin. I tried to dig deep within myself, tapping into the energy I had locked away for so long, trying to find a way to use it, to wield it to my own needs.

"I can't let them die from me," I muttered under my breath, watching as blood began to spill from Pollux and Lucas as they tore into each other, and Loki and Inanna as they went after my friends. Even Silas lay battered and bruised against the cobbled rubble that fell upon the floor from where he hit the wall, cuts on his face and arms, his shirt ripped—it was too much for my heart to bear.

If my mother had been able to get rid of Loki once upon a time, then that power in her now runs through me, and I could do the same. I simply had to find a way to use it.

Remembering something my mother had told me long ago, I closed my eyes and felt the gentle hum of power cascading through my body, touching the part of my soul I had no control over.

Are you finally willing to wake up my child? It has been so long since we met.

The voice that echoed through my mind when I concentrated on that power scared me slightly. I didn't understand who it was talking or where it was coming from, but with slow admission, I whispered its response.

"Save them, and you can have me."

It was all that was needed for an abrupt power to course through my veins. My eyes flew open to see the surrounding dungeon area in a complete and utter mess vibrating in a variety of colors as if every single object in the room, including every person, created their own color from their bodies.

The dark mass that surrounded Loki accented the dark violet blues that surrounded Inanna. They were the reason for the pain I had felt since I had gotten here, and knowing that made my blood boil.

With all of the sudden strength that I had, I ripped my hands-free from the silver shackles that had bound me to the wall. My heart raced as I watched Inanna prepare to throw a massive punch of power towards my brother.

There was no way he would be able to overcome something like that, and in a split second, I dove in front of him, throwing my hands out to watch the powers she had cast rebound straight back at her as if bouncing off the palms of my hands.

As she fell over onto the floor, her body caught fire as her screams of agony flowed through the air I couldn't help but smile. It was wrong, perhaps, but after what she had done both to my mother in accompanying Loki and to me and my friends now....she deserved it.

It was clear Loki had realized he had met his match because no longer did he have a sinister smile on his face. Instead, his eyes were wide, and fear filled them as his lips parted open. "That's not possible."

No longer did I feel like the girl who couldn't control herself. No longer did I feel as if I was a ticking time bomb waiting to explode. Instead, I felt in control, and I felt powerful.

Both of which I loved.

"No longer will your reign bring fear to the people of these realms. I banish you, Loki, back to the prison world you came from." I had no idea where it was I was sending him, but with a flick of my wrist, I opened a portal. A looming black sky of celestial matter and white tundra rock cascaded through the distance of the portal, and as Loki stared at it, he began to shake.

"You can't send me back there. I refuse to go. Your power is no match for me, I'm a god!"

Loki didn't hesitate to slowly bring the source of power from within himself, forming the core energy of who he was within the palm of his hands, and as he attempted to launch that power directly toward me, I simply tilted my head and watched him.

It was pretty the way the voided strings of black matter flowed within his fingertips, but with a snap of my fingers, the power left his hands and came crawling to me. Dancing within my own hands before seeping into my skin as if finding me a better host.

"That's not possible—" he gasped as I stepped closer to him.

"A lot of things aren't possible, but it's time for you to reconsider the choices you have made."

With a flick of my wrist, his body was cast into the void before it slowly closed behind him. The last I heard were the cries of his anger as he attempted to proclaim his revenge. Yet, even though the portal closed, those were the only sobs and tears I heard.

Slowly turning around, I realized that there was a bigger problem.

There upon the floor laid my body cradled within Silas' lap. Tears flowed down his face, and Trixie, Sansa, and my brother. They wept for me, but what I didn't understand was how my body was there, if I was here. Blood seeped from the wounds and onto the floor, and as my body paled, I realized they had no idea I was standing right here.

"What the fuck?" I muttered in confusion.

Was I a ghost? It wasn't possible, and yet it was like they couldn't see me.

As confusion filled me, I heard the thundering approach of footsteps, and turning to look out the hole Silas had created when he burst into here, I saw my grandfather—Odin—standing amongst the rubble.

Odin's gaze fell soft as he glanced at me and then at the body on the floor. A look of sorrow and regret seemed to fill him as he realized what had happened.

"Where were you? You should have saved her," Pollux screamed, jumping to his feet as he stormed toward Odin. "She died because of you."

"Am I dead?" I asked, watching as he refused to acknowledge my brother but instead turned to me and slowly nodded his head with a heavy sigh.

"Yes, Cassie... your mortal life is gone as you know it."

An Heir To a new Dynasty

Cassie

Death was something I hadn't expected to see so soon. Yet as my grandfather explained I was dead, or at least my mortal life was, I couldn't help but suddenly feel a hollow pit within my stomach that screamed at me to say everything I wish I could have said.

They never tell you when you're at the end, you're filled with regret over everything you wish you would have done differently. It doesn't matter if you lived a good life or if you lived a bad one. Everyone must feel some kind of regret in some way or another.

"How can I be dead? I wasn't supposed to die."

Nodding his head once more, he held out his hand and gestured for me to follow him. But as I gazed at my brother and my friends, who were staring at Odin in confusion, I couldn't help but wonder if there was somewhere else I was supposed to be.

"Are you even fucking listening to me?" my brother snapped and, Silas laid my body on the floor and stood to his feet, grasping my brother's arm to stop him from approaching Odin.

"Don't. He's trying to help her," Silas said softly trying to make my brother understand what was going on.

As Pollux knitted his brows together, two guards entered through the same hole my grandfather had come in and quickly went to my body, collecting it from the floor before carrying it out.

Disbelief fell upon the faces of Trixie, Sansa, and my brother. But with a gentle gesture, Silas ushered for them to leave as he stayed back watching them go. I wasn't sure what it was that Silas was doing, but when his eyes cast to the space where I stood—I could have sworn he was looking right at me.

"Everything will be okay, Cassie."

I didn't have the slightest clue what it was he was talking about, but before I could open my mouth to ask, Odin placed his hand within mine and gestured for me to follow him. "You know, I never thought this day would come so soon…"

The trailed-off statement he made had my mind spinning, and as we stepped through the rubble near the opening, I tried to make sure I didn't trip over it. Even though I saw my body on the floor, and I was told I had died, I didn't feel any different than when I was alive.

"None of this makes sense. Why am I still here if I'm dead?" I asked as we stepped into the clearing outside. My eyes scanned my surroundings in shock as everything around me seemed so much brighter and clearer than I had remembered it being.

"Because technically, you're not dead."

Odin's comment made no sense. You couldn't be dead, and not dead. That was physically impossible, wasn't it? "What do you mean… you either are or you're not."

"Typically, yes," he replied, our footsteps in sync as he pulled me forward across the courtyard of the school and toward the direction of the arena. I hadn't realized the underground area I had been in before was beneath the schools, but looking around now, it made sense.

The school, from what I had learned since my time being here, was one of the oldest buildings in this realm. It was the first place in which Odin and the other gods and taken up home, but over the years, as more half-breed children were born, they built their new home and transformed this one into a school that could protect and teach the children.

"I'm guessing I'm not a typical situation then?"

Laughter echoed from him as he shook his head. "No, you most certainly are not."

"So what am I then?" I asked, my feet hitting the vibrant green grass with ease before Odin finally let my hand go, and turned to face me.

"You are part of me, Cassie. My blood runs through your veins, and because of that, you have a celestial soul. It was bound in your shifter body, but when you were injured, the shifter side of you died."

The shifter side of me died? What the hell did that mean? Am I not a shifter anymore?

"That's not possible... that would mean I'm—" I gasped, thinking of what he was saying. I wouldn't technically be human, because that wouldn't be possible, but as he stared at me, I watched his smile fall.

"It is possible, and you're not human, child—well, not exactly. You actually have a choice to make right now, and it's completely up to you what you want to do. You can remain as you are and rest in Asgard for eternity, but be a soul in limbo, or you can accept the proclamation of being my heir apparent."

Odin was a god and for him to need an heir didn't make sense. It wasn't like he would eventually die or anything. Unless there was something I missed in my history classes that I should be worried about. "You can't die though."

"No, I can't." He chuckled. "But one day, I hope to... retire, I guess is what you call it on earth."

"Retire? Is that even possible... you're a god."

I was stating the obvious but as I watched his twinkling blue eyes stare at me with so much intensity, my heart wanted to burst from my chest. It wasn't anything loving as one may think. I was nervous as hell to be around Odin, even if that wasn't something I would admit to my brother or anyone else.

"I am a god, but eventually, I would like the chance to teach someone else to do what I do. To rule by my side, but as my successor." I wasn't sure what to say to what Odin proclaimed. I had never thought it possible, but yet standing here now talking to him, I realized he wasn't the egotistical man I thought he was.

He was far more caring, and the guilt of what happened to me still lingered in his eyes.

"Can I ever go home?" It was the one question I had that I needed answered, and with a sigh, he shook his head no.

"Unfortunately, Cassie, you're bound to this realm now. However, if you accept my offer, you can go to visit your family, eventually. Of course, it would only be for a short time but you could go and visit them or any of the other realms."

To hear I would never be able to go home again brought tears to my eyes. I didn't want to rule a realm or anything like that, but the thought of never seeing my family again was a thought I couldn't manage. "Okay... but I need something if I agree."

Glancing up into his eyes, he hesitated for a moment. "Okay... and what would that be?"

"My little brother..."

"The one who's sick?" he said cutting mid-sentence.

"Yeah, the one who's sick. I want him cured... Pollux will return home one day, but my mother will never be able to live through losing two of her children. Can you heal him?"

Odin paused for a moment as if contemplating what I asked of him, but after a moment, he nodded. "Okay, I will see to it our healers tend to him."

"Wait... you have healers? You could have healed him this entire time?!"

I wasn't sure whether to be shocked or angry that he could have healed my little brother a long time ago and didn't. Yet, as he held his hand up shaking his head with a smile, I quickly found myself calming down.

"It isn't that easy, Cassie. We don't mess with fate, but I'm sure, under the circumstances, he would prefer to have you agree to be here over the fate of your little brother. He will simply rewrite his future as he has done for so many others."

Opening my mouth, I tried to find the words to explain my shock over hearing Odin talk about fate as if it was an actual person, but by the look on his face and the amusement in the corners of his wrinkled eyes, I already had my answer.

"There is really someone out there who decides our futures... that's brilliant." Sarcasm dripped from my remark causing Odin to laugh a little harder than he had before.

"You will meet him eventually. He will partake in the Solstice games as a judge, of course. It's an essential part of your succession. It's where you will pick your mate or mates if you choose to have more than one."

I had agreed to the succession in order to see my family, and of course, save my brother, but to hear that there was some kind of games that would be held in my honor to determine the man or men I would be forced to spend my life with was beyond crazy.

"Excuse me? First of all, I will never take more than one mate... I have seen what that has done to my mother... and second, why do I have to participate in games?" I had so many questions, and the more I thought about them, the more I felt crazy in my current situation.

Odin was calm, his eyes cast from me toward the direction in which my brother had gone, and with a deep breath, he smiled at me. "We need to find your brother... all of your questions can be answered at a later time. I think you have had enough excitement for one day."

I wasn't sure why he needed to find Pollux, but Odin's entire demeanor changed, and as it did, I realized that whatever was going on with me had to deal with my brother.

Crossing the grassy field that laid outside the school, we headed towards the backside of the gardens that surrounded the main building of Asgard. The same building in which the gods resided, but also where my room and Pollux's room were.

The moment our feet hit the steps of the building, I couldn't hold back my questions anymore. "Where are we going and why do we need Pollux?"

Looking over his shoulder, he sighed again and kept walking. "He has to help with your succession."

Door after door, we passed until we stopped outside Pollux's room. The soft sobs and whispers coming from the other side made me stop in my tracks, and as Odin opened the door, all eyes turned to us—or him, because they couldn't see me.

"What the fuck are you doing here?" Pollux snapped, standing to his feet. "Haven't you done enough?"

Narrowing his eyes, Odin groaned, and it was the first time I heard a normal sound come from him. At least that I could remember. "I'll ignore your outburst for now, but on another note... would you like to see your sister again?"

Pollux froze in his place, and as he did, Trixie stepped forward. "Of course he does... we all do, but that's impossible. She's dead."

"No, she isn't," Sansa breathed out softly, "I can feel her."

Stepping forward, I made my way closer to Pollux, and as I did, he shuttered. "Explain, I don't have time for riddles and games."

Glancing back at Odin, he smiled. "Very well. If you want her back, revoke your celestial side, and give it to your sister. With her Celestial form and yours combined, she will become a god completely and will then take her place as my successor."

My eyes widened in shock, realizing what it was he was asking my brother to do, and as I turned to gaze upon Pollux, his, Trixie's, and Sansa's expressions all matched mine.

"You want me to do what?" Pollux muttered in disbelief. "I can't just give it up... it doesn't work like that it's in my DNA."

"Actually, it does. Your twins, Pollux. All these years, you have regretted not being there for your sister when you should have. Now is your chance."

It didn't make sense what Odin was saying, and even though I didn't want to believe him, the distant gaze in Pollux's eyes let me know that what he was saying was true. Pollux did feel guil,ty and with a deep breath, he nodded his head.

"If I'm no longer a Celestial, I will be forced to go home?"

"Yes," Odin replied, "but she will be able to visit you. With Loki gone, the veils can be much lower than they have been over the past few decades."

My mind swirled with the information being passed around, and as I tried to process it all, Pollux opened his mouth and began to speak. "I, Pollux, revoke my Celestial rights and transfer them to my twin sister, Castor. Let her be whole once more, and take her rightful place on Odin's throne."

A surge of power rushed through me, causing a pleasurable hum I had never felt before, and as the high began to settle, I realized that all eyes were on me. Literally.

"Cassie—" Trixie choked back as she threw her arms around me. "I thought I'd never see you again."

The reunion with my friends and my brother was wonderful, and as I glanced back to look at Odin, I realized he was gone. I had signed my fate, and though my brother didn't know of the conditions of my agreement or what I had done for our younger brother, I knew one day he would understand.

One day he would be able to forgive me for leaving him.

"Where's Lucas?" I asked as the three of them pulled away. "And where's Silas?"

"Silas said he needed time to himself for a while. We aren't sure where he went," Trixie replied as she glanced at Pollux.

"As for Lucas..." my brother said, letting out a heavy regretful breath. "He disappeared after the battle. Odin told the guards to let him go... or so they said. Said he wasn't a threat because it wasn't him making those choices. It was his father and Inanna. We don't know where he went, and honestly, I don't care where he went."

Unsure of what to make of my situation I sat on the edge of my brother's bed taking it all in. I had lost not only my mate but Silas my companion and on top of that, my mortal life as I knew it.

If I was ever going to survive what was to come, I was going to have to stop my childish ways and grow up quickly. I wasn't just some young girl, rebellious and trying to make a stand in life. I was now the heir apparent to Odin's throne, and I had no doubt that people would be gunning to get rid of me.

This time though, I'd be prepared for whatever shitstorm blew my way.

Cover Design by Natasha Art

Editing Services by Aimee Ferro

Interior Header & Breaker Design by Leigh Cadiente